THE FIRST SONG

Selected and Translated by Miriam Morton

FIERCE AND GENTLE WARRIORS, *stories by Mikhail Sholokhov*

SHADOWS AND LIGHT, *stories by Anton Chekhov*

THE FIRST SONG

THE
FIRST
SONG

By Semyon Rosenfeld

Translated and Edited by

MIRIAM MORTON

Doubleday & Company, Inc.

GARDEN CITY, NEW YORK

Translator's Preface

The First Song is a novel for young readers. It is about a Russian boy who had a passion for music, showed very promising talent, and dreamed of some day becoming a great cellist. Written by Semyon Rosenfeld, (1891–1959), a Soviet writer who spent most of his life in Odessa, the narrative is in the first person and is obviously a fictionalized autobiography. (The translator has obtained the author's autobiographical notes which corroborate this.) Like the book's hero, the writer was thirteen years old at the time of the story's beginning.

The book was first published in Leningrad, in 1959, only a month after Semyon Rosenfeld died.

The First Song unfolds in the teeming southern seaport of Odessa, on the shores of the Black Sea; the city is also Russia's musical center. Kolya Orlov, the story's hero, lives there in times when a young person from a poor family like his faced endless obstacles in his strivings to reach goals requiring an education or training in any art. Kolya repeatedly experiences disappointments and frustrations. But he also enjoys many unusual encounters and blood-chilling adventures, as he earns his living and seeks to fulfill his musical ambitions in the vital city caught up in social upheavals.

The events in which Kolya is embroiled take place in the

first years of this century, in the setting of the disastrous
Russo-Japanese War and the ensuing partial Revolution of
1905. In that historical year, Odessa was the stage for the sav-
age suppression of popular protest against hunger and tyranny.
The whole country was seething under the cruel autocracy.
The people wanted the basic freedoms and a constitution.

Kolya is an eyewitness to many dramatic scenes. He
gradually begins to understand the feelings and heroism of
his countrymen.

In the end, from his city of Odessa, named after the Greek
epic wanderer Odysseus, Kolya embarks on his own long
journey. His "Odyssey" is to the promised land of fulfillment
as a musician, along the road toward the liberation of his
nation from the Czarist despotism.

Noted works of literature and works for the stage and screen
have been inspired by Odessa's ordeal in those early years of
the twentieth century, by her brave sailors and her celebrated
musicians and poets. *The First Song* is a moving and enter-
taining work of this kind for the young reader.

The translator has edited the book slightly. In the main,
only those paragraphs and phrases have been omitted which
refer to obscure and confusing details.

A pronouncing glossary of the names of Russian characters
is provided, with their identities. It is hoped that this will
make it simpler and more enjoyable for the reader to get acquainted with the story's many people.

MIRIAM MORTON

The People in the Story

A Pronouncing Glossary of the Russian Names

This glossary does not attempt to give the full phonetic equivalents of the Russian sounds. To make this pronouncing aid very simple, we suggest that the reader remember the following: the Russian "a" is pronounced as the "a" in the word *car*; the Russian "I" like the "ee" in *peek*; the "e" as the "*ye*" in *yes*; the stress falls on the syllable in capital letters.

Aleksei (Alek-SEI) — a fisherman

Anka (AN-ka) — Kolya's friend

Avdeenko (Av-DE-en-ko) — a censor

Beklemishev (Bek-le-MI-shev) — Reggio's real name

Chaliapin, Feodor (Cha-LIA-pin, Fe-O-dor) — a famous Russian basso

Chekhov, Anton (CHE-khov, An-TON) — the author

Egor Egorov (Eg-OR Eg-O-rov) — a stoker; Kolya's good friend

Gregory Mikhailovich (Gre-GO-ry Mik-HAI-lo-vich) — cellist and conductor; Kolya's relative

Katya (KA-tya) — the wounded girl

Kolya Orlov (KO-lya Or-LOV) — the hero of the story

Kolka (KO-lka)
Kolenka (KO-len-ka) } — his nicknames

Krukovsky (Kru-KOV-sky) — a journalist
Kukharsky (Ku-KHAR-sky) — a censor
Lenka (LEN-ka) — a newsboy
Lesha (LE-sha) — nickname of Aleksei the fisherman
Matiushenko (Ma-tiu-SHEN-ko) — seaman-leader on the
    battleship *Potemkin*
Motka (MOT-ka) — a newsboy
Nikolai (Ni-ko-LAI) — Kolya's formal name
Orlov (Or-LOV) — Kolya's surname
Petrov (Pet-ROV) — a seaman
Prokopii (Pro-KO-pii) — prisoner who helped Kolya escape
Pyotr Ivanovich (Py-OTR IVAN-o-vich) — a university
    student
Rimsky-Korsakov (RIM-sky-KORsa-kov) — a composer
Sashka (SASH-ka) — Kolya's buddy
Senka (SEN-ka) — a newsboy
Shlemka (SHLEM-ka) — a newsboy
Spirka (SPIR-ka) — Kolya's buddy
Trepov (TRE-pov) — a notorious chief of police
Tsenovsky (Tse-NOV-sky) — music critic
Vakulenchuk (Va-ku-len-CHUK) — the sailor killed by his
    naval officer
Vitka (VIT-ka) — Kolya's buddy
Volodya Rensky (Vo-LoD-ya REN-sky) — the cello student and
    Kolya's instructor
Zagrabsky (Za-GRAB-sky) — cellist who gambled away the
    money for Kolya's cello

THE FIRST SONG

1

THE WIDE OVERGROWN COURTYARD was the battlefield. The high piles of wood were the fortress. The old caved-in cellar served as the commanding officer's dugout. Pieces of waterpipe were our cannon, and sticks of all shapes and sizes our rifles and sabers. And the low gray fence marked the boundary of our territory, on the other side of which the enemy forces were deployed.

The foe had just been repulsed, and we were busy counting our losses.

It was then that the stocky figure of a stranger appeared at the wicket of the dilapidated, warped gate. The man was tall and handsome. His large hazel eyes were friendly and took in the scene with interest. His dark beard rested cozily on his wide cream-colored bow tie. He wore a brown velvet jacket trimmed with black silk braiding, which fitted his stately figure well. Wavy locks of black hair fell to his temples from underneath his wide-brimmed hat.

Approaching me, the man assumed a stern expression and asked angrily: "Why aren't you in school?"

"Who is he?" I thought, fearing the worst, but than I recognized him. "I remember you!" I announced boldly. "You are our relative!"

He was, in fact, a relative—my mother's second or third

cousin. But how did he get here? What could he possibly want in our small town when he resided in the important city of Odessa, where he played in such a famous theater, a theater so remarkable that my parents often lacked words glowing enough to describe it?

"Why aren't you in school?" he repeated even more sternly.

"Let's hurry to our place . . ." I said briskly, shrewdly avoiding answering him as I wondered how in the world he knew that I had played hooky that day.

I soon found out. Trying to locate us, he asked the first boy he met in our neighborhood whether he knew where the two brothers Lyova and Kolya lived. And the boy replied without hesitation:

"Yes, I know where. Over there, in that house. Lyova was in school today, but not Kolya."

This is the way my secret was disclosed to the visitor.

As the two of us were walking across the large courtyard, my distant cousin said:

"But how did you recognize me?"

"I remember you—you used to come to our house and play on the . . ."

"The cello."

"Yes, that's right."

"But that was long ago, when you were very little."

"I do remember it. Your name is Grisha . . . Gregory Mikhailovich."

"That's all very true. But, just the same, I'll take Lyova to the opera this evening, but not you."

"Why?" I asked in great distress.

"Because he went to school today and you didn't."

I was despondent. Gregory Mikhailovich had arrived this day with his opera company. Tonight they would present their first performance, *The Queen of Spades*, the only opera I knew anything about and which my parents had praised so often.

From early childhood, ever since my parents took my brother and me to a morning musical show, I had loved the theater, especially the singing and instrumental music. Now, suddenly, there was the chance to hear *The Queen of Spades,* and I wasn't going!

I remembered everything that Gregory Mikhailovich had played for us. One of the songs was "Thoughts of a Wanderer," another . . . the title of this other song I couldn't recall but I could still sing it. Mother often said that I had a good ear and a good memory and that Lyova didn't. But now *he* was going to the opera while I was staying home. That wasn't justice! I was about to cry with disappointment.

Gregory Mikhailovich kept his word and didn't take me. My parents went, my older brother went, but I was left at home to choke back bitter tears. In my helplessness and rage I tried to draw a caricature of the heartless distant cousin, but instead of a human face I somehow drew a hideous mask.

To ease my grief, I played an ardent game of "Friday" with the old woman who roomed with us, telling her that Gregory Mikhailovich was an old fool, that I detested him despite the fact that he played the cello so well, and that he was conducting the orchestra in that evening's performance.

Remembering afresh what I was missing at the opera, I nearly cried again, and it took all my self-control to hold back the tears. Soon I fell asleep right there, at the table.

Next day I made sure to be at school, and that evening, in a state of great excitement, I sat on the lowest step of the conductor's podium and listened to the opening measures of the overture, waiting impatiently for the curtain to rise.

My eyes roamed over the performers and I tried to identify the sounds with the instruments as they came from one or another part of the orchestra. The curtain went up, and I was immediately lost to the real world. The set was radiant with the spring sunshine that filled the garden, some children were playing soldiers, a fairly convincing officer in a gray wig and a shako appeared—I was utterly captivated. And when the gray officer, in the midst of thunder and lightning, raised his arm and, turning his face to the audience, sang out: "Oh, Thunder, Lightning, and Wind! Before you I solemnly vow—she'll be mine! mine! or I'll forfeit my life!" I was seized with rapture. I was even more strongly moved, and scared, by the scene in the Countess's bedroom. At the sight of the old woman falling dead from fright when the villain threatened her with his pistol, I almost screamed with terror.

Of course I knew that all this was happening merely on a stage, that it was "not for real," and I tried in every way to control my emotions. But when, in the last scene, from behind the props representing a barracks, the moaning wind carried the sound of funereal chanting, a blast of wind tore open the window extinguishing the candlelight, and clouds of snow whipped into the room now eerily bathed in moonlight, and the ghost of the dead Countess appeared, I fell to the floor for safety and closed my eyes as I listened to the voice of the insane Germann repeating in his delirium: "Three, Seven . . . Ace . . ."

I couldn't fall asleep all night. I tossed in my bed and saw, as if in a nightmare, the corpse of the old lady, the drowned Liza, the dying Germann, and I heard their voices and the beautiful and terrifying music.

From that day I could think of nothing else but the opera theater.

Every evening I waited at the performers' entrance for Gregory Mikhailovich to arrive and begged him to take me in with him. After a prolonged and strict cross-examination: "And did you attend school today? Have you done your homework? Do you have your mother's permission?" he finally, believing or pretending to believe me, allowed me to follow him into the auditorium where I'd hear a new opera.

Evening after evening I took delight in the performances. And life seemed impossible now without the theater, and I'd be upset when I'd overhear conversations about the approaching departure of the company.

This sad event soon actually took place. One Sunday Gregory Mikhailovich came to us earlier than was his custom and informed us that they were giving their last performance that evening and would leave the next day, early in the morning. This was a great blow to me. Our town would be empty and dead without the opera.

I watched for an opportune moment and with emotion disclosed to Gregory Mikhailovich that I just couldn't learn a thing in school, that I had no talent whatever for books. At the same time I complained about my teacher, who had informed my father that I was an incorrigible idler and that I would never amount to anything. I begged him to take me with him and find me some sort of job in the theater, assuring him that I would conscientiously carry out any task—pasting up posters all over town, sweeping the stage—anything, if only he took me with him.

Gregory Mikhailovich looked at me with astonishment:

"What's the matter with you?" he said severely. "You don't know what you're babbling about. You're just a kid, not even thirteen, right?"

"I'll soon be."

"What'll you think of next! Quit school! Forget it, kid."

"I want to study music."

"That's fine. But after learning grammar and arithmetic."

And Gregory Mikhailovich looked at me closely and with a no-nonsense expression:

"Forget it! When you are grown-up—no, don't you dare think about the theater even then. The stage is fascinating only from a distance. In reality there is nothing cheerful about it. Anyway, first you must finish school."

The opera company was leaving our town. I went with my mother to see Gregory Mikhailovich off. I watched the singers and musicians arrive at the dock in horse-drawn carriages, saw them mount to the deck and wave their hats and handkerchiefs to the people as the ship slowly moved away from the shore.

Mother's cousin was also waving his hat. Then, seeming to remember something he had wanted to say, he put his hat on, leaned over the railing and, cupping his hands, shouted:

"Hold on to him or he'll throw himself after us . . ."

My mother tightened her grip on my hand and wouldn't let go of me, as if afraid that I'd really throw myself into the water.

The ship increased its speed and before long turned into a dot and disappeared.

2

AFTER THE DEPARTURE OF THE OPERA, life became very
dull. Somehow all the fun went out of the usual adventures—
secret excursions to the seashore, fishing, forbidden trips in
the rowboats, shooting arrows. My childhood games—leap-
frog, warfare, jumping over fences, wandering over roofs—
somehow suddenly became things of the past. I began to study
more diligently, and maybe I would have calmed down altogether had not an unexpected change—not for the first time,
though—come into the life of my family.

My father was transferred to a job in Odessa, from where
we had migrated several years before. In the end of September,
on a bright sunny morning, my mother, brother, and I—my
father had left ahead of us—went to the docks and boarded
the same ship on which the visiting opera company had left a
month ago. It was a freight ship. It carried coal and iron from
Mariopol to Odessa, and from Odessa to Mariopol it brought
roof tiles and other merchandise. Despite the coal cargo the
ship was clean and comfortable, and it was interesting and
lively on its decks. But when the propeller began to turn, and
the green water was whipped up noisily into spraying foam,
cutting a long white pathway in the wake of the moving
ship, and, when I saw the familiar shore slowly disappear from
sight, I felt very sad.

I had spent most of my life here, in Mariopol. In the summer I would virtually live on the beach, baking myself on the hot bright-yellow sand, and when I was overcome by the sweltering heat, I would throw myself into the transparent green water of the Azov Sea to swim and dive. Here also, only a short distance from the city, was the Kal'ka—a river of many legends about the clashes long ago between the Russians and the marauding Mongols. We boys often crossed it in a flat-bottomed rowboat. Tall reeds grew thickly on the opposite shore. This was almost the beginning of the Don Cossack region. And on this very spot we had made the important decision to explore this wild country of the Cossacks for buried Mongol treasure. Perhaps we would find a caldron of gold, a trunkful of ancient weapons, or magnificent saddles and harness. Yes, I was leaving a great deal behind me, and my heart was heavy.

But the captain was soon shouting into the loudspeaker down to the engine room, "Full speed ahead!" and the steamship, gathering momentum, quickly left my city far behind. Its outlines became dimmer and dimmer, and soon it disappeared altogether as the sky merged gradually with the green sea.

After a while my sad thoughts left me. Many other ships were on the sea. Some passed us carrying nothing but coal—the white *Emerance*, followed by the bulky black *Pyotr Karpov*, then came an unusually long one, the *Maria Regger*, and the fat and ugly *Taras Bulba*. Our vessel, the *Pyotr Regger*, properly saluted them all with her flag, and they answered courteously. All this was new and interesting to me. Cupping our hands into a make-believe telescope, my brother and I scanned the sea, and the one who was the first to spot a ship when it was still no larger than a dot on the far horizon, felt very superior to the other.

Although it was already autumn, the weather was dry and

brilliantly clear. It was as warm as summer. The calm water was a smooth blue-green. The gold of the sun flashed on it, forming an interminably long fiery-golden carpet across the immensity of the sea, and its million sparkles were blinding.

Everything on board was unfamiliar and intriguing. I felt an uncontrollable desire to touch everything, to feel the shape of every strange object, and to examine it. The gear which rested in the prow and at the stern, the large coils of thick hemp rope, the heavy chains that stretched along the sides of the ship from the captain's bridge to the helm, all were intriguing. Nor did I ignore the huge windlass. The signal lanterns also arrested my attention, with their bright colors and beautifully shaped glass—green, white, and red. And within reach was a box with a large assortment of the flags of all countries.

But most interesting of all was the engine room.

With great curiosity we looked down below through the open hatchway and saw the large engines breathing heavy steam and the thick steel pistons, covered with thick oil, going up and down with a strong and regular rhythm. Knowing that these engines moved the enormous ship's propeller which, turning so lightly in the water, made the ship move forward so steadily, caused one to regard all this machinery with great respect, as one would a very powerful and competent person.

A man in a striped sailor's jersey often looked up at us from the engine room as we stared down. His face was nearly black, but his eyes stood out sharply from this blackness, like two white circles, and they seemed to shine like lanterns in the darkness. He often wiped his hands on a piece of sackcloth, and kept looking up. He smiled at us, showing a row of snow-white teeth. And he was singing some song, but the thud of the engines drowned out his voice.

At sunset, a cool breeze suddenly passed over the deck, and

the ripples on the water's surface looked like shimmering many-colored dabs of paint as they reflected the setting sun. But the sea soon became noticeably darker. The seamen who were off duty now gathered at the ship's stern. They came from all over the ship.

The stoker whose acquaintance we had already made, was among them. Now his face was not at all black, he had scrubbed it. And his eyes were now not white but light gray, and friendly. He was wearing a clean sailor's blouse and a muffler of sackcloth. He held an accordion in his hands. At first he tinkered with it for quite a while, loosening this and tightening that, checking the various parts. Then, resting for a few moments as if to gather the energy for it, he began to sing, lowering his head toward the instrument until it nearly touched it. He did this, it seemed, in order not to miss a single sound. He played a sorrowful song, keeping his eyes closed. When he finished playing the melody, he opened his eyes, raised his head, and smiled in a self-conscious way. The sea breeze blew against his heavy locks, and this made his face look even more pleasant and good-natured. But soon he hid his face again, lowering it almost to the accordion. He now played something unfamiliar to me, wonderfully moving.

The other seamen stood or sat around him. A little farther away some passengers had made themselves comfortable on coils of cable, and still farther off, on a reclining deckchair, sat the captain's mate, and near him stood the fat ship's engineer. Everyone listened attentively and with obvious enjoyment. Some even with rapture. I, too, was absorbed in Egor's singing, and I watched the fingers of his coarsened hands run lightly over the keys, and drank in the slightly hoarse music of his old accordion.

A blue twilight soon enveloped us. Green, red, and white lights appeared on the stern and on the bridge. The sea became even darker, and soon looked like a gigantic pool of ink on which played the reflections of the colored lantern lights and the yellow-blue stars. The breeze had become chillier and was now blowing up our sleeves.

Twice my mother had sent someone to get me to go down for supper and to put on a jacket. But I couldn't even think of it. How could one leave when Egor was still playing!

Annoyed with my stubbornness, Mother came herself to get me, but she stayed on and listened with great enjoyment. Then, feeling too cold, she left and sent my brother with my coat and cap.

Egor played on for a long time. His skillful hands, completely invisible now in the darkness, continued to draw wonderful melodies from his instrument.

He interrupted his playing abruptly, rose, and said in a pleasant, light tenor voice: "Well, enough! Must get some sleep. Have to work tonight."

And closing the accordion carefully, fastening it with a leather strap, then throwing it over his shoulder, he made his way among the piles of rope, commenting: "Too much carousing today and carousing on the morrow, and a kopeck for bread you'll have to borrow."

Egor, as I soon found out, liked to talk in proverbs.

He now started down the fo'c's'le and I followed him.

"Egor, may I come with you?"

"Why not? Welcome to our 'tent.' "

The fo'c's'le was poorly lighted and was full of the stale smoke of cheap tobacco. There was a smell of coal dust, cigarettes, whisky, and black bread. Someone was snoring with a startlingly different, rolling snore. And someone else was lying awake on a nearby cot, almost invisible in the semi-darkness and smoke haze of the crowded quarters.

Egor wrapped his accordion in a large flowered peasant kerchief and put it away in a green trunk with iron fastenings. Then he took a guitar from the wall, sat down at the table and

began to loosen its tuning pegs, adjust the strings, and fix
other things with his knowing hands. But, no sooner did I
begin to question him about what he was doing with the
guitar, than my older brother came and announced that unless
I went up to supper at once, Mother would send a seaman for
me.

"Don't worry, Kolya," my new acquaintance said. "Come
back tomorrow and I'll show you a few things. There are many
days of this trip still left to us and, fortunately, tomorrow is
Saturday."

I left Egor reluctantly and consoled myself with the thought
that I would see him again tomorrow and would then, without
fail, ask him to teach me to play the accordion.

But next morning I managed to see Egor only through the
hatchway. Passengers were forbidden to go down to the engine
room, and for some reason Egor worked all day even after
working the night shift.

We soon came to the end of the Azov Sea and entered
the Kerchinsky Strait, and, after passing one more floating
beacon, we were on the Black Sea. But I experienced a great
disappointment now—this sea was not at all black. And no
one was able to explain to me why it was called black. I even
thought the Azov Sea darker. But when I found out that the
Black Sea was deeper and larger, that its water was bitter
and salty, and that it never froze over, whereas the water of
the Azov Sea was sweet and fresh and it froze over for several
months in the year, I grudgingly admitted the superiority of the
Black Sea. Fantasy now took over, and I imagined that the
Pyotr Regger had entered the ocean and was carrying us to
unchartered shores. Any minute now I expected the captain
to look through his telescope and announce, in a voice shaken
with emotion, that he had spied the barely visible outline of
a new continent. The ship's passengers and crew, crowding
at the rails, were about to watch eagerly the silhouettes of

blue mountains emerge from the foggy horizon. But one of the crew cruelly shattered my dream when, in passing, he said casually, pointing to the shore:

"Look, there is my birthplace, Feodosya, a golden city!"

We were merely passing the Crimea.

The ship moved on, keeping closer to the shore, as if the captain was intent on showing us the many lovely places of the Crimean Peninsula. We passed Aluyshta! Yalta! and Alupka! We could see not only the white houses, the tall cypresses, the winding ribbons of the roads not far from the shore, but even the dark figures of the people on the beaches. We passed white yachts with billowing sails, sturdy fishing boats, and small rowboats with vacationers. It looked to me like a fairy-tale scene in an azure kingdom. The light-blue clear water, the strong smell of sea salt, the faint scent of flowers and sun-baked earth, the calm, cloudless sky—they all seemed full of magic.

But we soon left the Crimea behind us. The shore disappeared, and we were aware only of the boundless sea, the blue horizon, the soft warm air, and the gay dolphins springing now and then from the water. They followed the ship and, seeming determined to amuse the passengers, put on a show of effortless and graceful leaps, making a semi-circle high in the air, then quickly diving into the waves like lively urchins.

The pounding engine made the ship shudder as it sped along, cutting a turbulent wake.

I waited impatiently for the evening, hoping Egor would again appear on deck with his accordion. But it was a long time till evening, an unbearably long time! Stealthily, so that no one would notice me, I went down to the engine room. It was almost dark in the long narrow passageway. I proceeded, feeling my way along the wall with my hands. I was somewhat scared and worried—what if Egor should get angry. With every step it became hotter. I put my head through a narrow opening and a wave of scorching air hit me.

I saw something that looked like the enormous jaw of a monstrous iron beast. Its mouth was full of flames and red-hot embers. And in front of this fiery monster stood Egor. I recognized him at once although he was half-naked and his face was invisible in the thick smoke. Bending over, he kept scooping up large pieces of coal with a wide shovel and throwing them into the furnace. The furnace hissed, smoked, and flared up as Egor fed it shovelful after shovelful.

I could hardly breathe in this choking heat. I began to cough, and felt as if my clothes were on fire. I quickly retreated and ran back to the deck.

There, after the heat of the furnace room, despite the blazing sun, it seemed as cool as under a sea wave. I relished the spaciousness, the clean air, and the ease with which I could breathe. And it made me sad to think of poor Egor spending days and nights in the inferno below.

That evening, when Egor came up on deck, I ran over to him and asked:

"How can you stand it down there?"

"Well, what can you do?" was his reply. "Do whatever work you can get, eat what they give you. Otherwise death will get you all right."

"But, can't you find other work?"

"There is no escaping this. It's all right," he added, laughing. "It will be easier in the next world."

As on the previous day when his work shift was over, Egor settled himself in his customary place on deck, amid the large piles of cables, put his accordion on his knees and began to tune it. Then, after pausing in thought for a few moments, he lowered his head to the instrument, stretched its pleats, and listened closely to the long chord. The many-voiced chords of the accordion seemed to me very beautiful, and I was ready to listen to them forever.

Again a crowd of passengers and crew gathered around him. Egor played on, but not for long. Rising suddenly, he said:

"I didn't get any sleep last night and was on duty all day— must catch a few winks now." And he went wearily below.

In the morning a large white city appeared on the horizon. It was Odessa. A little later a tall white lighthouse came unexpectedly into view, as if it had sprung out of the water, and from the lighthouse to the shore a semi-circular breakwater opened its passageway to us. We entered its wide gates, and the ship glided noiselessly through the glass-smooth surface of the water, cautiously nearing the pier.

I didn't manage to see Egor again. As soon as the ship docked, my father came up the gangplank and led us ashore. I kept looking up for as long as I could, keeping my eye on the opening to the engine room, but no one appeared.

The driver was soon through putting our things in the horse-drawn carriage. My brother and I climbed up and sat on a narrow bench facing my parents who were installed in the wide seats of the phaeton, which smelled of leather and of the stable. In another minute we would be on our way, and still there was no sight of Egor. The driver pulled on the reins, turned the carriage toward the city, and the ship disappeared from view.

3

I COULDN'T PUT EGOR and his music out of my mind.

I couldn't sleep that first night in my new home in Odessa. I kept thinking of the ship and felt as if I were still on it. I heard the shudder of the hull, the thud of the engine, and the sound of the accordion.

Then, suddenly, an idea struck me—after all, the ship was still in port!

In an instant I decided to go down to the waterfront and find Egor.

Very early next morning, the moment my father left for work, I got up quietly, dressed, and slipped out of the house. I soon turned down a street leading to the Nikolayevsky Boulevard and reached the wide sweeping stairway leading down to the harbor. I skipped down two steps at a time, glancing back now and then at the statue of Cardinal Richelieu overlooking the steps. I did this to see what progress I was making down the seemingly endless stairway.

The wharf stretched along the entire length of the harbor. It was lined with shops, warehouses, and travel agencies, and behind these were the moorings and stone jetties. A short distance out in the breakwater were rows of ships and boats of all shapes and colors. They were moored, and their flags of many countries fluttered in the strong breeze and made one think of mysterious distant worlds.

I crossed over to the mounds of coal at the refueling dock and went on through the narrow walks to the quay from which we had left yesterday for the city. The walks were crisscrossed with steel cables and hemp hawsers with which the ships and boats were moored to the iron bitts, and they were cluttered with unused gangplanks. The lines of longshoremen carrying heavy loads up and down gangplanks and along the dock moved slowly. But I dodged all this and hurried on to the large warehouses for Marseille tiles. Near one of them a ship was being loaded.

There it was!

I recognized it even from a distance, its high hull with the familiar inscription in silver letters, *Pyotr Regger.*

I dashed up the gangplank, yellow red with tile dust, and found myself on the familiar deck. I sneaked down the ramp leading to the engine room. It was weirdly quiet down there. The engines were silent, the pistons were still. I ran down the steep steps to the seamen's quarters. The place was deserted. I was about to return to the deck when I heard Egor's voice from somewhere.

"Hey, Kolya, where are you off to?"

In a tiny cabin dimly lit by a kerosene lamp, Egor was working over the small parts of a disassembled machine. He didn't look as black as usual when at work, but his face had dark smears over it and his hands were covered with machine oil.

"How did you manage to get here?" he asked, putting aside his work. "How did you find your way to the ship?"

I didn't say anything for what seemed like quite a long time, then I explained haltingly:

"I came to ask you . . . Won't you please teach me how to play?"

"So that's it! You don't give up, do you? You know, there's a proverb: 'Learn before your young bones stiffen.' Well, let's go to it while the 'crocodile'—I mean the captain—is still out on the town. Let's have a little lesson."

Egor showed me how to work the keys of his accordion. He did this in a relaxed way. He picked out some chords, slowly drawing out each one, explaining patiently what he was doing. He had me sing the same chords. Then he offered me his seat, placed the heavy instrument on my knees and said:

"Now, my boy, go to it. Pick out some simple tune . . . Go on. Begin . . . 'Oh, the endless steppe . . .'"

Egor sang the tune in a low tenor voice, helping me pick out the melody. This was hard, almost impossible. I lost the rhythm, couldn't find the right keys, forgot to stretch the pleats, or, stretching them, failed to press the keys at the same time.

I was about to give up, but Egor wouldn't hear of it. "Go on, keep trying. Don't be easily discouraged."

After many attempts and failures, I finally succeeded in playing a few decent sounds and, to my delight, heard the beginning of the familiar song. I repeated the tune many times, and when Egor left for a few minutes, to go up to the deck to see if the machinist was coming, I began to sing to my own accompaniment. I was amazed at how good my voice sounded and how well it blended with the sounds of the accordion, and I kept repeating the refrain, "Oh, the e-en-nd-less steppe . . ."

Egor returned, and praised my progress. "You can't graft talent onto your skin if you weren't born with it," he said, "but anyone can see that you have some! As water is to a ship, you might say, talent is to a musician." His eyes shone, his white teeth glistened, a slightly wavy lock of hair fell across his forehead. He was handsome, despite the greasy black smears on his face, the worn rag around his neck, and the soiled sweatshirt he was wearing.

"Come, let me play something for you now, before we have to say good-bye. The crocodile will soon be back." He picked up the instrument carefully, sat down, and, as usual, lowered his head to the accordion. He played something very moving. He played it softly, as if only to himself. Then he stopped for a minute, and, without raising his head, sat there lost in thought. When he resumed his playing, the chords poured forth and the passionate music sounded like a huge chorus.

I thought Egor played beautifully and wondered how he had learned to play so well.

Once more Egor passed the accordion to me. With impatience I felt the keys, picked out another song—much faster than the first one—and began to sing. The melody came all at once, as if without my bidding, and my voice followed it freely.

I was happy and proud—my fingers were playing a real tune, they were making real music. Within a few minutes I had sung the entire song, and each time I played the refrain with greater assurance.

"Good boy, Kolya, well done!" Egor exclaimed. "Some day you'll amount to something, mark my word. You have, my young friend, the soul of a minstrel."

And pausing for a moment, he continued: "If someone will take an interest in you, you'll be a musician. But, my young friend, you'll have to study. Without studying, nothing will come of it. I know this from my own experience. As the saying goes: 'To avoid failure, start learning in your youth.'"

He stood up suddenly. "The crocodile is back, I hear his voice. Have to go now. Well, chum, you and I will not see each other so soon again. Tomorrow we sail with some tiles for Sochi, Pati, and Batum. Then we go to Mariopol, and only after that will we sail back here. If you'll write down your address, I'll drop by to see you when we dock here again."

Walking me to the pier, he said: "The accordion is all right, you can learn a bit on it. But it isn't for you. You should play the violin or even that . . . how do you call it? It's like a violin only about four times as large and it stands on the floor when it is played . . ."

"Do you mean the cello?"

"Yes, that's it, that's for you! I'd gladly play one myself. It sounds so good! But it isn't for the likes of me, lacking talent . . ."

I protested: "You'd play the cello better than anyone!"

"Kolya, my boy, you're a good kid!"

I insisted: "It's true, I mean it. If only you took lessons . . ."

Egor broke into a thunderous laugh: "If only I took what? And with whose money, if you please? The English king's, I suppose! What's more, I'm illiterate—went to primary school for three months, and that was the end of my education. After that I had to follow my dad to the city— to work. I read syllable by syllable and write with a child's scrawl." He kept laughing, then went on: "You flatter me. 'Take lessons,' you say. 'The bear would buy some honey if he had the money.' Talent is not enough, not when the pocket is empty."

Then Egor raised his hands and examined his fingers closely. They were discolored, coarse, and massive. "Such hooks are good for pulling barges, not for plucking cello strings."

I liked his proverbs and the way he chose his words. I could have listened to him some more, but I had to go.

Egor led me across the railroad tracks, and offered me his strong hand: "Well, good-bye, Kolya! In two weeks or so I'll come to see you, will bring you a treat. But don't forget

what I told you—for you, it's music. It's in your head, in
your heart, in your fingers."

Then he left, and I ran along the now familiar route to
the city, to my new home. And in my ears, without pause,
echoed Egor's encouraging words and rang the melody of the
song about the endless steppe . . .

4

MY FATHER WAS DISMISSED from his job soon after we settled in Odessa. Left without earnings, he could no longer pay the tuition for my older brother or for me. Both of us had to drop out of school.

But we did not loaf for long—we soon found jobs. My brother went to work for an export firm, Jacob Owen and Company, and I in the main office of the important newspaper, the *Odessa News*.

My brother's wages were five rubles a month, mine, three.

Each of us left home for work early in the morning and returned late in the evening.

I liked my job. I liked hurrying across town to the printer, counting off two hundred copies of the freshly printed newspaper and rushing back with them to the office, where the manager and some of the subscribers who came for their copies personally were waiting for me. The incessant running to the editorial room, or to the post office, or to the journalists' homes, and going on personal errands for the staff—I found it all very interesting. My duties gave me a legitimate excuse to roam the city nearly the entire day, and to ride on the horse-drawn trolley or on the bus, and even, whenever I had to deliver heavy bundles, in a cab. I enjoyed peering into the store windows, watching street incidents, and once in a while stopping at the bakery to buy myself a pastry for a few kopecks.

I liked to meet the people whose names were known all over town from the by-lines in the paper. Always having at my disposal the latest issue, I read not only the news but also the articles and columns. I knew the writers by their names and imagined them to be quite out of the ordinary, not resembling others at all. I met some of them in the flesh, and at times I even chatted with them. Occasionally I delivered their salaries to their homes or brought them books. I particularly liked the very tall and thin Andrei Krukovsky, with his massive turned-up nose and long limbs. He wrote literary pieces that I diligently read through several times, although I didn't quite understand them.

I treated the author of these challenging articles with awe, and I would look at him from the bottom up, tilting my head back to see all of his tall figure. I listened with pleasure to his youthful and bantering voice. Adapting himself with ease to my age, he talked to me simply and amiably.

"What are you finding so interesting in that paper?" he asked me with exaggerated surprise one day when he saw me reading the *Odessa News*. "What are you reading?"

"Your literary column," I answered, sounding more bold than I felt.

"Do you think it's any good?"

"Very good."

"I wrote the piece all by myself," he said, assuming a ridiculous air of importance and pointing proudly to his chest with his thumb. "All by myself! No one helped me. I'm pretty great! Others couldn't do as well! How old are you?" Krukovsky asked rather unexpectedly.

"I'll be fourteen soon."

"That's great! But why don't you attend school?"

He then asked many questions about my father and the family, and in the end advised me to go back to school without fail as soon as my father found work again.

Sometimes I took the journalist Sig's salary to him at the Hotel France. His room was always full of gray cigarette smoke that filled every part of it, obscuring the window and surrounding the lamp with a yellow halo.

There were small piles of cigarette butts all over his desk. It looked as if no one ever cleaned it. There were butts on the floor as well and on the window sills and chairs. There was an empty cigarette box on the bed and near it lay a chewed cardboard cigarette holder. There were ashes on everything, the tablecloth, quilt, pillow, and even on his coat that was hanging on the wall.

Without removing the cigarette from his mouth, Sig would ask me to run down and get him a hundred "Gypsies," his favorite smoke. He wrote on long narrow sheets of paper, taking a sip of cold dark tea from time to time, then he would resume his smoking and writing.

Sig was a man of medium height, dark, hairy, unshaven, and it seemed strange to me that from the pen of this gloomy and unkempt person and in this dreary, smoke-filled room, emerged such gay, witty articles. He had to write one day after day, without a break, without any rest. And when Sig was late with an assignment, a boy was sent to his room from the newspaper office and he was to remain there until the piece for that day's issue was done.

I was proudly aware that I was in personal contact with a famous journalist and that in my very presence were born works that, it seemed to me, were awaited by thousands of eager readers. But I was sorry for the smoke-soaked Sig, doomed to sit in that stuffy hotel room without sunshine and without fresh air, and to write, write, write.

No, the life of an author didn't appeal to me. It was far better to be a musician.

I kept thinking about music. I listened to it hungrily whenever I got the chance and believed that sooner or later I'd learn to play some good instrument, preferably, by far, the cello.

I waited impatiently for Gregory Mikhailovich to return. He was still traveling with his opera company. I kept hoping that he would not refuse to obtain an instrument for me and that he would agree to be my teacher. I planned to ask him. But there was no word from him, and no one knew when he would be back.

Nor was there any sign of Egor.

And while I was waiting for them to come to Odessa, the idea occurred to me to make the acquaintance of the music critic of our paper, Dr. Tsenovsky. Perhaps he would give me some good advice. I waited for the chance to meet him—after all, he would come to the office sometime, as every member of the staff did sooner or later. In the meantime I kept reading his articles about the opera, symphony concerts, and music schools. His writing was simple and clear.

I imagined the author of these articles to be very wise and, without doubt, also very kind. After all wasn't he a writer about music?

Finally came the day when I succeeded in meeting Dr. Tsenovsky. He was a man of more than medium height, vigorous and serene. He had a small dark beard, dark eyes, and thick eyebrows. He spoke softly and unhurriedly. Now and then his face lit up with a good-natured smile.

That day, as he was about to leave the building after calling for his salary at the cashier's window, I went up to him and said that I wanted to study music but that my father was unemployed and couldn't afford to buy me a cello—not even a violin—or to pay for lessons.

"But do you have a good ear for music? If it's as good as your complexion, then indeed you should take up music."

His remark about my complexion made me blush even harder.

He promised to have a talk with a friend of his who was a cellist and to let me know the result when we met again.

From that moment I lived with renewed hope. My goal now seemed to me quite near to realization. The prospect gave me wings, and I ran around town doing my errands with even greater enthusiasm. The newspaper office, the printer's shop, post office, harbor, railway depot, the errands for the newspaper staff, the numerous brief contacts with the many errand boys working for nearby offices, stores, and steamship companies—all of this I found very exciting. And I liked everything and everyone at my newspaper, the employees, the visitors, the whole atmosphere, especially the talk about papers, magazines, books, authors.

I disliked only one person, the office manager. He was a hard mean old man. His steely eyes stared piercingly through his gold-rimmed glasses. He was tall, slightly stooped, and he moved about briskly on his long legs, thin as stilts, and it seemed that he managed, in some way, to be present simultaneously in every part of the large establishment. Whenever he saw me, he would ask the same questions:

"Where've you been? Why were you gone so long? How come you hang around without doing something useful?"

All this was unwarranted. No one got around as fast as I, since I never walked but always ran. And I was never without some work, constantly carrying out someone's orders. I resented the injustice of his remarks.

"I wasn't gone long . . . I got there fast . . ." I'd say in self-defense.

His picking on one of the young clerks whom he obviously,

for some unknown reason, disliked, increased my bitterness toward the mean old man.

This clerk was a very pleasant youth with a pale face and gentle eyes. He and I had a good relationship. At noon he would usually give me some money and I'd run to the delicatessen store right near the office, in the arcade off Preobrazhenskaya Street. He always shared with me, in brotherly fashion, the ham, cucumbers, rolls, and pickled apples that I bought for him, and we'd lunch together. From time to time, he brought me books from home—most of them were from the Golden Library series—*Little Men, Lord Fauntleroy, Tom Sawyer, Huckleberry Finn.* Evidently he had many books. And once he gave me, as a gift, a book of poems that I had long dreamed of possessing.

I was convinced that Boris was a very good person, better than anyone else in our office. I therefore always felt like throwing something at the head of the old manager whenever he came over to the young clerk and shouted at him angrily:

"Again your report isn't ready! You good-for-nothing! You're a mama's boy! You're a jellyfish, not a worker! I don't need the likes of you! Get out!"

I couldn't understand how one could put up with such a humiliating scolding. Was it possible that when I grew up and someone dared yell like that at me, an adult, that I'd listen and keep silent? Not for anything!

Then something happened that unexpectedly brought to an end my employment in the office of the *Odessa News.* It was already evening. I had come running in the rain from the post office, carrying a bag full of letters and newspapers. My short, threadbare fall coat, made from my father's old one, was wringing wet, my torn shoes were full of water and made an unpleasant squishy sound with each step. Little cold streams ran down my neck from my rumpled wet cap.

I happened to bump into the manager as I came running in with the heavy bag.

"Where have you been so long?" he asked me rudely, staring at me with his piercing, evil eyes.

"I wasn't gone long at all," I replied.

"Don't you dare talk back to me!" he yelled. "What insolence!"

"But you asked me, so I answered."

He said no more, looked at me savagely, and walked away. But I continued to feel irritable from the disgusting sensation of cold dampness inside my torn shoes, and the unfair treatment from the old man—I felt very resentful and outraged. And when I descended the spiral staircase to the basement quarters where Boris worked and heard the shouting of the manager, I suddenly began to choke with indignation.

The old man was examining some papers. He flung them down on the table and picked them up again, looked at them through his nearsighted eyes and flung them down once more.

"You are a blockhead!" he shrieked. "You can do nothing right! You are an idler!"

Boris, dismayed, listened in silence. His face was very pale, his eyes had darkened, and the pencil shook in his hand.

Finally he permitted himself to say timidly: "I did everything as you told me to."

"I didn't tell you, I ordered you! But you didn't do it right and spoiled everything. You are a parasite, you are an idiot!"

I could no longer control myself.

"You're an idiot yourself!" I cried out before I knew what I was doing. "You're an old parasite yourself, a blockhead, a mean old sorcerer!"

I even ran over to him to strike him, but he caught my arms and held them with such force that I cried out in pain. I tried to hit him with my leg, but he held me off and, startled, hissed with fright:

"What? What is this? Are you out of your mind? You've gone mad!"

"You mean sorcerer, sorcerer, sorcerer!" I repeated in my rage, "I'll kill you, kill you!"

Someone caught me from behind, carried me upstairs, and threw me out into the street. My coat and cap were sent flying after me.

It was dark and cold outside. There was a drizzling rain. My feet were soaking wet, and I felt a dull pain in my chest.

I had far to go before reaching home. I had to cross the huge, gloomy and muddy Old Sennaya Square, and this seemed harder now than usual.

What was I going to tell them at home? They were expecting me to bring my first month's wages today—three rubles.

At that moment I felt that I was no longer a youngster, that all at once I had become a grown-up, that life was full of injustices, and that it had just placed a heavy load on my inexperienced shoulders.

But, of course, I was far from grown-up. I walked along the hushed, dark, quiet streets feeling wronged, insulted, lonely, and my throat was choked with misery, the tears flowed freely down my cheeks.

5

Months passed and my father was still without work. The family lived in poverty and subsisted on the help provided by two brothers.

My mother explained to us children that our father was a sort of helpless person: he was a conscientious and capable worker, performed his duties on the job diligently, but as soon as he lost his employment he at once lost his spirit. He didn't know where to turn or to whom to offer his services. Extremely self-conscious, modest, and, also perhaps, proud, he was unable, as others did, to go from office to office, from store to store, and from bank to bank, asking for work. Knowing bookkeeping well and how to run an office, and understanding commerce, he could even be a manager of a warehouse of building materials—after all, he had been, for several years, in charge of the Mariopol division of the Russian distributors of Marseille tiles. A gentle and sensitive man, he got along very well with people. But all these qualifications, it seemed, no one needed, and my father remained without a job. His brothers, engaged in similar occupations as he, but more energetic and worldly men, would from time to time find a job for him, and then he would work industriously and devotedly.

But the same story would repeat itself. Having lost his

job several months ago, my father left the house daily, in the morning, and went off somewhere, evidently to see some acquaintances who had promised to be on the lookout for work for him; then he dropped in at his brothers'. On the way he picked up some books and returned home by noon. Stretching out on the living-room couch, or leaning over the table supporting himself on his elbows, he read for hours on end, unable to tear himself away from his book, and reading on and on with great avidity. He read with incredible speed. And whenever he no longer had new books to read, he would drag out some old ones that had been read to shreds; in some of the tattered books the beginning and the end were missing.

"That's enough!" my mother pleaded, "you'd do better to go down to the docks to see about work."

"In a moment, in a moment," he promised, without interrupting his reading.

Father had large gray—no, rather, faded blue—eyes, a trimmed brownish goatee beard, a tobacco-stained mustache, hollow cheeks, and nice, though noticeably thinning, slightly wavy hair. He had an uncommonly mild look about him, and his face had a kindly and melancholy expression. He submissively did as my mother asked and would go off somewhere to offer his services, with reserve. And somewhat relieved that no one, thank God, needed them, he would return home.

Chekhov was the Russian author Father admired most. He always spoke of him with awe not only to adults but also to us children. And when of an evening he would read to us his most loved Chekhov stories, he would be as pleased and proud as though they were his own creations. It was on evenings such as these that I heard for the first time "The Boys," "The Noncommissioned Officer Prishibeev," "The Flatfish," and excerpts from "The Steppe." And when Father

read to us "Oysters" and "Grief," I myself fell in love
with Chekhov, and within a short time devoured volumes
of his short stories.

I was also fascinated by everything my father so en-
thusiastically told us about the author himself—about his
purity of heart, his outstanding humaneness and compassion.
I also liked Chekhov's picture, his gentle eyes, soft damp-
looking hair with the one curl carelessly falling to the left
side of his forehead, his clipped beard, and his pince-nez
with its double black cord. The fact that Chekhov had the
same pleasant and quiet look as my father, whom I loved
very much, that their little beards and mustaches looked almost identical, that they wore nearly similar stand-up starched
collars with pointed ends, narrow bow ties, and even the same
striped suits—all this made the author near and dear to me,
as if I knew him personally.

I began to work again, and spent from twelve to fourteen
hours a day on the job. The office where I was now employed
did not resemble in any way the one where I had found
my first job. There were no newspapers or magazines here,
or the tumult of the editorial room, all of which I had liked
so much.

This company called itself the Southern Commercial
Agency. It did business with hundreds of firms all over the
country. It bought produce and goods from trading centers
in the Caucasus and in the Crimea and dispatched them
to the central provinces of Russia, to the Urals, and to
Siberia. The merchandise arrived in ships, was unloaded on
the docks, transferred to freight trains, and transported by
rail to the interior. I learned the ins-and-outs of the business
fast, and soon personally handled the transfer of large ship-
ments of Brazilian coffee, coconuts, and pistachio nuts. I
purchased for my firm many crates of figs, dates, Málaga

wine, prunes, dried apricots, raisins, barrels of herring, Caucasian salted cheese, olive oil, and wine.

Although I was now in my fourteenth year, my monthly wages were only five rubles, despite the fact that I was doing the work of an adult expediter. Nevertheless, I was very proud of the importance of my job, and worked with great enthusiasm. I got much satisfaction from presenting all kinds of shipping documents at the transport agencies, weighing in the merchandise, bargaining with the drivers, and accounting to our bookkeeper.

My bosses were shrewd men—they knew that bright boys could easily be trained to do any work with dispatch and to carry out instructions efficiently; that they worked eagerly and expeditiously and, usually, for five, seven, or ten rubles a month a boy accomplished no less, and at times even more, than an adult assistant or expediter did for a monthly wage of thirty or forty rubles. For this reason there were boys like me working for all the offices, stores, warehouses, banks, and steamship companies throughout the city.

The boys liked their exciting jobs—running errands on foot and in carriages, going to the docks, to the railroad depots, on board the ships, and they liked the constant dealings with adults.

Just the same, I didn't experience a full measure of satisfaction. I felt a nagging desire to read, to finish at least the one book that I constantly carried around folded in my pocket, in the hope that I could snatch a few free moments in the day to enjoy it. I grieved even more from the constant awareness that the days were passing and I wasn't making any headway in music. I had neither the time, nor an instrument, nor a teacher. My hopes for the future had waned.

Only in the rare moments of leisure did I manage to read a little and, even more rarely, to listen to music. At ten or eleven o'clock at night, free finally from work, I would run across the whole city to the Aleksandrovsky Park. There I would wriggle my way through the crowd to get closer to the stand, whose ceiling resembled a gigantic shell, and listen to the large symphony orchestra.

I loved to listen to the "William Tell Overture." I liked the quiet opening chords played by the cellos, the sounds of the violins, and the high notes of the flute. My imagination painted sunny green meadows in the hills, or a peaceful morning on a calm lake. I had once seen *William Tell* on the stage and knew the story. I now imagined William himself, hunting, and his son with him, a red-cheeked little boy with an apple on his head. And the father was being ordered by the cruel land overseer to aim his arrow at the apple.

The serene music gradually changed to one full of foreboding. You could hear the wind, the rising waves, the rush of the downpour, the clap of thunder, and the roar of the storm breaking over lakes and mountains. I listened, seeing it all vividly, and was transported by the frightful majesty of the scene, depicted with such force by the simple and familiar instruments. Gazing at the conductor leading the orchestra with such authority, I vowed for the hundredth, for the thousandth time, that no matter what, I was going to study music and would become at least a cellist.

The symphony concerts in the park would end at midnight. I would then start on my way home, feeling cheated that I had heard only a small part of the program. I had very far to go, but I hardly noticed the distance—I kept hearing the music, and the opening passages of the cellos repeated themselves endlessly, to my great delight. I hummed the melody and even "conducted" as I walked, waving my arms with abandon. Luckily it was dark in the streets at night.

6

A GREAT DEAL OF MY WORK for the Southern Commercial Agency had to be done on the waterfront. The docks were in a constant uproar of activity. Life was never at a standstill there. The sounds of the various steam whistles were mingled with the squealing of the loading cranes. Swinging in the air and clanging their chains, the cranes filled and emptied the huge ocean-going ships. Their holds, deep and dark as catacombs, were constantly changing cargo. Into the bottomless pits of the foreign ships poured endless streams of golden wheat, corn, and barley from freight trains, and some were loaded with alcohol, sugar, and wool. Up and down the numerous gangplanks moved crowds of passengers of every nationality, occupation, and age.

All this fed my imagination. I would hear foreign speech and would be transported by it to some distant land, trying to picture the African, Australian, or South American forests—familiar to me from books—with their tall, broad-leafed coconut, banana, and "pineapple" palm trees. I wandered either among black-skinned Negroes or handsome and stately Hindus, or found myself among tattooed and painted Indians wearing feathers in their hair and with ivory rings hanging from their noses and lips. The Indians danced and hopped to the beat of tom-toms.

In my imaginary wanderings I saw the fantastic scenes at the seaports of the whole world—Shanghai and San Francisco, and Constantinople and London, Marseille and Naples. And in each place my boyish daydreaming brought me into contact with music. I saw myself not as an ordinary traveler but as a famous musician sailing across seas and oceans to move the hearts of men with my art.

But my wild fantasies would soon be mercilessly shattered against reality. Again there would arise the pitiless old quandaries about how to obtain an instrument, an instructor, and the time for studying. For the hundredth time I examined all my resources and all possibilities. This did not take long. There was still no sign of Gregory Mikhailovich. Egor seemed to have disappeared into the sea. As of old, Father had no money to spare. Although he was now working by the day, there was hardly enough for bread. I couldn't ask my uncles for help, as it was they were always called upon to aid the family to survive.

But I felt I must do something! Find a way! I decided one day to stay away from work for an hour or so and go visit Dr. Tsenovsky in order to ask him to get me into a music school. He had promised to help. Maybe once I enrolled in a school they would also give me a cello. And perhaps they would allow me to study at night. Maybe it would all somehow be free?

Dr. Tsenovsky lifted the lid of his piano and pressed down some of the keys, one at a time. I sang the notes he played, and he seemed pleased. Moving the piano stool into place, Tsenovsky seated himself, played a whole musical phrase and asked me to repeat it, vocally. When I did this, he said:

"Good boy! That was perfect. And what tunes do you know?"

"All kinds."

"All right, for example?"

I was not sure that the doctor would care for the ones I knew and kept an embarrassed silence.

"Do you ever listen to the singing on the boulevards?"

"Yes."

"Do you know 'Autumn Song'?"

"Yes, I know it."

"O.K., sing it."

I sang. He smiled at me approvingly and said:

"Very good . . . I'll have a talk with Kaufman, the director of the music school, and you go and see him Wednesday."

And Wednesday the director and I had the following conversation:

"What instrument do you play?"

"So far . . . none . . ."

"How's that? Then what for did you come here?"

"To study."

"To study what?"

"How to play the cello."

"But where is your cello?"

I was at a loss to know how to answer him. Was it possible that he didn't understand that my need of an instrument was exactly what had brought me to him.

"Where is your cello?" Kaufman asked again, with noticeable annoyance.

"I thought . . . that . . . in your school . . . there is . . ."

"It doesn't matter what there is in my school! You have to have your own instrument."

Then, giving the matter a moment's thought, he asked, looking at me quizzically:

"And the tuition you'll have to pay here—do you know the amount?"

"No."

"Twelve rubles a month, payable six months in advance."

I stood there, petrified and wordless.

He waited for my reaction.

I continued to stand in silence.

"So," he summarized, "tell your father to bring twenty-five rubles for a cello and seventy-two for a half year's tuition in advance. Then you may start your studies. All right?" These last two words he uttered a bit more gently.

"All right . . ." I replied, ". . . I'll tell my father," and I left.

Not knowing what to do next, I hung around for a long time outside, at the school's entrance. The fantastic sums mentioned by Kaufman depressed me. A hundred rubles! I thought—why my father didn't even earn this sum in three months! And I had been so sure that they would accept me at the school. Now, suddenly . . . What could Dr. Tsenovsky possibly have said to Kaufman? What had he asked him to do for me?

I had no desire to return to the office of the Southern Commercial Agency, or to the waterfront.

That's the end of music for me! The fateful thought filled my whole mind—that's the end of music for me!

I turned my steps reluctantly toward the office.

When I passed a store of musical instruments on the way, I stopped to examine the display of pianos, violins, flutes, accordions, guitars, and mandolins. I was, of course, especially taken with the cello. It was exactly the kind I could have used—a three-quarter size. I had noticed and admired it in the window before and had chosen it for myself. In my imagination I was already holding it in my hands, tuning it, and playing it. A price tag hung from the scroll of the cello, and I knew only too well that it would never belong to me. Today I understood this particularly well. I kept looking at the cello with the gloom of hopelessness. Tearing myself away with an effort, I continued on my way.

A burning sense of outrage welled up in me. As on that

day when I was thrown out bodily from the building of the
Odessa News, I now walked the streets, this time sunny and
noisy, feeling wronged and lonely, and the familiar lump rose
in my throat, and tears dimmed my vision.

I wanted to tell someone very wise and kind how exasperating and unfair my circumstances were. But to whom could I
tell it? To my father? No. He had gotten used to things as
they were and seemed indifferent to everything but books. I
had had a talk with Krukovsky, but all he offered was the
wise council: study! I had turned to Dr. Tsenovsky, but he
had not even been able to make himself clear to the director
of the music school, Kaufman.

No, all this had been useless! But to whom could I turn
now? Then, suddenly, the wonderful idea hit me: to Chekhov!
It was he who was the most wise, the kindest, the most
understanding. Yes, he understood absolutely everything! How
wonderful were his stories about children—about boys, about
girls, as though every one of them had opened his heart to
him.

Yes, but Chekhov lived far away. Father had told us that
he lived in Yalta. It was impossible to go to him. Perhaps
I should write him?

Having hit upon this idea, I calmed down and hurried on
to the office. But there a new disappointment awaited me.

"Where have you been?" the senior expediter asked angrily.
He was a short man, his face was narrow, his very large ears
stuck out, and he had a remarkable resemblance to a cat.

"Where have you been hanging around?" he flew at me.

"I had some business to attend to."

"What kind of business?"

"Personal."

"How's that . . . what do you mean personal?" He was
horrified. "On working time? You attend to personal business
on working time?"

"I had to."

"Why did you have to?"

He repeated this question several times, but I refused to tell him the facts. I considered it degrading to talk to one like him about music.

The manager appeared on the scene. Trusting his sense of justice, I told him the truth. But this truth upset him terribly. His full, ruddy face became purple-red. He screamed at the top of his voice:

"You receive a salary here, and you go to study music there?"

"I was only hoping to study, but . . ."

"On working time?"

"I work from seven in the morning to ten at night . . ."

"Oh, so you're a socialist! You count the hours!" He exploded like one set on fire. "Are you an anarchist, a progressivist? You argue like those bums, the revolutionaries! Get out of here! Out! Out!"

All of him swelled with indignation and he seemed about to burst.

"Get out of here! Out! Out! Out!"

He stamped his feet with rage, and his potbelly shook.

Like a pig in a poke, I thought to myself. Unexpectedly I felt like laughing. The wild scene seemed to me strangely amusing, the mad rage and, above all, the stupid tangle of thoughts in that large and foolish head of the manager. Without intending to, I found myself taking the same pose, and I began, like him, to stamp my feet, and, trying to mock him with an exact imitation, I shouted:

"You're an anarchist, you're a socialist, you're a progressivist! Bow-wow-wow!"

I mimicked him so faithfully that the manager, somewhat uneasy, began to retreat to his office, begging the employees:

"Take him away, take him away! You can see he's mad, he's gone mad, he'll bite me!"

But the employees didn't touch me. I stopped the act and, realizing that all was lost, said calmly:

"I'm not a mad dog, I merely imitated him." And lifting my cap, I bowed with a theatrical flourish to the astounded employees and quickly left.

7

 AGAIN I WAS ON MY OWN from morning till dark. I'd find my way to a quiet alley in the public park and spend long hours there lost in my fancies or in Chekhov's stories, or Tolstoy's *The Cossacks*. Or, idling along the waterfront, I'd approach some seamen and inquire about the *Pyotr Regger*, hoping to learn something of Egor's whereabouts. But my chief occupation was the building of castles in the air, to which I surrendered myself with my former zeal.

Seated on an iron kevel for fastening the heavy lines of a ship, or on a coil of heavy rope, I observed the colorful life on the docks, as I daydreamed for hours on my favorite themes of sea-roaming and music. But more and more often the scenes taking place around me interrupted my imaginary journeys. I sat gazing one day at a large ocean-going ship. I saw myself on its deck, the ship bearing me to a faraway land. And at the very moment when I stepped onto the unfamiliar shore, I, a renowned musician, and was surrounded by a crowd of admirers, at a short distance from where I was sitting a scene, not at all imaginary but quite real, was taking place. A dock policeman was hitting a drunken tramp on the head with the sheath of his sword, attempting to sober him up that way.

The tramp, a husky, barrel-chested, broad-shouldered fellow

in blue seaman's trousers full of holes and a torn shirt open
at the neck, kept waving away the blows as though they were
a tiresome fly.

"The devil take you . . ." he muttered in a low bass voice
through his drunken drowsiness, then he turned over lazily
on the dusty ground and fell asleep again.

The policeman, also large, and tough, kept hitting the
sleeper on the head, and after a while began to pull the
man's swollen ear with his rough, heavy fingers. Moving his
woolly mustache fiercely, he kept shouting:

"I'll wake you yet, you'll get up for me . . . I'll shake you
up . . . you . . ." and he continued to pull at the drunken
man's ear, to beat him over the head. Then he dug the tip
of his boot into the sleeping giant's back. But the tramp
only squirmed, drew up his knees to his stomach, and kept
muttering:

"What's eating you? . . . Leave me in peace . . . Get away,
you pestering Satan . . ."

I meant to get away from there as fast as I could, but
when I heard the piercing whistle of the policeman and saw
people come running from all sides, I remained to see what
would happen. It seemed that the policeman was as good
as his word, for he finally managed to get the drunkard on his
feet. Springing up, the tramp socked the policeman in his
ribs so hard that he flew sideways, fell against a pile of
wood, and lay there with his face bleeding.

The giant stood there, stretched to his full, immense height
—heavy, broad, with a large shaggy head, and bare, almost
black sunburned chest. He stood still, his fists on the ready,
as if he were waiting for his opponent to respond with an
answering blow. But the policeman was now obviously far
from this intention. Bloody and disheveled, he clung to the
woodpile and kept blowing his whistle frantically. No one,

however, came to his aid. The tramp then lowered his arms and said good-naturedly:

"Why do you carry on like this, you fool? What'll you gain from it?"

The policeman continued to blow his whistle.

"Give up, why don't you?" the tramp tried to persuade him. "I won't touch you. Who needs you? . . . Go back where you came from."

The tramp's round face had the brightness of youth, his large nose tilted innocently upward, and his soft lips seemed about to stretch into a friendly smile. His bloodshot, drunken, and bleary eyes, which had lost their color, were fixed on the policeman.

"Beat it!" he insisted, irritation mounting in him.

Now in a rage, he raised his fists again. "Beat it!" he roared, re-enforcing his order with strange sailor's curses. "Get going, or I'll knock your block off!"

The policeman reached for his holster, but the tramp instantly dealt him such a blow that he doubled over and helplessly dropped his arm.

"Now, will you go?" the tramp asked the policeman almost in a whisper, bending over him and gazing into his eyes.

Without answering, the policeman, stooping and holding his painful right hand with his left one, quickly skirted the woodpile and scurried off.

"Hey, there, Alesha," a Tatar longshoreman called to the tramp. "Now it won't be safe for you to hang around here any more. Hey? Don't you think so?"

"The devil with him," Alesha answered simply, "I'll leave for Kherson."

"Kherson, Nikolaev, Ochakov," the Tatar listed the cities like a teacher, "they're all near here, too near—you can reach them with a finger. Any dog can smell you out in Kherson.

You've got to get away to the Caucasus, to the Volga, the Kama . . . You mustn't remain near here. Do you hear?"

"So what?" Alesha said with even greater indifference. "If it has to be the Caucasus, let it be the Caucasus, if it's the Volga, so it's the Volga. It's all the same—it's all Russia. As long as you have your native soil under your feet and your own sky over your head . . . Trouble on my hands I'll always find—there's always trouble for my kind . . ."

"You'd better go now," the practical Tatar urged him, "go in that direction . . . Hurry . . ."

"Let me shake your paw," Alesha said, moved by the man's concern, "and here is mine."

He smacked hard the toil-hardened palm of the Tatar, patted him affectionately on the back, and walked off in the opposite direction from the one taken by the policeman.

The Tatar's eyes followed his huge frame; he looked around for signs of danger, and kept urging him on loudly:

"Go faster!"

"That's all right!" Alesha called back. "Don't worry! I'll get away."

Climbing into a swiftly moving empty cab, the tramp quickly disappeared from sight at a nearby turn in the street.

Somehow Alesha reminded me of Egor—I didn't know why—maybe it was his simplicity, his good-natured smile. Maybe it was the same casual but common-sense attitude toward life: "If it has to be the Caucasus, let it be the Caucasus, if it's the Volga, so it's the Volga. It's all the same—it's all Russia!" I kept thinking about Egor and Alesha and didn't realize that I was walking toward the coal docks.

As always, when I found myself here, I was fascinated by the sight of the coal stevedores. Along the steep gangplanks, they descended with their loads, one behind the other. They were half-naked, wearing only tattered trousers cut off at the knees, which stuck to their perspiring bodies. The men looked like Negroes—they had the same dark brown bodies, the same faces in which, like in the illustrations in *Uncle Tom's Cabin*, the whites of their eyes stood out sharply and their white teeth gleamed. On their left shoulders, supported by the right arm, rested, as though riveted to their flesh, heavy baskets of coal.

The sun beat down pitilessly on their tanned skins, making the sweat stream down their faces and chests, down their caved-in stomachs and bent backs. The coal dust hung in the air and settled into the pores of their overheated bodies, into their eyes, their mouths, and when the men spat, their spittle was thick and black, as through they had swallowed soot or tar and had drunk it down with ink. The file of black men with the baskets on their shoulders moved endlessly—up and down, up and down, from five in the morning till seven in the evening, with a short break for a meal.

Other ships, anchored nearby, were being loaded with huge, bulky crates, unwieldy bales, L-beams and rails, two-hundred-pound sacks of sugar, slaughtered pigs, tin, brass, steel posts— and all this was being carried onto the ships on the backs and shoulders of human beings bent double under their burdens and bathed in sweat. The stevedores' muscles looked like springs, like taut, heavy springs, the calves of their legs bulged under the strain, looking bloated and as if about to burst, and their veined necks were tensed with blood, the tight skin looking as though it was about to break under the pressure of the load. And they labored this way twelve or fourteen hours a day, going up and down the very steep and long gangplanks until the vessels lay low in the water with their freight.

Not far away, in the shade of the large warehouses on the Tiamozhnaya Square, near the booths of the shipping agencies, ragged, barefoot, unshaven, and emaciated men sat, lay, or leaned against wooden stockades. People would refer to them with contempt as "the tramps," and even more bluntly as "the savages." They were merely the unemployed. They hung around for days, waiting for the arrival of ships to be loaded or unloaded, and roamed the length and breadth of the harbor that stretched for several miles, looking for work. Weakened by hunger, they became quickly exhausted when they chanced to get a job. Then they would be cruelly chased away, and again they would remain without food or shelter. There were no free lodgings for them near the docks or in the city.

That day there were many of them lying around on the cobblestones near piles of tile, patiently waiting for a freight ship from Marseille. Some of them had their eyes glued to the blue line of the horizon—watching for the appearance of the dark dot of a ship. Others sat around listlessly, with their eyes staring hopelessly at the ground. Still others, stretched out on the pavement, lay sleeping, their unkempt heads resting on their large, rough fists.

A crowd of unemployed dockers had gathered near a makeshift little office where stevedores were being hired. Only forty men were needed for the job and almost all of them had already been picked. The rest—there were no less than a hundred of them—were wearily shifting from one leg to the other, damning everything on earth and cursing roundly, and they did not disperse only because they had nowhere to go.

"We don't need anyone else," the hiring agent cried, standing on the doorsill of the shack, "we've hired all we need."

"May you be damned, you accursed one!" said a no-longer young, wrinkle-faced, bony man, flinging his old, crumpled, torn seaman's cap to the ground. He was still wearing the gray striped vest of a seaman. He was evidently an aging stoker or machinist who had been fired from his job.

"What can a man do, hey? Where can he turn?" the man said bitterly.

"That's how it is," said another with quiet despondency.

He too was shaggy, with graying hair and beard, a squat, short man, probably very strong at one time but now a defeated person with gray, resigned eyes that had become used to everything. "I'd spit at it all . . . but my mouth is too dry from hunger."

A little to the side of this group stood a youth from the countryside, about eighteen, with a sun-bleached mop of blond hair and a peeling sunburned face. He stood gazing about him with a perplexed and forlorn look, and his innocent eyes seemed to ask: "How can this be? They'd told me in the village that things were good in the city . . . that there was as much work as one could want . . . and now . . . what can all this mean?"

Entering the passengers' dock, I saw a large steamboat of the Russian Steamship and Trade Company. There was an uninterrupted flow of passengers and their porters laden on all sides with suitcases and boxes. They were ascending the wide gangplank to the deck. The blackboard on shore, placed near the ship, was inscribed: "The S.S. *Yalta*, on its Crimea-Caucasus route, with stops at Evpatoria, Sevastopol, Yalta, Sudak, Feodosia . . ." Before I finished reading the list of places in the Crimea and the Caucasus, someone's loud voice made me turn around. Very near to where I was standing, a crowd of people were watching a strange sight with amused curiosity. One behind the other, three camels were lumbering down the gangway.

"Could God have created such monstrosities?" one of the spectators said.

The face of the speaker seemed very familiar to me. Then I recognized him in an instant, but I didn't believe my eyes. It couldn't be! It just couldn't be!

Nevertheless it was he—exactly the same as I had always imagined him and the way he appeared on numerous pictures —the pleasant face with the rather sparse little beard, the gentle look, the tiny wrinkles around his eyes, the severe pince-nez with its double black cord.

Yes, yes, it was Chekhov!

Astounded, delighted, I couldn't turn my eyes from his face, his tall figure in its long black coat, his soft black hat.

"Just look," he was saying to his companions in a low, very modulated voice, laughing good-naturedly, causing the wrinkles to spread out from the corners of his eyes like tiny rays, while his pince-nez shook gently, "Yes, these are real freaks of nature. Only monkeys are more grotesque." His manner of speech was uncommonly friendly, simple, the way very kind people talk to little children whom they love very much.

I was spellbound and didn't know what to think—why was Chekhov here? How did he get here? What was he going to do next? I began to surmise vaguely that he, as many others who were on their way from the north to the Crimea, had arrived from St. Petersburg or Moscow on the railroad, and from here would go on to Yalta by sea.

I was examining him with such unconcealed interest and so insistently that he finally noticed it.

"My dear young man, why do you look at me that way?" he asked pleasantly, and my heart was moved by the friendliness in his gray eyes, by his deep gentle voice, and by the novelty of the words "young man" and the formal "you" addressed to me for the first time in my life.

Embarrassed, I remained silent for a long time, then I blurted out:

"I know you."

"You don't say!" He pretended to be extremely surprised. "How do you know me?"

"From your pictures."

"Where did you see them?"

"In books."

"So, that's it. And where do you obtain those books?"

"At home. From my father."

"Tell me, I beg you, which of my works have you read?"

"'Oysters,' 'The Boys,' 'The Cook's Wedding.'"

Chekhov smiled. Evidently I was blushing deeply for, turning to his acquaintances, he said in a whisper:

"What an enviable complexion!" Then, turning to me again, he asked: "I suppose you don't smoke?"

I felt the blood rush to my face, probably making me redder than ever.

"No."

"You're probably fond of chocolate. You love it, isn't that true?" he insisted. "Confess!"

"Yes, I do."

"Well, here is some. Eat it in good health."

He reached for a bar of chocolate in his carpetbag and offered it to me. I was paralyzed with self-consciousness and stood there like a block of wood, without even thanking him.

"Here, take it, take it," he urged me gently. "I warn you, I'm the sort that changes his mind, I may keep it."

"Thank you," I mumbled indistinctly, and accepted the chocolate.

"Just look at his color!" he gushed, and was about to pinch my cheek fondly but changed his mind, resisting the temptation.

"And how about Mayne Read and Jules Verne? Have you read them?" he asked, smiling.

"Yes, I have."

"And would you like to run away to America?"

"Yes, I would," I pretended.

"Is that why you hang around where there are ships?"

"Yes, that's why."

"That's right, one can see that. It's quite obvious. And what is your name?"

"Montezuma Hawk-Claw," I answered, daring to pass myself off in jest as one of the characters in his story "The Boys."

"So, that's the kind of fellow you are!" The author laughed with amusement. "And what about a traveling companion— do you have one?"

"Yes, I have."

"And what's his name?"

" 'Paleface—my palefaced brother . . .' "

Suddenly we were deafened by repeated blasts of the steam whistle, and someone said:

"We must go aboard now."

Chekhov coughed softly, turned away covering his mouth with a folded handkerchief, and didn't speak for a while.

"Come, Anton Pavlovich," one of his fellow travelers urged him. "The second whistle will blow soon."

"Well, good-bye, much esteemed Montezuma," Chekhov said quite simply, and, as though we were very good acquaintances, offered me his hand.

I transferred the piece of chocolate quickly to my left hand and with my right I lightly squeezed the long thin fingers of the author.

"To read Jules Verne is very useful," he said to me, "but you shouldn't run away to America. It's always better at home. Here you have your father and mother. Do you love your father and mother?"

"Yes."

"There, you see! But in America there's no father or mother. At home it is quite better." And then he suddenly asked: "Do you go to school?"

"No."

"Why not?"

I explained the situation in a few words. Looking at me closely, he said with seriousness, as to a grown-up, and, at the same time, in a specially friendly way, as to a child:

"That's a shame . . . But, what can you do? It means that you should turn to learning a trade . . . or get work in an office or a store . . . get training in some sort of occupation. And in the evening you should study, read . . ."

The words then began to flow about my desire to study music and about . . . but then all sounds were drowned in the loudness of the second steam whistle, and Chekhov, taking leave of those who had come to see him off, turned to me once more:

"Don't lose hope, my dear young man. Go after what you want. You'll succeed."

He waved his pale hand in parting, walked slowly up the long gangplank onto the deck and stopped at the railing.

Soon the steam whistle sounded for the third time. Noisily parting the waters, the ship cast off. Then it gradually turned its prow away from the shore, slowly bringing into view its wide, high, and ample stern, and I noticed that Anton Pavlovich was moving along the railing as the ship was turning, so as to continue to face the wharf. Stopping midway, Chekhov removed his hat and waved it. But I couldn't be sure to whom. Some people on the quay responded as I looked enviously for some sign that Chekhov was waving specifically to me and not to them, or at least not only to them. I ran quickly to the side hoping to see him better. I noticed that the author, turning in my direction, put his hat back on his head and waved his hand.

That *was* for me! Only for me! Now I was quite sure! There was no doubt whatsoever! I was ecstatic. I felt an uncontrollable urge to tell everyone about my meeting with Chekhov. I wanted to get home immediately to share the great event with my father. But I didn't want to lose sight of the great man, of the ship on which he was standing, right there in the middle of its stern.

All at once a sadness came over me. The ship was in full

pace soon. It began to grow smaller and smaller. The figure of Anton Pavlovich merged with the others and I could only surmise where he was at that moment. And I could only pretend that I could still distinguish him from the other passengers. Actually I no longer saw him. The ship was nearing the end of the breakwater and it soon disappeared behind the tall, white lighthouse.

8

SOMEHOW TO OBTAIN A CELLO, I thought up all kinds of cunning plans. I offered my services as an errand boy at a musical instruments store. But the manager—a stout, purple-cheeked German—said to me in broken Russian, "We only German boys hire. Russian boys are sloppish boys."

I hated to leave that store. There was everything there that anyone could possibly need for sharpening his ear—small, gentle violins, singing cellos, dignified bass viols, dainty flutes, sleek black clarinets with their shiny metal keys, oboes, bassoons, all kinds of brass and wind instruments. There were guitars, mandolins, balalaikas, and even hand organs made by the famous firm of Nechada. The salesmen were playing various instruments to demonstrate them, customers were trying them out, and sounds in a variety of tones and pitches came from everywhere. A medley of melodies blended into a continuous cacophony, straining the ear, but, at the same time, it was somehow pleasant to listen to. I hated to go away empty-handed from this vast storehouse of music, and I tried desperately to persuade the horrid German that I was a "neat" boy.

"I'm smart," I assured him, recalling the praise with which my former employers had spoken of me. "I can do anything! You'll see!"

"No, Russian peoples we need not," the German repeated. "We only Germans need."

And when I was about to leave, as final proof that he couldn't possibly take on a Russian boy, or perhaps on purpose, to insult me, he added, "Russian person—loafer."

I flared up. A burning indignation took possession of me. I thought about my father, about Egor, about all my unfortunate friends, and I felt an uncontrollable resentment.

"You're a loafer yourself," I said, looking him straight in the eye, and with a voice that sounded not like my own, "You're a loafer yourself, you sausage!"

And turning from him, I ran out of the store.

Toward evening I went to the shop of the Czech Palechek who repaired string instruments. The old man's mouth was twisted as a result of some illness, his eyes were teary, his gray mustache yellowed at the lips from tobacco, and his little beard tapered to a sharp point. He was tall and very stooped. He spoke in a friendly way and sincerely offered me a seat. When he found out what made me so anxious to find work in a music store, he removed his chewed cigar from his mouth, patted me on the head with his discolored roughened fingers smelling of tobacco and glue, and said:

"Come back in two or three weeks and I'll give you a cello and teach you myself."

Despite his ugly, twisted face, his swollen eyelids, there was something appealing in the old man's appearance. He was especially nice when he spoke or smiled—he had a soft old-man's voice that had a pleasant warmth in it, and he was friendliness itself. I left feeling comforted and full of hope.

But ten days later I found the door and shutters of his workshop locked. On the heavy iron lock hung a square piece of cardboard on which was written: "Because of the illness of the proprietor, the shop will be closed for an indefinite time."

I continued to apply at offices, stores, and warehouses for

work as an errand boy, and evenings I looked around for a chance to listen to music.

I discovered that the School of the Russian Music Society had an orchestra class. Its instructor was the Czech clarinetist, Kuteel. Posing as a student, I sometimes managed to get into the auditorium, where I watched with secret envy the boys and girls sitting at the wooden stands awaiting the cue from the conductor to begin. Kuteel, in his teacher's uniform with gilded buttons, would tap his baton against his stand, raise it, wait until there was complete silence, and, finally, wave his arm. At that moment the boys and girls individually became unnoticeable and a large symphony orchestra appeared instead, the same kind as played in the civic theater or under the white shell in the Aleksandrovsky Park. For me this was not a group of students but a real symphony orchestra, and I listened to it not only with delight but with genuine respect for the musicians. I experienced envy and regret that I wasn't one of them, that I was on the wrong side of the platform, and not a performer but a listener. The free-flowing melody seemed to mount ever higher, as up a steep stairway, and, having reached the summit, it started its descent to the very lowest step—then it began its climb again. It all sounded wonderful.

Kuteel would often stop the orchestra to point out errors, would ask different sections and even individual players to repeat this or that passage. Then he would tap impatiently, giving the signal once more for the orchestra to start from the beginning. I found all this extremely fascinating.

I was not always alone in my musical adventures. Anka was frequently with me. As her good-natured mother often put it, we "hung around music" together. Anka was the same age as I, and my neighbor. Her father was an educator —the director of a secondary school—and she herself was a high school student. She loved music and was glad to accept my invitation to any kind of rehearsal. She stayed out of school occasionally, was late to dinner, but she couldn't control her enthusiasm for music.

She was now sitting near me in the auditorium of the School of the Russian Music Society, listening with the same rapture as I. Her large eyes had darkened. Her short black ringlets and tawny skin made her resemble the portrait of an Italian youth that I had seen in the window of an art gallery on Deribavskaya Street.

"It's great!" she would whisper excitedly into my ear, "isn't it?"

"Wonderful!" I would answer with equal enthusiasm.

"Who's the composer?"

"I don't know."

Next they played "Scheherazade," and again we were lost in the music. We particularly enjoyed the solo parts as they were more understandable to us because of our limited knowledge of the score. Our beloved violins led in the telling of the fascinating tales of Scheherazade, with the oboe or the English horn—I couldn't always tell them apart—speaking for Prince Kalender. The clarinet's long notes seemed to us sweetly wistful, and the dignified, elderly voice of the serene and wise bassoon reminded us for some reason of the composer of "Scheherazade," Rimsky-Korsakov, whose portrait hung right there on the wall in the auditorium. Seeming alive, the gray-bearded composer condescendingly listened to the rendering of his work by the youthful musicians.

Several days later, we gave a five-kopeck piece to the ticket man at the Civic Theater and he let us into the concert hall to listen to the rehearsal for a recital of Mendelssohn's violin music that was to be played—as it seemed to Anka and me—not by an ordinary human being, but by some kind of a fairy-tale magician, the violinist Aleksander Fedelman. We soon made a discovery that astounded us greatly.

Fedelman was rehearsing some short piece for an encore. He was alone on the stage except for his accompanist, but suddently Anka and I distinctly heard the sounds of a second violin coming, obviously, not far from the one the famous violinist was playing.

"There is another violin," the puzzled Anka whispered, "do you hear it?"

"Yes."

Both of us looked around to locate the second performer, straining to the utmost our hearing and sight—but we saw no one else. Then we each caught on at the same instant that it was Fedelman, that he was playing in such a manner as to produce the sounds of two or three violins simultaneously. He was playing double and triple notes. This was explained to us in a whisper by another music enthusiast, a little older than we, himself a violinist and student at the music school. We had no idea that one could play on several strings at once and we now listened to the virtuoso with ten times as much interest.

Next day was Sunday. We went to the Catholic Church. I refused to walk alongside of Anka—she was wearing a new school uniform, light brown shoes, and a pretty little hat, while I was in my old threadbare suit that I had noticeably outgrown, and on my feet I had on a pair of patched boots, crudely cleaned with sticky shoewax.

"You walk ahead of me," I said to her, "and I'll follow you."

"No, you walk right with me," she insisted.

"But, look how well dressed your brothers are," I pointed out stubbornly. "I feel embarrassed. People will laugh at you."

"All right, then would you like me to go home and change into something old?" Anka offered.

"No, don't you do that."

"Then stop arguing. Come on, we'll be late."

The organ was already playing when we entered. We halted right at the entrance, overwhelmed by the powerful flood of the music. We got the impression that an immense symphony orchestra was hidden in a vast closed closet, that the sounds were reaching us through the countless large, medium-sized, and small pipes installed throughout the amazing architecture.

When the organ music stopped, a wonderful silence reigned in the church. The yellow light from the candles flickered and fluttered over the large crucifixes, and purple flowers gleamed everywhere. The old priest was uttering some words indistinctly, little bells rang from time to time, and the parishioners were singing off key. All this was forbidding and saddening. But as soon as the sounds of the wonderful organ again ascended to the high vault of the nave, it became cheerful in the church, as at the opera or in the best concert hall.

The music that was being played was not only unfamiliar to us, it didn't at all resemble anything we had heard before. The tones were high, pure, tender, like the voices of young girls, of flutes, and of birds, and it seemed that they were pouring down from above, from the sky, and penetrating into the church through the stained-glass windows together with the slanting rays of the sun.

I stole a look at Anka. Her large dark eyes, shaded by her long eyelashes, were fixed on the organ, and she was listening avidly. Her face was pale.

Never before had we heard such music!

"What are they playing?" a woman who was standing near us asked her neighbor.

"A Bach chorale," her neighbor answered barely audibly.

We left the church, forever captivated by the new instrument and the composer Johann Sebastian Bach.

From that day on, whenever possible, Anka and I ran to the Catholic Church to listen to the organ.

9

ONE EVENING, when I got home, my mother greeted me with the news that Egor had come by. His ship had arrived from overseas the day before, and he had come to "ask about his young chum."

"I brought a present for Kolya," he had informed my mother with an air of mystery. "Tell him to come and see me as early as he can tomorrow morning."

I was restless all night. I was tormented by curiosity. What kind of present did Egor bring me? What could it be? Was it a model of an ocean steamer about which he had spoken to me with such eagerness? Or was it a marvelous fishing rod with twelve different hooks and colored birds' feathers? Or, maybe, it was a magnificent parrot—some kind of many-colored cockatoo from Australia or from South America, or a red-green one from New Zealand? Perhaps he brought a miniature camera? Or . . .

I remembered every object that Egor and I ever spoke about—I had always listened carefully—but I couldn't decide definitely on any one of them and finally fell asleep.

As soon as the first rays of morning penetrated into my room, I got up, washed quietly, and buttoning my jacket on the way, rushed out of the house.

It was very pleasant early in the morning on the spacious

and clean streets of Odessa. The houses looked freshly washed —white, light blue, bright yellow—and their closed inside shutters made them resemble sleeping creatures with tightly shut eyes. Everyone was still asleep, and only the yard porters were up, standing at the open gates, holding the stretched, long rubber hoses as they watered the streets generously. A cool dampness rose from the smooth, handsome pavement laid out in regular diabase squares and the asphalt sidewalks. A tiny man was scurrying from street lamp to street lamp extinguishing the gas lights with a thin, crooked pole.

On the corners stood open carriages with drooping horses and dozing drivers. The grocers were opening their doors and neatly piling heaps of large, round, dark-green watermelons, baskets of roseate grapes, crates of Crimean apples and large yellow peaches to the sides of the store entrances. Then they made a fire under the huge tin kettles in which they cooked tasty corn-on-the-cob—the famous golden Bessarabian corn.

And over all this hung the slowly rising disk of the purple-red sun, affectionately embracing everything in its soft rose-yellow light.

Descending from the avenue down the wide and steep flight of stairs, I caught sight of the stack and mast of the *Pyotr Regger*, Egor's ship, and of the lines of men unloading Marseille tiles.

With impatience and with a fast-beating heart, I approached the ship, breezed up the gangway covered with the rose-colored tile dust onto the familiar deck, and hastened straight to the machinists' quarters. There was the seamen's cabin and the narrow stairway leading directly to Egor's tiny cubbyhole.

And there he was himself!

Sprawled on a long narrow cot, his head resting on his

raised arms bent at the elbow, he was sleeping soundly and
snoring loudly.

"Egor," I shook him lightly by the shoulder.

"What? What is it?" he jumped up to a sitting position
and stared at me for a few seconds. Then, recognizing me,
he came alive and got up to greet me.

"Kolka! Hello, boy! What a present I brought you! Just
wait and see!"

He pulled his small dark-green trunk from under the cot,
took a small key from his pocket, and opened the lock.

I watched Egor with great excitement, waiting breathlessly
for him to reveal the mysterious treasure. The key clicked
in the lock, Egor turned it a second time, and, finally,
the trunk was opened. First he removed some soft things,
then small envelopes with strings, then parts for a guitar,
and only when everything else had been taken out did he
lift out a strange-looking object carefully wrapped in glossy
yellow paper.

He undid the wrapping with nimble fingers, and I recognized
at once what it was.

"It's a mandolin!" I exclaimed.

"Nothing else but!"

It was new, handsome, with a shiny dark-brown sounding
board and four pairs of metal strings.

Was it possible that it would belong to me?!

"Why don't you take it?" Egor asked, holding the mandolin
out to me. "Here, it's yours."

I took the instrument, examined it, found the pick stuck
between the strings, and sat down at once on the cot and
tried to play. This proved not so simple to do. But Egor
showed me how.

"I wanted to buy you a cello," he explained, "but I didn't
have enough coin. They wanted eighty francs for one in
Marseille—that means thirty rubles in our money; in Toulon—

seventy, which comes to twenty-six rubles. But this thing I bought in Naples—they call it 'mandolin' down there—for fifteen lire—about six rubles. This price is still pretty steep for the likes of us, but more reasonable."

At last I regained my speech: "Thanks a lot, Egor . . . You're so generous . . ."

"I may be generous, but my purse, dear fellow, is lean."

"You shouldn't have spent this money on me . . ."

"That's nothing, it was only a small amount. It's too bad I didn't have enough money for a cello. That's a real instrument! A mandolin—that's more like a toy—in Naples every swarthy urchin plays one."

"Egor! Hey, there, Egor!" someone shouted from above. "Hurry, the overseer wants to see you."

"They're calling me," Egor said with annoyance. "Well, there's no helping it. I'm sorry we must part so soon, as sorry as if you were my real brother. But I must go now, Kolenka. When I get back from this next long trip, I'll visit you first thing."

We went up to the deck, and Egor, stopping for a hurried minute, looked me over. "You've shot up, Nikolai. Not bad! You've gotten husky and have filled out. There, go now and play the mandolin. And when I have the cash I'll dicker for a cello."

He stood there for a while. When I reached the gangplank he called out: "Give my regards to your father and mother," and disappeared behind the gear.

I was touched by Egor's interest in me. Why was he being so nice to me? Maybe for no special reason, simply because he was lonely and had no family. His parents had died long ago. His only brother—called Kolka, like me—had drowned when still in his teens. He had played the reed pipe well.

Perhaps Egor cared for me because he, too, loved music

and because he could have been a musician but hadn't studied due to poverty, and therefore hadn't become one. Maybe for all of these reasons? Yes, most likely that explained it.

I remained for a long time on the wharf, looking up at the ship. But realizing that I stood no chance of seeing Egor again that day, I went away reluctantly, looking back every few steps. I walked on, hugging with delight the precious gift from Egor.

10

I LEARNED TO PLAY THE MANDOLIN very soon. Whenever I visited Anka, she accompanied me on the piano and I played our favorite songs; I even learned how to play Tchaikovsky's "Barcarole."

Moved by my show of talent, my mother pointed out accusingly to my father: "If need had not forced us to sell our piano, the boy could now be studying music. You see how gifted he is!"

"If he's really so gifted," my embarrassed father answered, "then let him find the way himself."

I regretted more than anyone the sale of that piano. It was a very old, broken-down, secondhand instrument—narrow, long, and old-fashioned. It had been obtained long ago by my grandmother for my mother when she was seventeen. It was her wedding gift. Although it was old even then, and in need of repair, it continued to be for many years the major ornament and pride of our household. Mother had often played romantic pieces on it and most often "The Maiden's Prayer," which I memorized so well that I could never forget it. "Prayer" was the first song I learned to play on my mandolin. It was hearing me play her favorite that kept reminding my mother of the sold piano. It even made her cry a little over its loss.

Nor had she forgotten how, as a little child, I used to pick out, with one finger, simple tunes, and how eagerly and quickly I had begun to learn and how I could already identify certain keys.

"The boy is very talented," she kept saying, "and how useful that piano would be to him now."

"All right, all right!" my father tried to calm her, "I'll find a position and we'll buy a new one!"

My father's words seemed to me purest fantasy. How could he seriously talk about such a purchase when there were days when we even lacked money for bread. Sometimes on such days women peddlers came into our courtyard carrying large round baskets in both arms and calling out in high-pitched voices:

"Buns, buns, fresh buns! Hot buns—with egg, mustard, sour cream, poppy seeds, or caraway seeds!"

In despair, my mother would then shut the windows and complain with tears in her voice:

"My God, never would I have thought that the time would come when I couldn't buy my children a crust of bread!"

"Right away, right away, in a minute," my father would say guiltily. He would quickly put aside his book and go off somewhere.

The peddlers—men and women—would continue to come into our yard, loudly proclaiming their wares with all kinds of refrains:

"Mackerel, mackerel, live mackerel! Last night it was in the Black Sea and now it's here for you and me!" Or, "Eggs, chicks, and hens! Buy one, buy tens! Grapes, apples, pears! We sell them here and at the fairs!"

My mother would be unable to resist, and, opening the window, would ask the price of the fish. Hearing the answer, she would sigh with disappointment:

"Just for spite, everything is so cheap today!"

And our neighbor, a wise old lady who also lived in poverty—her ailing son had been unemployed for over a year—remarked grimly: "When there is no money, it makes no difference—cheap or expensive—it's all the same."

An old-clothes man would come into the yard calling out in his mechanical singsong way: "Old clo-o-thes! We buy-y-y old clo-o-thes."

"This is for us," the old lady would mutter irritably. "We can do business with the likes of him."

My mother would then try to find something around the house that the old-clothes man might want to buy.

"Wait," she'd beg him, "just a minute."

She'd search in the chest of drawers that had already been gone through a number of times before for the same purpose, she would open the old trunk for the hundredth time, would look around the kitchen just in case something or other had previously escaped her notice, and at last find ing some object or other, she'd carry it out to the old man. He would take the thing indifferently from her, examine it critically, and either reject it or reluctantly give her a few sorry kopecks—enough only for a loaf of bread.

But money was needed not only for bread—the rent hadn't been paid for some time, the grocer had been insisting that we pay a much-overdue bill, our clothes were completely worn out, and our shoes were falling apart.

In view of all this, could anyone hope for a piano?

So I continued to play the mandolin. Only occasionally, when I was visiting Anka, and only when her father was not at home on such occasions, did I try to pick out some simple melody on her piano. She had taught me how to read music, to tell a minor key from a major, and the melody from the accompaniment.

I continued to look for work with even greater determina- tion. But I still hoped to find a job where I'd be in contact with musical instruments, and I continued to apply at stores, the shops of tuners, and at concert halls.

I was practically grafted to one of these places. For quite a long time I had been drawn to the building of the City Theater. Its façade was on Richelieu Street, one of Odessa's main thoroughfares. Its side entrances were: one on the elegant English Square, landscaped lavishly with flower beds, and another on the old, staid Palais Royale Street, shaded by chestnut and acacia trees and rendered charming by the tiny Pechessky Cafe, with its small, babbling fountain and the swans swimming in its basin.

The employees' and players' entrance to the theater snuggled on the incline of the short, narrow Theater Alley, at least a whole flight of stairs lower than its neighboring streets. Many was the time I tried to sneak into the theater through this entrance, but the forbidding doorman stubbornly refused to let me pass. No matter how hard I tried to explain that I simply had to see the Director, he would not pay any attention.

"We don't need any boy helpers," he rudely interrupted me. "Go on, on your way!"

Then I tried to outsmart him. Three successive days I made my appearance at ten-thirty in the morning and patiently waited for the Director to arrive, the old man Reggio. I approached him when he was still half a block from the building, in order to have time to speak to him before he disappeared into it. Tall, erect, with a neatly trimmed silver beard, he wore a wide-brimmed black hat, carried a heavy cane in his hand, and walked like a military man—with measured steps, holding his shoulders proudly. Gathering courage, I walked up to him and blurted out before I had a chance to lose my determination:

"Excuse me, please . . ."

Reggio stopped, willingly:

"What can I do for you, young fellow?"

"I want to ask you to hire me . . . to work for you . . ."

"How come—for me?"

"At the theater. In your decorator's workshop."

"And what will you do there?"

"Everything."

"Everything?" he questioned me, and a glint of amusement shone in his eyes. "You'll paint scenery?"

His question baffled me; I lost my poise, and fell silent.

"You don't answer—smarty? You want to get rid of the old man and take his place? Yes? Admit it!"

I realized that he was joking, but in my embarrassment I forced myself to inject into my reply all the sincerity and seriousness of which I was capable:

"No, I don't even know how to paint."

"You don't? Then what do you want with the decorator's workshop?"

His good-natured laughter heartened me.

"I'll mix paints, wash brushes, clean up . . ."

"We hire a workman for this—a paint mixer."

"I'll help him."

"But we don't have such a job."

"I'll work without pay."

"Why?" he asked with surprise.

"To learn."

For a moment he looked intently at my flushed face, then he told me to follow him.

Triumphant, I walked nonchalantly past the hateful doorman, keeping close to Reggio—just in case. The doorman looked at me suspiciously, but the Director reassured him:

"He's with me."

I walked up the stairs with him to the second floor. We entered a huge stage, crossed it, and took a narrow passage along a brick wall at the end of which a ridiculously tiny elevator was hidden—it had room for only one person.

"I'll go up on this thing, and you use the stairs over there," Reggio said.

The old man then shook his stick threateningly in my direction as he was being lifted by the elevator, and shouted to me from above:

"When you finally manage to get rid of me and to steal my job, you scoundrel, then it will be your turn to go up on this contraption."

Upstairs, in his studio filled with sketches, model stage sets, easels, Reggio questioned me about my parents, why I wasn't attending school, and when he found out in the end of our conversation that I didn't have the least inclination toward painting and dreamed of becoming a musician, he had a fit of laughter again, an old-man's wheezing laughter.

"Then why in heaven's name did you come to me?" he asked, wiping away the tears.

"To get into the theater."

"What a young scoundrel you are!" Reggio said, still doubling up with mirth. "What a swindler, what a villain!"

Having had his fill of laughing, he added:

"Very well, go to the auditorium now, pay attention to what goes on around there."

As I was nearing the door, he called out:

"So, do I understand you correctly—you'll work without pay?"

"Yes."

"Don't you forget it and keep your word, but, in the meantime, here is an advance on the deal." And he held out a blue bill—five rubles.

"What's that?" I asked, puzzled.

"Money."

"But . . . without pay . . ."

"Here, take this on account."

"But . . ."

"Take it, take it, don't argue! My arm isn't made of iron—it's getting tired. Take it!"

"Thank you," I said, accepting the money.

"Eat it in good health!"

When I was about to leave the room, he called to me once more:

"Now, there, hold it, you bandit! Hold it! Are you going to spend all this money on sweets? Don't you dare! Give it all to your mother."

"I will."

"Exactly! Now tell me, how many pastries are you capable of gobbling up in one session?"

"Three."

"Not more than that?"

"Maybe four."

"And how many with a drink?"

"With water? Five."

"There, here is some more money—for five pastries and soda pop with syrup. Be careful, don't swallow it all at once but in five parts. And the five-ruble bill give to your mother. Will you?"

"Without fail!"

I fled down the broad staircase on my eager way to the bakeshop, but I stopped at the stage, spellbound by the sounds of music coming from somewhere in the depths of the auditorium.

At first I couldn't figure out what was going on around me. For the first time I was now seeing the theater not as a spectator but in reverse order: first the stage, then the orchestra, then, facing me, the conductor Pribik with the baton in his raised hand, next the first rows of seats dimly lit by the footlights, and, finally, stretched the rest of the large auditorium, sunk in darkness.

But I soon came to and realized that a rehearsal was in progress. I remembered that an Italian company was currently giving performances at this theater, and that I had seen the posters with the names of the celebrated singers—Anselmi, Titta Ruffo, Santorelli.

I now heard someone's lovely singing voice. Who could it be? Was it possible that it was Anselmi? Was it possible that I was hearing that very same Giuseppe Anselmi about whom articles were appearing in all the newspapers, and whom people were so anxious to hear that many have stood in line all night to obtain tickets? I approached the open window of a small summerhouse—part of the stage set—and saw a slender young man in an elegant costume with a high double, stiffly-starched collar, and heard his clear, magnificent voice—like the sound of a cello.

He repeated the same phrase three times, and I recognized it—it was from an aria in the opera *Tosca*, which the whole town seemed to be humming at the time. And, although he was not singing in full voice and did not render the entire aria but sang in "pieces," with pauses, it all sounded so good that I was rooted to the spot. The music and the singing suddenly stopped. Anselmi crossed his arms on his chest, bowed low to the conductor, and said:

"Thank you, maestro, many thanks. That was very good."

He had a thin, dark-skinned face, large dark eyes, thick black brows, and lots of black wavy hair, combed back. Smiling pleasantly, he also thanked the orchestra, complimenting them:

"Russian orchestras are the very best."

Then he left the stage.

As I walked down to the first floor, a plan was forming

in my mind with the speed of lightning—tomorrow evening I must remain after work and hear the opera.

Passing the mean doorman, I said to him casually:

"I now work here."

"For whom?"

"That hasn't been settled yet."

"Tell me, if you don't mind," he mocked, "when will this matter be settled?"

"Tomorrow evening."

"Aren't you an important personage now! A regular governor. If that's the case, then I may let you in," he said condescendingly.

Feeling delighted about the turn of events, I rushed for the horse-drawn trolley, to get home the sooner and tell my family everything.

11

IN THE STAGE DESIGNER'S STUDIO everything was very interesting. The room was immense, the canvases were huge, the paintbrushes large—the whole place was wonderful and unusual. The canvases were spread right on the floor, and everyone walked over them freely. They were painted with long brushes, like those used by house painters, but exactly what was painted on them was hard to tell at close range—all one saw was patches of many colors, circles, lines, crude flourishes, and nothing else. But from a distance, and when one squinted— as the scene designers always did—everything became clear: here was a door, there a window, a wall, a tree, or a column.

Reggio himself came there seldom. Ordinarily he worked in his private studio, drawing sketches, examining model stage sets and discussing them with the technicians, the decorators, and the chief stage manager. Occasionally he would make an appearance in the main workshop, looking tall, erect, and elegant. He would look intently and severely at the canvases being painted and order changes that he wanted made, pointing with his rubber-tipped walking stick from which he was inseparable.

His Russian speech was clear. I was surprised that there was not a trace of accent in it, since he was an Italian. I decided that he must have lived in Russia for a very long time. Perhaps he was born here. There were many Italians, Frenchmen, Czechs, Greeks, Turks, and Englishmen in Odessa. These people had long ago mastered the Russian language. Most likely Reggio was one of the Russified Italians.

I found out by accident that he was a native Russian. I overheard the studio director, Sadovnikov, tell Reggio's story to a visiting friend of his:

In St. Petersburg, in a famous guards regiment, there once served a handsome officer by the name of Beklemishev. He had been a favorite among his fellow officers, for he was clever, good-natured, friendly, and a wonderful artist. But the authorities did not approve of him. They considered him a liberal, a fault-finder, a mocker, and a sharp-tongued critic of his superiors. Those whom he disliked feared especially his cartoons. They enraged those who recognized themselves in them.

On one occasion, over a bottle of champagne with his brother officers, Beklemishev incautiously said that he respected the memory of the Decembrist Rebels (a group of young noblemen and poets who had staged an uprising against the Czarist autocracy in 1825, demanding democratic reforms). Saying this, he/rose to his feet, saluted, and added that sooner or later their cause would rise again. Someone reported these words to his superior. Beklemishev was discharged from the regiment. Soon after, some "incriminating documents" were found; he was charged, convicted, and sentenced to hard labor.

He lived through all the horrors of prisons, chain gangs, and convict labor in the mines of the Siberian wilderness. Only after many years of untold hardships did he succeed in escaping from his Siberian exile. He fled the country to Italy. At first he lived in a small town called Reggio, in Calabria, on the shore of the Gulf of Messina, and later in other cities. He studied and became a professional artist. He re-

turned to Russia when he was already middle-aged. He settled
not in St. Petersburg but in Odessa, and never again used
his real name. He established himself first as one of its
stage-set designers and later became the chief designer at the
Civic Theater.

Now he was close to seventy. He was completely gray, pale,
and wrinkled, but, nevertheless, he had the handsome face
of an elderly scholar, physician, or artist. From a distance
he resembled the writer Turgenev or the Italian patriot
Garibaldi, whose portraits hung in picture galleries.

"Why are you staring at me like that?" Reggio once asked
me unexpectedly when I brought him some clean brushes
and was staring at him without being aware of it.

"For no reason . . . just . . ." I mumbled.

"Really? I don't allow people to look at me free of charge.
Pay first, then look. Do you have a ten-kopeck piece?"

"No, I don't."

"How about five kopecks?" he bargained.

"Two kopecks?"

"That I have," I said.

"Hand it over."

Laughing, I gave him the coin.

"Now, don't you laugh, it's not a joke," he said, and,
taking the money, put it in his pocket. "Go ahead and
look—but not for a long time. Only two kopeck's worth.
That's all. Now go."

Then he had an afterthought:

"There are many of you around here wanting to stare at
me. For forty years now they've been doing it, and still
they've not had enough."

He was a pleasant and friendly person, a gentle grandfather,
and I always basked in his sensitive kindness.

The same day he called me in, made me sit down in
his studio, and, screwing up his eyes shrewdly, asked:

"How are you going to listen to the music around here when you work upstairs and the music is downstairs?"

"I don't know."

"But I know."

"How?"

"You'll go down at once to the auditorium, you'll sit down in the last row, you'll watch the rehearsal, and then you'll come and tell me whether or not you liked the stage sets. Understand?"

"I understand."

"Even better than is necessary . . ." Reggio laughed merrily and with great good nature. "Even more than necessary— you're a tricky one! Now get down there or you'll be late."

My heart did a happy somersault. I sped down the stairs, two at a time, and wished I could reach the auditorium in one jump.

I found the last row in the dark theater and made myself comfortable in the soft velvet seat. I heard someone whisper— a few people were seated in the same row, some in front, in back, and in the loge. I was burning with impatience. Why don't they hurry? I regretted that Anka wasn't there with me, and I decided to arrange soon for her to come to a rehearsal. Meanwile, I'd tell her about everything I was now going to hear and see. If they'd only start!

At last the light went on in the orchestra pit, the first sounds of tuning of instruments could be heard, and among this medley of sound I could distinguish the cellos.

Suddenly the silhouette of the conductor loomed in the semi-darkness. He tapped the tip of his baton against his stand, there was complete silence, and into this silence rose, like a sunburst, a lovely melody—the one I had heard during yesterday's rehearsal. This melody recurred in every scene of this opera *Tosca* and the tenor sang it in the last act, at the close of the performance.

The curtain was finally raised. Anselmi was Cavaradossi. Santorelli was Tosca. She had a very high and pure voice. When she and Anselmi sang together, their voices rising above the orchestra and pouring into the auditorium, it seemed to me that the torrent of their song would not have room enough within the theater and would push asunder walls and ceiling, overflowing into the street. The chorus joined in, the church bells rang, the orchestra played, but Anselmi and Santorelli, with the force and beauty of their voices, could be heard above the chorus and orchestra. A man entered—Scarpia—in a short cloak and three-cornered hat. He began to sing, and I realized at once that he was Titta Ruffo.

Titta Ruffo!

How fiery were his young black eyes; how freely and handsomely he carried himself on stage. He uttered only a few phrases, but his voice was deep, passionate, strong—it came forth like the sound of ten cellos playing in unison. And each of the phrases he sang was so well rounded and melodic, like a complete song.

The curtain was lowered and the auditorium was again in darkness. I sat there, excited by the drama and the beauty of the singing, but the impression of the opera's plot was soon dimmed, and only the voices resounded in my head— the high and resonant soprano of Santorelli, tender and warm, resembling the violin, the vibrant tenor of Anselmi, and the deep, rich baritone of Titta Ruffo. They rang in my ears separately and together, as if they were all still singing, and I were still listening to them with eyes closed.

The intermission lasted a long time. I walked onto the stage and at once saw Titta Ruffo. He was fussing around a table set on the stage for dinner. He didn't seem to approve of the place where the stagehands had put it and was moving it closer to the forestage. He rearranged the plates, the vase

with flowers, moved the knives and forks. Only the chairs
were still in their former position. Then, to my own surprise,
I busied myself and lifted the two chairs and placed them
at either end of the table, according to the settings.

"O-o, gud, vere gud," Titta Ruffo said pleasantly. "Thank
you."

His swarthy face broke into a flashing smile, his dark
eyes merry with warmth, his white teeth gleaming.

I returned to my seat after the curtain had already been
raised.

The second act was in progress. Throughout this part of the
rehearsal I could hear my neighbors whisper their praises of
the singers. During the second intermission they all walked
out into the foyer, but I remained glued to my seat for the
remainder of the performance, afraid to lose the sensation of
delight that I had just experienced if I moved.

Overcome by the tragic end, I roamed upstairs in a trance.
When I entered Reggio's studio to tell him how wonderful
it had all been, I saw that he had a visitor, the star singer
Titta Ruffo.

I retreated in awe and started to go away.

"Where are you off to? Come back here!" Reggio called out.

I came back. Reggio laughed and said something to Titta
Ruffo in Italian. The singer looked at me with a smile and
said in broken Russian:

"Vere good. Vere good. You will want be artist? Yes? Vere
good."

Evidently he didn't know any other Russian words, for he
kept repeating the same ones mechanically.

"Were you crying?" Reggio suddenly asked me, peering into
my face.

"No," I denied, blushing.

"That's not true. You did cry, I can tell from your eyes."

Again he said something in Italian, and both men laughed gaily.

"By the way," Reggio said, turning to me, as if he just remembered something, "here is some money, run down to Franconi's and get a dozen pastries and bring them back here, quickly."

"What kind?" I asked.

"All kinds. The kind you like best."

I rushed headlong to one of the best pastry shops in the city, at the Franconi Cafe.

Within a few minutes I was back, carrying carefully a pretty box wrapped in white paper and tied in a bow with pink string. I went up to Reggio's room, but he was about to leave.

"Have you bought them?" he asked sternly.

"Here they are."

"Are they good ones?"

"The best."

"Then keep them."

I was sure he was kidding and continued to hold out the box to him.

"Why do you stand there like this?" he said angrily. "Go home and give them to your mother."

"What about you? Don't you . . ."

"I don't need any. Do you want me to overeat and get sick and die so that you can take my place? What a sly one! You'd better be on your way, pronto, before I warm your back with this stick! You miserable plotter!"

He shook his stick high in the air, assuming an outraged look, and quickly departed.

Half an hour later, I tore into the house and told my family about Reggio as I impatiently tore the pink string from the white box with the large round trademark, "Cafe and Pastry Shop Franconi."

"He's a good person," my father said. Father was lying on the sofa reading, for the tenth time, the novel *Money*, by Émile Zola. "A good person and an eccentric one."

My mother prepared the samovar, and I ran to get Anka. Soon we were all seated around the table, abandoning ourselves to the feast. My mother, smiling sadly, said:

"Well, in the absence of dinner, pastry will do. The first dish will be an éclair, the second, a napoleon."

"Especially, since such a dinner does not require bread," my father added in the same vein.

After eating his pastry, my father returned to the old sofa and his book. He had worked the whole night unloading bricks from freight cars at the Odessa Freight Station and was now groaning with the pain in his back and arms.

Later that evening he was going down there again to do the same kind of work till morning.

12

THOSE WINTER MONTHS at the theater passed in a sort
of happy dream. I was glad to get up early in the morning,
hurry across the large Old Sennaya Square, walk the entire
length of Richelieu Street, and, turning down the very narrow
Theater Alley, make for the stage entrance.

"Ha! the head director has arrived!" was the doorman's
daily sarcastic greeting. "May we now start the rehearsal,
Your Highness?"

Sometimes he altered somewhat the words of his mocking.
Removing his cap with its gold braid, he bowed low and
in a fawning manner saluted me with:

"I bid you good-day, sir chief conductor. What is your
pleasure—is the rehearsal to start at once, or would you, perhaps, prefer to rest awhile?"

I'd quickly mount the stairs. Everything up there, in the
theater, without any exception, gave me genuine pleasure.
I'd get from the designers a list of needed paints and pig-
ments, relishing the sounds of their names: zinc white, white
lead, baryte, bright ocher, gold, Prussian blue, malachite green,
emerald green, ultramarine, cinnabar vermilion. What new,
interesting, and unusual words, how nice they sounded—especially umber, cobalt, carmine. I jotted down with an equal
sense of discovery the sizes and variety of brushes, palette

knives, canvas cloths. Then I took the horse-drawn trolley to the Old Market on Great Arnatskaya Street and to the whole-sale candle shop, and, making the necessary purchases, piled them in the high two-wheeled carriage of the red-faced old coachman Mendel-Berel, and brought the supplies to the thea-ter.

But the brightest moments for me were, of course, at the rehearsals and the performances. Within a short period of time I managed to hear a number of the most famous operas, and some of them several times.

Anka and I were now the most frequent visitors to the theater. I found secret ways of sneaking Anka backstage, where we both installed ourselves on a narrow workman's scaffolding suspended from the ceiling, high above the stage.

One day Reggio found us there:

"Haven't you gone home yet? Why are you still here, so late?"

"I'm listening to *Traviata*."

"How many times have you heard it already?"

"This is the fifth."

"And who is this girl?"

"This is . . . the daughter of a neighbor of ours . . ."

"So-o-o . . . is she a music lover too?"

"Oh, yes."

"All right, go on and listen, go on . . ."

He walked away, then came back, saying:

"It's not very nice of you, Kolya, to entertain such a pretty young lady on a scaffold. Come with me."

He led us to the fireman and said to him: "These are special guests, find a comfortable place for them here in the wings."

Reggio socialized with the Italians in the company and they often exchanged visits. The musicians probably found it pleasant to be able to converse with him in their own tongue.

One day he sent me again to Franconi, told me to buy the best cake and to deliver it to the soprano Santorelli, at the London Hotel. In a large room whose windows opened on the Nikolayevsky Boulevard, revealing a wide view of the harbor, the sea, and the shore of Peresyp, I found Titta Ruffo, Anselmi and his wife—a pale, unattractive woman—the chief conductor Pribik, and other artists of the company. The party was noisy and gay. Someone was playing the piano. There were numerous bottles with beverages of different colors on the table, open boxes of chocolate candy, and goblets and wine-glasses filled with drinks of all colors.

Titta Ruffo stood at a window, and with raised glass and a good deal of laughter was recounting something with great animation, causing the others to laugh, too.

"Ah, Kolya, welcome!" he greeted me boisterously. "Welcome, Kolya! Welcome, my dear boy of Russia!"

He took the box with the cake from me and, holding it on the wide palms of his hands, his arms outstretched, carried it pompously to Santorelli. Going down on one knee, he bowed his head solemnly, and Santorelli, with the proud mien of a queen and with a theatrical flourish, took the cake from him and royally carried it to the table.

I was about to leave, but the hostess, taking me by the hand, led me back into the room. She insisted that I drink almost a full glass of sweet wine and that I eat a slice of the cake. I said, "Thank you," and Santorelli answered in very funny Russian: "Welcome you please be." Again I made for the door, but this time it was Titta Ruffo who wouldn't let me depart. He led me to the piano and, after saying something to the others in his own language, installed himself on the round stool and began to test my ear for music. He had me repeat individual notes and then, in order to see if I could sing in tune, he played whole phrases. I repeated these too without any mistakes. Then he deliberately played something complicated and long, and I, trying to repeat it, stumbled on the fifth or sixth note. Blushing darkly, I got hopelessly confused and stopped when Titta Ruffo broke into merciless laughter.

Santorelli and Anselmi fell on him with reprimands. They were supported by the Czech Pribik:

"You mustn't do this," the conductor said softly, "this way anyone can get mixed up."

Then I, too, flared up—evidently the wine had done its work:

"I could sing everything, everything that has been sung in the theater! Everything, everything! I could even sing *Siciliana*."

"Yes, I want, I want!" Anselmi exclaimed.

"Please to do," Santorelli asked with delicacy.

"You can't do it," the mischievous Titta Ruffo said, challenging me cunningly. "You are said a joke."

"No, I really can," I repeated heatedly. "I can, I can!"

Pribik sat down at the piano and began to play.

"All right, let's hear it, let's hear it," he said, smiling, and nodded his head, giving me the sign to begin.

I assumed the typical singer's pose and began:

> O, Lola, in your eyes I see the azure sky,
> Your face is like a blooming rose in May!
> He who has ever kissed your rosy lips,
> Will never for any other blessing pray!

My voice was thin and weak, it shook and wavered. It seemed to me that any moment it would break. But I continued boldly and without embarrassment, for I knew that I sang absolutely in tune. And Pribik—the chief conductor—confirmed this! He continued to play, nodding his head in rhythm, which signified—I was certain of this—approval as well. Otherwise, I reasoned, he would simply have stopped playing. Following the second stanza, when I had to repeat the refrain in a higher scale, my voice suddenly cracked, and I rendered the classical rooster's crow. Mortified, I stopped and looked helplessly at the maestro. He, too, stopped, and, to the accompaniment of Titta Ruffo's wild laughter, said, accentuating the words in a manner peculiar to him:

"Ha! you've just done it like a typical good singer. Good singers always give a crow once in a while—bad ones never."

"That's right, that's right," Titta Ruffo agreed—"Anselmi, Colombini, Garulli, Gillion—they all crow well! In Italy they receive for this talent rotten eggs, soft tomatoes. No, Kolya, you have a very short range—you stumbled on 'la'!"

I broke into tears and rushed for the door. But Titta Ruffo caught me, took me in his arms and tried to console me.

"Don't, Kolya, don't. You are good, you are vere good! You no real rooster, you small child's size of one."

Santorelli also tried to reassure me:

"You later was be a good singer."

"Not 'was'—'will be,'" Pribik corrected her.

"That's right." She laughed. "Russian languages, hard languages."

"Then, when you 'will be' singer you give a real big crow," Titta Ruffo couldn't resist saying, "like our Caruso and Gillion."

"I'll never be a singer," I announced importantly. "I don't have a voice. I want to be a musician."

"Oh, fine, fine!" the Italians approved in chorus. "Yes, yes, a musicians."

"And are you taking lessons?" Pribik asked, seriously.

"No, my father has been unemployed for a long time. I don't have money for a cello."

"And do you insist on playing the cello?"

"Yes."

"Why?"

"Because it is the very best of all the instruments."

Pribik adjusted his pince-nez on his nose, straightened the double black string, smoothed his small graying beard with the tips of his fingers, and said slowly:

"Very well. Come and see me tomorrow. In my studio. After the rehearsal."

"Oh, thank you!" I said, expressing my gratitude with great sincerity. "Good-bye."

I bowed, and left.

My heart was filled with hope and good cheer as I turned my steps homeward.

No less a personage than Pribik told me to come and see him tomorrow. Pribik himself!

Then I noticed an unusual excitement in the streets. Groups of pedestrians crowded around the newspaper vendors who were waving the papers and shouting:

"Surprise attack on Russian fleet!"

"Military clashes in Far East!"

People snatched up the papers, turned to the "extra" and quickly scanned the news. They remarked to each other: "Imagine, such vile trickery!"

"Sneaking up, like thieves!"

"Like bandits . . ."

I didn't understand a thing. The hubbub in the streets stirred in me an uneasy feeling—I knew that something big and serious was happening.

I bought for a kopeck an "extra" edition of the *Odessa News* and ran home with it at full speed.

13

THE IMMINENCE OF WAR with Japan caused the Italians to leave the country. They were replaced by a Russian opera troupe. And the opera enthusiasts of Odessa would stop to read on the posters the long-familiar names of their favorite singers, with the approval of old admirers.

Within a short time I succeeded in hearing some of the most magnificent voices in all of Russia.

"Well, how are things?" Reggio whispered when he stumbled on me one day backstage, my mouth wide open with wonder. "Are you enjoying yourself?"

"Yes, sir!"

"Do they sing well?"

"Very."

"Not worse than the Italians?"

"It seems to me . . . not . . ."

"It 'seems to you'? You're afraid to admit that you prefer the Italians, you rascal!" He mussed up my hair with his long thin fingers, laughed softly, and walked away.

Next day, when I brought him some white cardboard paper for his easel, he at once remembered yesterday's remarks and resumed the discussion with obvious eagerness:

"So, tell me, who is better—the Italians or the Russians?"

"The Italians," I answered with feigned conviction.

Reggio turned sharply in his armchair, flung his pencil on
the table so that its pin-sharp point broke in pieces, and
looked furiously at me with his large eyes, all, of course,
jokingly:

"You are lying, you wretch! Lying! It's from grown-up
blackguards that you've learned this nonsense. Everything
Russian is not as good as what's foreign—is that right? Isn't
that what the grown-up morons tell you? Well, they're wrong!
Hose, gloves, perfume, face powder—those things may be better than ours—everything else we do better! What books we
have! What music! And painting, and theater! And our people! . . ."

Seeing me grin, Reggio continued even with greater indignation:

"Why are you laughing? Do you think I'm joking? Listen
to this: over here, right on our corner, we have a barber.
He's a plain everyday Russian with the plain everyday name
of Grisha—and he's a wonderful barber, a master at his craft.
But the sign over his shop reads: 'Coiffeur Grégoire de Paris
et Bordeaux'—otherwise, no one will believe that he's a good
barber! And next door to him you will find 'Tailor John
Basil Creckon.' This one—the so-and-so—had been a tailor's
apprentice, right here at our theater, the son of our fireman
Ivan Vasilievich Krikunov, if you please! They don't approve
of themselves, have no confidence in themselves—'everything
from foreign countries is superior.' Take, for instance, pastries:
they are prepared by Russian bakers, from Russian flour,
sweetened with Russian sugar, and baked with Russian butter,
but they call them 'éclair,' 'napoleon,' 'bouchée,' 'petits
beaurres,' 'petits fours,' and the devil knows what else!"

Then, having warmed up to the subject, Reggio recited a
long list of delicious Russian dishes turned into fancy French
specialties, in name only. He pronounced the unfamiliar foreign words with a special comic intonation and very fast.

I was bursting with laughter. He kept pouring out, as from a bottomless sack, more and more, stranger and stranger, names of French recipes, and then, beside himself with exasperation, he ended up banging the table with his fist and shouting at me, as if I were to blame for it all:

"Why are you laughing, you wretch? What's so funny?" His sharp little gray beard shook, his eyes, circled with a web of wrinkles, looked furious and determined, his thin, tapering fingers were clenched in a fist, and he insistently tapped his knuckles against the table, as he said:

"They have Bottistini, Caruso, Adamo Didur, but we have even better ones. In Moscow I recently heard a singer, our own Feodor Chaliapin. This—mark my words—this is the King-of-the-Bells! The world has never before heard the likes of him! Don't you forget this, you nasty boy! And don't you ever again dare to lie that the Italians are better singers! Now, get out!"

After such discussions, I listened with even greater attention to every opera that was new to me and to every singer whom I had not heard before. My new musical explorations resulted in many unforgettable discoveries. The opera *Carmen* was one of them.

From the moment when, at the end of the overture, I heard the short motif—it consists of only five notes—I was all attention. I felt that it would be repeated. And, indeed, it was played again and again. Reggio later explained to me that this motif, this theme, foretells the gypsy Carmen's inevitable death. These few notes are woven into the music, now openly, now hidden in a new, changed harmony. They mingle with another theme, one that sings of the love of Carmen and José, and which is played in the high notes of the string section of the orchestra, or, at times, only by the violins—I couldn't quite tell. The love theme, like the ominous one of the first five notes, is heard repeatedly throughout the

entire opera. And as the story unfolds, other themes flare up
—the music for Escamillo's victory, the fiery dance tune of
the *habanera*, and the lively *fandango* dance music. All this
made my head spin. In the end, when José actually pulled
the huge knife from his belt and ran with it toward Carmen,
I nearly screamed with horror. I wanted to run to her rescue
and kill José with his own knife. But I was restrained by the
music. From the full orchestra the familiar five notes suddenly burst forth, now sounding prophetic in a kind of pa-
thetic sob of all the instruments, a sob that seemed to mourn
and mock all—the living and the dead—Carmen, and José,
and Micaela, and their unfortunate love.

14

I HESITATED FOR A LONG TIME to ask Reggio for help in obtaining a cello. In a way, it was his very kindness and friendliness that made me feel reluctant to turn to him for still another favor. But one day, when I felt very keenly the hopelessness of my circumstances, I went to him with all the courage of a person who had nothing to lose.

"Alexander Nikolaevich . . . may I ask you . . ."

"For money for vodka? I certainly won't give it to you. I can't stand drunks!"

"No, I don't need vodka, I need . . ."

"Tobacco? Nothing doing! I can't stand smokers . . . I'm a blue nose. Or, perhaps, you play cards and need money to pay your debts?"

"No . . . but I want to play . . ."

"You see? What a scoundrel of a boy you are! You don't play cards, but you want to start . . ."

"I want to play the—"

"I'll have nothing to do with it! Get out!"

"I want to play the cello."

"I didn't know you could play the cello?"

"I can't, but I'd like to learn."

"Oh! you'd like to learn? That's splendid!" He became serious at once, and interested. "So, what about it?"

"I don't have a cello."

Understanding at once the whole situation and asking for no further explanation, he said:

"How much does a cello cost?"

"About twelve rubles."

"Do you have an instructor?"

"No."

"Tomorrow you'll have an instrument and an instructor."

"Thank you!" I said, hardly believing my good fortune.

"You're welcome. But if you don't do well, I'll flay you alive! I'll have you whipped! I'll put you in irons! Will send you off to Siberia! Do you understand, you bandit?"

"I understand."

"Exactly! Now, go."

I left him feeling happy and full of hope for tomorrow. I already saw myself as a grown-up cellist, thin and interestingly pale, with rich wavy hair like that of the poet Lensky in the opera *Eugenii Onegin*, handsome in a frock coat, a snow-white shirt front, and a large carnation in my buttonhole. In my hand I held an ancient Stradivarius. I appeared on a brightly lit concert stage, and a storm of applause met me. I responded modestly, with a barely perceptible nod of the head, and took my seat. I waited for silence, and, giving the accompanist the signal to begin—of course, the accompanist was Anka—I commenced. Then, quite unexpectedly, someone hit me in the back.

"What do you think you're doing, you fool?"

The water in the sink at which I was washing some paintbrushes was running over, narrow streams of dirty colored water were spreading toward the doorsill of the designer's workshop. Quickly turning off the faucet, I grabbed the swollen brushes out of the basin and in doing so, to my dismay, splashed not only myself but also the person who had hit me—the director Sadovnikov. A man of average height, fat and round, he sprang away from the sink like a tight ball, and scolded me harshly:

"Have you gone stark mad, you blockhead? Are you out of your mind?"

"It was an accident."

"An ac-ci-dent," he mimicked me meanly. "The water is running over and he turns on the faucet even stronger! I'll get rid of you, you nasty kid!"

My heart was about to burst from the insult. My face was burning, as if hundreds of hot pins had been stuck in it. I was ready to flare up with rage and say some insolent things to the director, but I clenched my jaws with a great effort of will and kept silent.

"You idler, you good-for-nothing . . ." he added, shaking large drops of water from his blue smock as he went off to another part of the workshop.

Next day Reggio called to me from a distance: "Next Saturday go see the orchestra cellist Zagrabsky, he'll give you a cello and will teach you."

I was happy!

To the end of that day I scampered up and down the stairs like a merry puppy, and that evening, after returning from work, I managed to arouse not only the family but the entire courtyard with the good news. I told my parents all about it, Anka, and my pals, Sashka, Vitka, and Spirka.

My excitement did not subside all week. Saturday finally came. I hurried to the orchestra quarters to find Zagrabsky. I found him in the large musicians' lounge but I didn't quite dare to approach him. At the moment, Zagrabsky, as was the case with the other card-playing musicians, was glued to his chair and did not take his eyes off the glossy bills which, together with a pile of coins, formed a small, loose heap in the center of the table.

I left, came back later, left again, and returned once more, but Zagrabsky was still playing.

Finally, he rose, stretched to his full awkward height, and looked at me inquisitively.

"Do you want me?" he asked, yawning. "What is it?"

"About the cello."

"What cello?"

"That Reggio asked you to buy."

"Oh, was that for you? All right, come on Saturday."

"Today . . . happens to be . . . Saturday."

"Next Saturday."

And Zagrabsky went away. I stood there, not knowing what to do. Some of the other musicians came over and surrounded me. They seemed to know something about the matter.

"About what cello did you speak to him?" one of the men asked me with concern. "The one for which Reggio had given him some money? He lost the money at cards."

"What do you mean . . . lost it at cards?"

"It's simple. He sat down to play, lost his own, then yours."

"But, what'll happen now?" I asked forlornly. My tongue stuck to the roof of my mouth and I could barely utter the words.

"Go and tell Reggio all about it," one of the musicians advised me.

I would have done so, but Reggio had in the meantime succumbed to a serious illness.

Grown-ups say that misfortunes come not one at a time but in bunches. On the same day, the designer Sadovnikov informed me with malicious spite that because of his illness Reggio was going to warm Italy and would not return for several months.

But even this was not the end to my troubles. Two days later when I came to work, at the usual time, I was not

allowed into the building. The same doorman who several
months before had stubbornly kept me out was doing it
again, on orders from Sadovnikov. He stood there, blocking
the door, and, as if seeing me for the first time, said:

"What do you want?"

"What do you mean? I want to go in . . ."

"What for?"

"To work . . ."

"As what?"

"As boy-helper."

"We don't need boy-helpers. Be off with you!"

"But Reggio hired me! Reggio himself! I've been working
here for months. Doing all kinds of things . . . running errands to the stores, buying paints, brushes, canvas, wood,
posters . . . I hauled these things in carts, carried them on my
back up five flights of stairs . . . I sawed laths, prepared the
canvas, painted boards, cleaned brushes, mixed paints. And I
was paid wages. Then why do you tell me all of a sudden
you 'don't need boy-helpers'?"

I refused to leave, determined to wait for Sadovnikov.

At last he appeared.

I said to him, "They wouldn't let me in."

"That's right. You don't work for us any more."

"What do you mean, I don't work here . . ."

"Just what I said. You're not an employee—you're not on
the payroll. Reggio paid your wages out of his own pocket."

"I'll work without pay."

"We don't need benefactors," he said, and disappeared
into the building.

I remained outside the entrance.

The singers, musicians, attendants, members of the chorus,
firemen, carpenters kept arriving. And I continued to stand
outside.

I felt cheated and cast out. But, somehow, from the depth

of my heart there arose an unexpected feeling of gratitude for the unforgettable joys I had experienced in this theater— things that no one could ever take away from me.

How could they deprive me of the music I had heard there? They could keep me from ever attending rehearsals again, even cheat me out of the cello gambled away at cards, but I would forever keep the gift of generosity from the good-hearted Reggio, and Egor's unselfish friendship and kindness, which warmed my dreams and ambitions.

It was late summer. The theater was closed.

I now spent most of my days with my friends from the courtyard, my neighbors.

Sashka, a short, strong fellow, the son of a locksmith, lived in the apartment next door. He always had color in his cheeks. He had friendly brown eyes and heavy black eyebrows. He loved to draw and had a reputation among us as a real artist. Every day he showed us new pencil sketches which everyone admired.

We inwardly rejoiced and were proud of Sashka's talent when we recognized in his drawings his father and mother. Sashka was a "khokhol," and when he got excited he spoke with a noticeable Ukrainian accent, pronouncing the sound "k" as "kh."

Vitka, a tall, thin, but muscular boy, we called "the engineer." He was forever building models of machines—locomotives, ship's engines, bicycles. His father, a carpenter, had apprenticed him to a shoemaker, where he was kept busy from dawn to midnight. But Vitka had recently run away from his master, and when his father was home he'd hide at the neighbors' houses.

And Spirka, the son of a part-time clerk, a sickly, silent

boy with a pale thin face and green eyes, was a poet. He loved poems and tried to write some himself.

We would all go together to the seashore to swim and fish. Sashka would draw while we stood behind him looking on with wonder as, with a few strokes, the sea, the sky, a sail, materialized. Vitka would launch his latest model—a tiny boat with a real steam-boiler engine and screw propeller. Smoke poured from the stacks, the propeller blades cut and sprayed the water, and the little boat sped forward pursued by the rail-thin, suntanned Vitka, ready to rescue his "offspring" in case of an accident. Spirka would mournfully read some verses, and I would play my mandolin and hum a song. The rest of the gang, endowed with no visible talents, served as our audience and spectators.

Anka continued to give me piano lessons. But this happened only occasionally—only when her father was not home—and I had to fall back on my small, simple, and docile mandolin, on which I had learned to play many waltzes, ballads, and other songs.

Thus the days passed. My father, after many disappointments, finally managed to locate a job as night watchman in a lumber yard, for which he was paid a pitifully small wage. My brother came down with scarlet fever, and I moved in with relatives. But I came to our home daily and carried out all the tasks assigned to me by my parents. I went in my father's behalf to ask for an advance on his wages, I ran for the doctor, to the drugstore, or to the grocery, or I helped carry in water for a bath, went to the houses of acquaintances for yesterday's newspapers and old, discarded books, which I handed through the window to my father.

Then, one morning, walking along Richelieu Street, I learned the awful news. I saw in the window of a newsstand the latest edition of the *Odessa News* and the report of Chekhov's death.

How could it be? Was it possible that Chekhov was no longer in this world?

I thought hard about what death was and why it existed in the world.

Others had died—the famous writers Pushkin, Lermontov, Turgenev, and the great composer Tchaikovsky—and now Chekhov. And I realized with horror that no one would escape —that sooner or later everyone dies, inevitably, and that Chekhov, since they printed it in the paper, must really be dead.

For one kopeck I "rented" a copy of the newspaper and read through quickly everything written about Chekhov, and without taking my eyes off his photograph, framed in black, I stumbled home.

Handing him, through the window, the freshly printed newspaper, still smelling of ink, I forewarned my father: "Do you know what an awful thing has happened?"

He turned his tired eyes on me in fright and for some reason quickly strightened the rolled-up sleeves of his shirt.

"Chekhov is dead!"

My father let fall the hand that held the paper, as if not daring to read it. He looked at me in stunned silence.

Then he unfolded the paper nervously and began to read rapidly, repeating softly:

"What a misfortune! What a misfortune!"

After returning the newspaper to the newsstand, I wandered through the streets for a long time, thinking about Chekhov, about how I had never written to him about myself, about other boys who wanted to study music and couldn't afford to, about children whom grown-ups beat over the head with their fists, about music stores full of cellos and pianos and children who could only yearn for them.

In the evening, returning home, I found Egor on the stairway. He was talking with my father through the half-open window. In his hand he held some object wrapped in a piece of cloth, and I at once recognized the outline of a small cello.

Running into Egor like that was so unexpected that I froze to the spot, standing there on the lower landing and looking in the semi-darkness at Egor's shiny gray eyes and white teeth showing in a wide smile.

"How goes it, Kolya?" he greeted me in a whisper, evidently afraid to disturb my sick brother. "Don't come too near, young one, it's dangerous for you here, you might catch the disease."

Telling my father that he would look in again tomorrow, Egor went down the stairs to meet me, both arms outstretched—one hand holding the cello and the other a tight small bundle crammed with something mysterious wrapped in a red kerchief.

"Here, Kolya, take the instrument."

"Where is it from?"

"The bottom of the sea."

I looked at Egor, at his smiling face, heavy locks of wavy hair peeking from under his seaman's cap edged with white, and he appeared to me as a truly rich guest from overseas, bearing generous gifts in his hands, hands strong as those of a valiant knight.

I took the cello possessively.

"And this," Egor said, holding out the full bundle.

"What's in it?"

"Take it, you won't be sorry. It contains nuts, a coconut, dates, pistachio nuts. All this, little brother, grows in places overseas."

I couldn't wait to remove the dusty cloth from the cello, to touch it, to examine every inch of it, to draw the bow across the strings. But where was I to take it? It was dangerous inside our apartment, and my relatives lived very far away.

We went to Anka's, but, alas, her grouchy father was home, and we had no choice but to leave the instrument in the care of Mote, the cook.

After that Egor took me to the big restaurant, "The Bear." At the very end of its longest room, almost underneath the organ erupting with deafening sounds, we sat down at a small table covered with a blue cloth.

"Hey, there, six-in-hand," Egor called to the waiter, using the familiar slang expression. "A pair of teas here."

The waiter, wearing a long, white Russian shirt with an embroidered collar fastened on the side, a man of about forty, short, round, with a shaven head, a yellow puffy face, and bluish bags under his dull eyes, rolled over to the table softly, like a ball.

"What would you like?"

"A pair of teas."

"With sugar, jam?"

"Raspberry."

"Right away."

Brushing some imaginary crumbs off our tablecloth with his large napkin, he rolled away soundlessly as though on air-filled tires, and in a minute he reappeared carrying two white teapots—one large and the other tiny. After pouring the tea essence from the small pot and the hot water from the large one, he placed before us two glass saucers with jam, and, pressing the napkin to his side with his elbow, he disappeared among the tables.

"Drink, pal," Egor said warmly, "we'll first wet our stomachs, then we'll eat something."

Untying the red bundle, he took from it a large brown coconut that looked as if it were wrapped in shaggy wool, a thick bunch of bananas, and something else "foreign," and arranged them neatly on the table.

"Fall to, Kolya, tuck it away. I brought all this across three seas for you—because you're so talented . . ."

He played the role of an attentive host, and with fatherly devotion kept putting generous helpings of the rich jam into my glass, stirring my tea himself, and he kept handing me a date or a nut.

Egor looked the same as he did when I first met him on the ship, when, after his shift in the engine room, he had come up on deck, washed and shiny.

"Have you finished? Here, have another."

Egor then asked me with concern whether my father was working, had my brother been ill a long time, what did the family live on?

As I talked to him, his expression became more tender and his face became sad.

"That's poverty for you, Kolya," he said, sighing. "You listen and listen to human woe but have no way of helping. I've seen plenty of grief in my day, and not only in Russia. You find the same order of things everywhere, there is injustice all over the world. But, never mind, my young friend, this won't go on forever."

Then he told me how he had bought the cello in Naples. Not having had enough money, he borrowed the rest, and to pay it back had arranged to put in extra hours of work on his ship, repairing the furnace.

"And so, you see, brother, I was not left altogether without money. These hands came to the rescue."

And he held up his dark, strong, coarsened hands, indelibly marked with soot and grease.

"I earned some money. And I can help out—I can give your parents some."

Before I realized what Egor was about to do, he took a

handkerchief from an inside pocket of his blue sailor's blouse, unfolded it, and, taking from it two red bills, held them out to me.

"Here, take them, brother, and give them to your dad."

"What are you doing!" I refused the money. "Don't, my father won't take it."

"What do you mean, he won't, isn't your brother ill, doesn't he need the doctor, medicine?"

"Just the same, Father won't take it."

"Then tell him that it is a gift from me to you. Get it? To *you!* Then, you can give it to him."

He pushed the bills into my hand, and, pretending to be angry, added: "Take it or I'll get mad, and when I get mad I become a ferocious, heartless beast."

The organ was playing a wistful tune. Egor's eyes became very dark, like two round dots, and there was a faraway look in them.

Neither the hubbub of the restaurant crowd, nor the incessant clattering of the dishes, distracted him from his private thoughts.

Then, looking at me, he gradually came to, and, smiling ruefully, said self-consciously:

"How I'd like to play! What a yearning I have for it! But what is one to do? There's no way out."

Egor's remark caused me to recall that from this day on I possessed a cello, and my heart filled with joy at the thought.

When the organ stopped playing, Egor began to talk about Italy.

"In Italy they sing many songs. Everywhere there's singing —on ships, in boats, on the streets, and in the market places, in restaurants and in their little cafes. Everybody sings— women, and men, and street urchins. You wouldn't believe it, almost everyone—except, maybe, nursing babies."

I laughed, and Egor, encouraged, tried to keep a straight face as he continued, jokingly:

"The baby stops nursing for a while and breaks into song—let's say, a boatsong or, possibly, a serenade—over there almost all songs are called either one or the other—then, after his performance, the infant goes back to sucking."

He was lost in reminiscence about the warm southern Italian nights, the guitars, mandolins, and, above all, the wonderful singers. It amazed him that these men, endowed with such splendid voices and a rare talent for singing, remained street tramps—poor, dirty, and hungry.

"Beggars—there are multitudes of them! They are in rags, barefoot, the belly empty, no roof over their heads. They possess nothing—nothing but their music. And I kept listening to their songs, picked some of them out on my harmonica, and now I can play them myself."

"Do they sound good?"

"I'll let you hear some, you can judge for yourself."

We went down to the docks. Taking advantage of not being expected at home, and knowing that my relatives would not worry about me, I accepted Egor's invitation with delight:

"First, I'll sing you some Italian songs," he said, "then we'll go down to the beach. We'll go night fishing for mackerel with my pal Lesha. On a barge."

16

A<small>T</small> NIGHT EVERYTHING LOOKED UNUSUAL on the waterfront. The small colored ship lanterns flickered in the darkness. One could only guess at the shapes of the ships' hulls,
masts, stacks, and rigging. The air smelled strongly of sea
salt, pitch, and fresh paint. The gangplanks and trap-ladders
creaked monotonously and comfortingly. The ships swayed
almost imperceptibly in the calm water, and the wistful
sounding of the half hour was heard from many of them at
the same time.

And when you looked up at the city, you saw thousands of
bright lights winking from the Nikolayevsky Boulevard, from
the windows of the London Hotel, the City Hall, the mansion
of the Army Commander, the huge terrace of the open-air
restaurant situated at the very end of the avenue, on a cliff
overhanging the sea.

Everything was asleep at the docks—the passenger, produce,
and watermelon wharfs. In a dead sleep lay the railroad
enclosures and the locomotives, the long freight platforms,
and freighters. The large custom, transport, and produce buildings and warehouses were dozing, and the tall elevators slum-
bered morosely. The vast pier, so noisy and palpitating with
activity in the daytime, so full of the racket of loading
cranes, the creaking of winches, clanking of trams, droning

of steam whistles, and the cries of the dockers—the pier now
slept, with the sleep of a giant workman who had toiled hard
and incessantly for sixteen long hours.

Only at one place in the long shoreline, at the Androsovsky
breakwater, where there were several passenger quays, was it
light and lively. At this late hour, on a daily schedule, two
small passenger ships left for Nikolaev and Ochakov—the
paddleboat *Express* and the new screw-steamer *Mikhail*. From
here also departed the tall, narrow steamers *Georgii* and
Orion.

I got to know these ships well, and the hours of their
departure and arrival, when I worked for the Commercial
Agency and had business to attend to on these quays every
day.

The steam whistles and the smell of the sea, the hurly-
burly of the hurrying passengers, the coming and going of the
porters in their white aprons, loaded down with luggage—all
this always stirred my excitable nature. And now as well, the
dim light over the passenger quay and the music of the
whistles over the quiet dark water awakened in me, with renewed force, my love for the beckoning, shoreless expanse of
the sea.

"There goes the naval ship on its Far Eastern voyage,"
Egor said, looking off into the distance. "It's taking convicts to the island of Sakhalin, in irons. And, maybe, some
down-and-out settlers, too. There—he who hasn't seen woe,
can have a look! Down in the hold there is darkness, filth,
anguish. They crowd them in like cattle. All in one heap—
old men, women, children. Hunger, sickness, disease. And
where are they taking them, what will they find there? Only
more of the same."

In the dark-blue darkness of the southern night nothing
was visible offshore except the green lantern of the lighthouse. And in the water, rows of the lights of floating bea-

cons quietly splashed in the black space, throwing shimmering yellow reflections on the slightly buoyant, dull sheen of the sea.

"How pleasant it is out there," I remarked. "Isn't it, Egor?"

"Y-es . . . For some it's pleasant, for others painful," Egor answered gruffly, even crossly. "Out there, on top, on the decks and in the first-class cabins it is very pleasant indeed to cool off, but below in the holds and in the engine room it is quite bad, and may God spare you that."

I felt uncomfortable before Egor because of my remark. "Of course," I corrected myself, "down below it is awful . . . I was talking about the way it is on top . . ."

"On top, brother, the likes of us will never find ourselves, unless we get there through our own efforts."

I sensed in Egor's words something left unsaid and, at the same time, something significant.

"What do you mean? What do you mean . . . 'through our own efforts'?"

Egor laughed. "How can I explain it to you? You're too young."

I was offended. "I was fourteen long ago . . . you just explain, I'll understand."

"Well, how can I explain it all," Egor seemed to strain for a way. "It's like this: the one who works below should, by rights, rest from his labor on top. Can you understand that? Everyone should work and everyone should rest. Right?"

"No," I answered deliberately, in order to encourage Egor to speak more elaborately, for I had a notion about which direction his remarks were taking. Among the books that I had already read, there were those in which I had already found out about the inequality among people, about the rich who spend their lives in having fun and the poor destined to spend their lives in ceaseless heavy toil.

"You didn't understand? Well, I said you're way too young.

And it's difficult for me to find the right words. But, generally, it's like this: if we, that is, we ourselves, the laboring people, with our own hands, don't shove off the idle ones from on top, then, that will mean that we'll forever remain on the bottom, to slave for the idlers till we die."

Not quite satisfied, I continued to ask Egor questions, and Egor, straining to find the exact words, continued:

"How am I to put it to you . . . some, let's say, work from dawn to night, till their calluses bleed. Others don't do any work, all they do is take it easy. Some, let's say, break their backs earning their crust of bread, they dig every seed from the earth with their bare hands, live in damp hovels, in rat-holes. Others indulge themselves in warm mansions, or, as you see, go on trips abroad in first class . . ."

I turned around compulsively and stared into the darkness at the dots of lights of the ships sailing away in the distance, as if I could, indeed, see on them both the stokers sweating at the furnaces and the carefree rich enjoying themselves in the luxurious cabins.

"The laboring people are numbered in the millions. Those who toil go about in rags, barefoot, poor, swollen with hunger, and the ones who do nothing but carouse—they own all the land, all the grain, all the goods, and mountains of gold. Now, do you understand?"

"I understand," I answered with conviction, as I saw before me, with amazing clarity, the picture that Egor had drawn.

"Now, then," he continued. "If you understand this, you'll understand what goes with it. Things cannot go on this way. There are some people—clever, honest, who care about the suffering of the poor. They have found out about each other and got together. Take a broom—every twig in it, separately, can easily be broken, but when tied together they cannot even be bent . . ."

We could now clearly see the outline of a ship approaching the dock. Egor hastened to finish what he was saying:

"So, that's how things are, brother, in this Russia of ours— and they have been this way now for hundreds of years. Do you see what I'm trying to say?"

The ship had landed now, and we walked toward the gangplank in silence.

All was so still on the deck, as if there weren't a living soul on board. Egor led me carefully by the hand as we crossed the deck together, avoiding the clutter of scattered chains, coils of rope, and cables. We soon reached the stern.

"Stay here," he said, "I'll be back in a moment."

A few minutes later he came back. Sitting down on a crate opposite the one on which I was resting, he gently stretched the pleats of his accordion and put his ear to it, as was his habit.

I sat there relaxed, thinking happily about the cello which I was going to hold in my own two hands tomorrow.

Egor played something beautiful. It stirred my heart with a warm and disturbing joy. Now and then he sang along with the playing. His slightly hoarse tenor blended so well with the accordion that it sounded as if voice and chords both came from somewhere inside the instrument.

The hour was struck on the ship.

"It's midnight," Egor said. "We'll go to the beach now, in a moment."

He stopped playing, then quickly entered a cabin and as quickly came out. He was mysterious and silent about this visit to the cabin. We carefully went down the gangplank, barely visible to us in the deepening darkness, and made our way to the beach.

The Langeron of Odessa!

What kid in this city did not fall in love with this spot! From the harbor it stretched along the coast to the summer

Villa Otrada (the Russian for "Consolation"), which, in its turn, spread over a wide sweep of beach till it touched the grounds of the Villa Arcadia, with its small, medium, and large fountains, and still farther was the summer estate of the Kovalevskys, then, finally, the seashore resort Lustdorf (the German for "Pleasure Village").

The rocky and sandy shoreline wound for fourteen miles, and above it, on steep hills, amid thick groves of acacia trees, were scattered the numerous *dachas* (summer villas) gleaming white in the dark-green foliage.

It was here, on this spacious beachfront, that boys played ferocious games of "sea pirates," had fist fights in which they won glory, bloody noses, and black eyes. Here, for hours, they baked themselves in the merciless heat of the sun, swam endlessly till seized with cramps, and dived under boats. At night they would row out to fish for chum and mackerel, and, imitating the fishermen who lived on the beach in makeshift shacks, they cooked a fish stew of mackerel and potatoes in iron kettles over an open fire, and though the stew always had the acrid smell of smoke, they ate it greedily.

I told Egor all about the Langeron, since he had not spent any of his boyhood here but in a faraway village on the shore of a small river.

"But why doesn't this place have a Russian name?" he asked.

Proud of my knowledge, I answered that this beach, like Langeronskaya Street, had been named in honor of Count Langeron, a French *émigré* who had settled in Odessa.

"That means it's the same as Richelieu, whose monument stands on the boulevard and after whom a street was named."

"That's it, that's it."

"That means the same holds for 'Deribas.' He was one of them."

"That's right."

"And why had these Counts run away from France?"

"They escaped from the Revolution."

"There you are, Kolya! Just you wait, young one, you'll see our Counts run away! They surely will! That's funny—those from France came here and those from here will run to France . . ."

He said these words very seriously and with utter conviction, but after a few moments he suddenly burst out laughing:

"We'll surely give them an opportunity to reciprocate our Russian hospitality to their Counts, and more."

And it now dawned on me that Egor knew perfectly well, without my explanation, the origin of French place names in Odessa, and that he had asked about the origin of "Langeron" only to test my knowledge.

At last we arrived on the Langeron beach.

The large pebbles crunched under our feet. To the left, two paces away, soft waves kept spilling over the sand. In the distance, to our right, glimmered the tall steppe grass.

How pleasant it was here!

A soft breeze blew from the sea, laden with a sharp smell of salt. From the hill there suddenly came a cool fragrance of new-mown hay, flowers, and some kind of bitter steppe grass. And all this mingled in the air with a strong odor of pitch, which was coming from the fishermen's barges scattered along the shore. The warm, light smoke of the bonfires and the vapor from the boiling kettles over the trivets tickled the nostrils pleasantly.

"Lekse-e-e-i!" Egor called loudly in an exaggerated drawl. "A-lek-ce-e-e-i!"

"He-e-e-re!" answered a deep voice from somewhere in the distance.

We quickened our steps, walking around the barges, fish-nets, anchors, oars, while we gazed into the faces of the people sitting around the fires. At last we heard, "Egor, over here!"

Egor's friend and buddy, Aleksei, nicknamed Lyosha, was formerly a stoker and now a fisherman.

In his loose homespun shirt, the tall, barrel-chested Aleksei, with his massive head, looked immense. He greeted Egor with outstretched arms, a resounding slap on the back, a smacking handshake, and a long bear hug.

"Egorii, my friend, you devil, where have you been all this time? Let me take a good look at you!"

He pushed Egor gently away from him, lit a match, and, for an instant, I saw Lyosha's face—its prominent cheekbones, heavy blond eyebrows, and the short and thorny untrimmed reddish beard that looked like last year's mown hay.

"You're the same as ever! You've not aged," he boomed, roaring with laughter. "And who is this? Did you get yourself a son?"

"Grandson," Egor laughed.

"I kept watching out for you. I looked yesterday—and there was the *Pyotr Regger* coming in. So I thought, well, now my chum will show up. I waited and waited, no sign of him. But here you are! Now let's have some supper, and then off we go, fishing!"

We sat down at the fire. Aleksei, after gulping down a glass of vodka with one swallow, handed each of us a painted wooden spoon with a golden design around the edge, then, cutting off thick slices of fragrant rye bread with his huge clasp knife, he passed them out to the people around his fire.

A long-legged, morose old man with a big nose covered with thin clumps of hair and with a gray Cossack mustache hanging down to his bare hairy chest, stared silently at the boiling kettle, waiting impatiently for his meal. Next to him sat a very young, suntanned, dark-eyed fellow wearing the same kind of homespun shirt as Aleksei. He was tapping his spoon against his hand with impatience.

Aleksei picked up a stack of tin bowls and filled them, one after another, with the delicious-smelling yellowish fish stew. He passed a filled bowl to each person, then he began to eat right from the kettle.

"I don't guarantee the taste, but it will sure warm us up," he tossed out between the first two mouthfuls.

"Come on, sit down and eat like us, from a bowl," Egor suggested.

Peals of laughter from Aleksei. "We eat from the trough and have enough, you eat from a plate but are never sate!"

"This is what the Cossacks wrote in a letter to the Turkish Sultan" (during the Crimean War), the young fellow explained to me. "Aleksei knows all kinds of popular sayings and funny limericks."

"That's true," Aleksei affirmed. "Enjoy your meal, kiss host Kiril, if he isn't there, kiss my mare."

I ate the stew with great relish. It smelled especially good and it was tasty, thick with potato and soft white mackerel, and richly spiced with laurel leaf, onion, and pepper.

"Now, off to the barge!" Aleksei gaily and noisily rallied us, and everybody obediently followed him.

The barge was already half in the water. Egor and I sat down in the middle. The young fellow and Aleksei slid our small craft into the sea and jumped nimbly onto its stern. We were at once enveloped by the damp darkness. The dying fires on the shore soon became distant, the flames dimmed and soon entirely disappeared from view. Carried along swiftly by the billowing sail, the barge listed, and in panic I grabbed both Egor and the side of the craft.

"Are you scared?" Egor asked solicitously.

"No . . . what do you mean . . . not at all!" I lied, but a new lurch of the barge forced me to grab Egor with both hands. I put my face against his shoulder and closed my eyes, convinced that we were all about to sink to the bottom of the sea. But the barge, as if nothing were wrong, continued on its way with assurance.

Small lanterns winked weakly on the prow and the stern. Inky waves rolled under us, and in their dark sheen played the faint reflections of the glimmering greenish yellow stars, now breaking with the water, now regathering into pale dots.

I soon began to watch what the fishermen were doing, though it was hard to tell in the darkness. Some were undoing the nets, others were slowing down the barge, turning it about. Then something was cast into the water and the barge was backed up a bit. But I couldn't figure out a thing, and was embarrassed to ask questions since everyone, including Egor, was busy.

The boat rocked. I felt dizzy. The cold of the breeze penetrated my light clothes, and I was shivering. Giving up hope that Egor would have a chance to pay attention to me, I lay down on the small bench and curled up.

I was freezing! I was on the verge of regretting having come along on the trip, when Egor came over to me as if he had heard my thoughts.

"What's wrong, fellow? Are you cold? Or are you getting sleepy?"

"I'm cold."

"Just a minute, youngster, wait a minute."

In a few seconds he was back, covering me with something heavy and warm, carefully tucking in the ends, as he said, laughing, "What a fisherman you'd make! The likes of you should go fishing only in their dreams."

And as I was falling asleep I heard, as if from a distance, Egor's words: "He's a good kid. And what a talent! You seldom meet such . . ."

Then I heard, as I was dozing off, Aleksei's muffled voice:

"The bundle isn't large. Two hundred leaflets. Take them in the morning. You'll distribute them on the ships."

My eyelids, now too heavy, closed tightly, and at the same time my ears stopped hearing—I heard nothing more and sank into a dark whirlpool of sleep.

I was awakened by a strong jolt.

Frightened, and blinded by the sun, I jumped up. Before me was the familiar Langeron beach. One end of our barge stuck in the sand bank, and a crowd of fisherwomen, holding large baskets, were waiting for the fishermen with their catch.

In the middle of our barge wriggled a whole mound of silvery, live mackerel. Graceful, slender, with a pretty blue stripe on their backs and silver tummies, the dainty fish filled almost the entire craft, and I couldn't understand how our few fishermen had managed to catch such a lot of them.

Egor, poking a hole through the gills of the still-live fish with the sharp point of a stick, strung some of the mackerel on a piece of rope—at least twenty—and held the lot out to me:

"Run home now, Kolya, and give these to your mother. Tell her that no matter how sick a child may be, it's all right to feed him this fish. It will only do him good. And let her have a feast on them with your father, and with you, too. Wait, I'll add a few more."

Handing the fish to me, he asked: "Have you hidden the money well?" and not relying on me, he personally checked the cash in my inside pocket—the red five-ruble notes.

"Well, Godspeed you! Hurry on home! I'll come by later —toward evening."

The night spent on the sea, the cheerful sunny morning on the beach, the money and mackerel that would be so welcome in our hungry household, the cello—the real, honest-to-goodness cello waiting for me submissively in the dark pantry of Anka's apartment—it all made me very impatient to get home, and, like a horse who had stood still for a long time and now felt the open spaces, I galloped home without catching my breath until I got there.

Very soon, within a few minutes, I'd be holding the cello in my own two hands!

17

SEVERAL MONTHS HAD PASSED since the day Egor brought me the wonderful present, but I hadn't been able to master it.

Day after day, for hours at a time, I struggled with the unyielding instrument. I'd take up the cello, set it down gently with the sharp point of its foot resting on the scratched-up floor, I'd carefully place my fingers on the strings, tilt my head slightly toward the fingerboard, but, alas, what issued at the touch of the bow was awful. It was a scraping, a squeaking, a shriek, a chirp—anything but music. I was ready to weep with frustration. I couldn't produce a single clear sound, much less play an ordinary scale.

No matter how hard I tried to find the needed note, the fingers of my left hand would not press the correct spot, and the right hand, acting independently, passed the bow crudely over the strings, drawing from them a vociferous protest.

I finally became convinced that a cello was not at all like a mandolin, that without an instructor I'd never learn to play this complicated instrument. But there was no hope of obtaining a teacher.

Could it be that I'd have to give up all thoughts of music and again hire out as an errand boy?

"No, no, and no!" I kept repeating to myself. "I will not give in. I must think of something. I absolutely must!"

And think of something I did.

Early one morning, I went to Yamskaya Street, to the familiar school of The Russian Musical Society, with the determined purpose of having a talk with a certain youth attending the cello class, whom I had noticed some time ago. I soon saw him approach the school, and, gathering courage, I went up to him resolutely.

"Are you studying to play the cello?"

"Yes," he answered, "why do you ask?"

"I . . . too, would like to learn . . . but I have no money . . ."

I was too excited to be able to utter anything else. I couldn't understand why I felt so self-conscious. The student had an ordinary and pleasant face, dark friendly eyes, and a warm smile. And, after all, he wasn't much older than I.

"Would you like me to give you lessons?"

"Yes," I said, my mood lifting at once.

"What about a cello?"

"I have one."

"Well, great! Come back tomorrow, at the same time."

Bitter experience had taught me to be cautious about mis-understandings. Did he understand in full the kind of favor I was asking?

"But . . . I have no money," I stammered, blushing.

"Why do you need money? Do you want to hire a carriage to get here, or to buy yourself a dress suit and top hat?"

"No," I answered, even more embarrassed, feeling my face burning, "money . . . for you."

"But you have already told me that you have no money," the student said. "Just come back tomorrow, at this time. So long."

He opened the door with the opaque windows and entered his classroom.

I was about to run home to tell my parents and Anka the

good news, when I heard, coming from the semi-dark auditorium, the sounds of instruments being tuned. Realizing that
they were about to start the lesson of the orchestra class, I
quietly slipped into the auditorium, and, trying to be incon-
spicuous, settled down in the most secluded corner.

Once again, as in the days when I often used to sneak in
here, I looked with envy at the boys and girls with their
instruments. There were slender light-brown violins, their
slightly larger and darker older brothers—the violas, and their
mothers—the dignified sturdy cellos, then the fathers and
grandfathers—the important-looking, mature, somewhat stern,
bass viols. And in the midst of these self-assured, serene string
instruments, here and there could be spotted the tiny black
pipes—the piccolos and the long, thin, comical flutes with
their many shiny nickel valves, or the rows of the altogether
frail-looking oboes, and the English horns with their flat,
toy-like reed pipes. Next to the oboes and English horns, somewhat larger, were the sturdy clarinets with their red "em-
bouchures," that is, mouthpieces, and, not resembling them
any more than a rich relative resembles a poor one, were the
haughty bass clarinets and the respectable, restrained, even-
paced bassoons.

On the left side of the orchestra stood out the triangular,
many-stringed harp. To the right of the harp glistened the
brass of the straight cornets, the round French horns, with
their wide flares, the oblong trombones, the huge, heavy
trumpets, and, right near them, just in back, were the neatly
placed percussion instruments—the tympani, cymbals, and
drums. And this assortment of instruments moving and
swaying in so many different ways and singing in such a
medley of voices, played hundreds of melodic fragments, weav-
ing them somehow into a single orchestral harmony.

The instructor Kutyl now walked onto the stage. When he
stepped up to the conductor's podium, total silence fell over

the auditorium, as if there were not a single person in the orchestra. And into this surprising silence, the instant the conductor raised his baton, an avalanche of impassioned sounds burst forth. A short pause—and the same melody, without any change, was played again, but as a distant echo, more quiet and more serene.

Kutyl angrily tapped the baton against his stand, and the orchestra stopped playing. A minute later, after the strict criticisms of the conductor, the orchestra, with fresh vigor, let loose into the auditorium a buoyant wave of the short melody, now so fiery and full of ardor that I strongly wished that the instructor would again stop the orchestra and repeat everything from the start.

But instead I suddenly heard someone's unpleasant, hoarse voice, and, turning around, I saw a yellow-bearded old man in the same kind of teacher's uniform worn by Kutyl.

"Boy, what is your name?" he asked me irritably, bending down to my ear.

I told him.

"Get up!"

I stood up.

"What class are you in?"

I didn't know what to say and kept silent.

"I repeat: what class?"

Choosing the words with difficulty, I tried to explain: "I don't study here . . . I'm here on business . . . I'm waiting for a student acquaintance . . ."

He stared at me suspiciously with his small, sunken, gray eyes.

"Who is he?"

"That one—the cellist." I pointed to the side of the orchestra where the cellists sat. "He promised to teach me . . ."

The playing of the orchestra drowned out my voice, and the old man shouted right into my ear:

"Follow me!"

In the corridor, fixing me with his gaze, he said fiercely, uttering each word slowly, in a low tone, but threateningly:

"Get out of here this instant! Do you hear? And if I ever catch you here again, I'll box your ears and take you to the police. Understand? Now, get out!"

"Why the police?" I asked, looking him straight in the face; I now found him contemptible.

"Ha, so, you're a fresh one, too! I'll teach you . . ."

He raised his hand with its long, dry, pale fingers to grab me by the ear, but I jumped away quickly, and, feeling even more deeply offended and with my heart bursting with indignation, I said:

"How dare you! I . . ."

"Guard! Guard!" the old man screamed. "Hey, who is here? Watchman! Inspector!"

Students and teachers came running out of the classrooms, aroused by his cries. I hurried toward the door, but the watchman was coming in my direction.

I tried to slip through between him and the wall, but another attendant flew at me from the side, knocked me down, and threw himself on top, pinning me to the floor with his weight.

"What are you doing?" I heard a soft female voice over me. "Stop this at once!"

"He must have done something," the one holding me down said. "Maybe he's a thief—they ordered us to catch him . . ."

He let me go. I got up. The woman, picking up my cap, asked kindly:

"What did you do?"

"I listened to the music."

"Where?"

"In the auditorium."

"Then, what?"

Pushing aside the students who crowded around me, the enraged old man appeared. Still furious, he began to explain in a voice breaking with wrath:

"Insolent street tramp! Good-for-nothing! He steals into the school! He sits there in the auditorium, stretched out like a lord! Listens!"

"And you pursue him like a thief!" the woman was appalled. "They knock him down, drag him . . . and for what? As if he were really a criminal."

"I know him," one of the boys spoke up. "He always comes around where there's music."

"Did you hear that! How can you do such a thing!"

From the insult and the pain in my back and arms, tears welled into my eyes.

"Don't, boy," the woman said gently, putting her arm around my shoulders. "Go home."

I put on my cap and mumbled: "Thank you . . . forgive me . . ."

And as I was leaving I heard her say: "You see! He's a decent boy!"

I looked around for a water pump in the school courtyard. After washing my eyes with the cold water, I sat down in a corner near a pile of lumber, and tried to pull myself together.

Then I walked out into the street and waited at the school, still hoping to see my young instructor. I waited one hour, another, a third—but he didn't come out. Evidently I missed him, or, perhaps he was going to stay on in the school till evening.

Hungry, tired, and embittered, I had to leave without arranging for tomorrow's meeting with my teacher, since going inside to look for him was now out of the question.

18

NEXT DAY IT WAS IMPOSSIBLE for me to try to contact the young cellist.

Early in the morning, just when I was about to leave the house with the cello, the mailman delivered a letter; it was the first letter ever addressed to me, personally. In a large round handwriting, which I somehow guessed to be Egor's, was written:

DEAR BROTHER KOLYA!

I swam and swam the seas and oceans, and fell right into the jaws of a powerful shark. Thus far I remain caught in his vicious teeth, and what will happen further only Allah of the Turks knows. Maybe he'll spit me out, or maybe I'll be swallowed alive—that's what a shark does. And some beast cut up my accordion, looking for hidden things in it, and ruining it for good. Also, whatever money I had was taken by a swine, and I now live on bread and water. That shark that nabbed me is not an ordinary one—he's made of bricks, his teeth are of iron, and his home is—you can tell where, just look at the postmark. But I have not lost heart, my young friend, though our life is tough and there's nothing to crow about. Much remains to be done . . . There are many of us here, some older, wiser, and better than me, but just the same such, too, wear iron rings and bracelets on their ankles—weighing up to twelve pounds—but neither do they lose heart . . . they even laugh at times and often sing brave songs. And how are *you* getting along—how are you doing with the cello, is the family all right, is everyone in good health? Be of good cheer and strong, study, and become an artist. I'm sure your name will some day be honored throughout Russia. As for me, if I get out of these jaws alive and healthy, I'll come back and will go on helping you. I hug you, little brother, and remain your big brother,

EGOR

My legs felt numb and my body as heavy as lead. I seemed to understand every word in Egor's letter, from the very first line to the last, but at the same time there was something that puzzled me.

What did it all *really* mean? Was it possible that Egor was in prison? And if so, why? "That shark that nabbed me is not an ordinary one—he's made of bricks, his teeth are of iron . . ." I re-read the crooked lines of the letter. "There are many of us here . . . such, too, wear iron rings and bracelets on their ankles—weighing up to twelve pounds . . ." No, of course, there was no doubt about it—Egor was in prison.

I kept looking for a long time at the blurred letters of the postmark and I finally made out the word Sevastopol.

Egor was in a Sevastopol prison! I pictured at once a dark, dank cell, the thick iron windowbars, the black bread and water.

". . . and what will happen further only Allah of the Turks . . ." They will probably send him in a convoy over thousands of miles into Siberia, in a gray convict's cloak and heavy irons, and will chain him there to his wheelbarrow to do penal servitude.

I clenched my fists with fury and despair as the thought bore into my mind that there was no way for me to help Egor.

If I were only a little older and if I had some money,
I would this very day get on the first ship to Sevastopol.
I'd rush to Egor, bring him food, clothes, books. I had once
watched our neighbor prepare a "bundle" for her imprisoned
son, and I had even helped her carry the narrow white sack
to the horse trolley.

Maybe I ought to sell my cello? Yes, I should take it at
once to the music store, get some money for it, and this
evening take the ship *Russian Company* to Sevastopol. The
following day I would at least be able to get bread and sugar
to Egor.

Early next morning I left home carrying the cello, as if I
were on my way to a lesson. Hurrying, almost running, I went
toward Richelieu Street, to the musical instrument store. Here
I encountered the first difficulty. The manager, resembling an
overfed tomcat, a stocky, red-faced, smoothly shaven, blond
man, examined the instrument and stated dryly that his firm
did not purchase goods from minors.

"Send an adult with it," he said indifferently, not even
looking at me.

I was told the same thing at the next store.

Without losing a moment, I rushed to a third one, on Big
Arnautskaya Street, near the Old Market. This wasn't really
a store but a repair shop, full of very old, beat-up, and broken
violins, mandolins, balalaikas, guitars. Behind the counter was
a man as old as the shop and everything in it—a sallow,
wrinkled old man, evidently the owner.

"What do I need with your piece of junk?" he grumbled
morosely. "I have a storeful of trash, and don't know what to
do with it."

At a loss, I remained standing on the sidewalk outside
the shop, unable to decide what to do next.

The pawnshop!—it suddenly occurred to me.

I knew only too well the way to this establishment. More

than once had I had occasion to take my father's only precious possession there—his old, dented, silver cigar-case, or my mother's ring, an heirloom worn thin over the years.

And now, carrying my own only precious possession, much bulkier than theirs, I hurried down Uspenskaya Street, tormented by the thought that they, too, might not take my cello.

The old pawnbroker, accustomed to seeing any object in the world placed on his table, looked at the cello without any sign of surprise. He did not even touch it, as if he meant to convey in this manner that it had no value to him. But in the end he decided to pick it up. He examined it carefully, turned it over twice, then squinting his left eye, stared through the curved sound-holes into the chest of the instrument.

"And what do you expect to get for this?" he asked.

"I don't know . . . whatever you'll give . . ."

"Three rubles."

I was horrified. What could I do with only three rubles?

"I want five . . ."

"No, three," and he started to hand the cello back to me.

"All right," I quickly agreed, "let me have it."

I left clutching in one hand a large, impressive pawn ticket and in the other a new green bill.

What must I do next?

I wanted to go home first, before going down to catch a boat, but what would I say to my parents if they asked me what I had done with the cello? Maybe it was better to confide in Anka—ask her to tell my parents what happened after I had gone. Or, maybe it was better not to tell anything to anyone and instead send my folks a postcard which they would get the following day, when I was already far away.

Yes, that was the thing to do. But what about the money for the card? No. As it was, I had little enough money, and I had to buy a ticket for the trip. If I spent money on things that weren't absolutely necessary, what would there be left for Egor? The boat fare was probably pretty high and would use up a large part of my funds. I decided then and there to avoid this expense, too, and somehow to make the trip without buying a ticket.

I had already walked three blocks toward the harbor when I remembered that I had taken along none of the necessary things for a journey—not even a piece of soap, a towel, a bag in which to pack the things to be left for Egor, nor did I have my mandolin with me. I certainly didn't want to part with it, and in an emergency I could sell it. Besides, the mandolin was a gift from Egor . . .

I immediately turned back and ran home. Fortunately my parents were out. Doing everything at top speed, and taking care that my brother should not notice what I was doing, I got an old flour sack from a kitchen closet, put the mandolin and a piece of bread into it, and, grabbing a change of underthings and my poetry reader, I was off.

On the way I stopped at Anka's. She met me with eyes wide with surprise.

"Where are you going? Why the sack?"

Lowering my voice, and feeling like a conspirator, I told her everything, including my plans to go to Egor's aid.

"You're mad!" she whispered with fright, and her big eyes became even bigger, and their dark depths even darker and deeper. "Where will you stay? What will you eat?"

"You must understand . . ." I explained in an undertone, although there was no one in the room to overhear us, "he's probably a revolutionary . . . He has nobody . . ."

"All right, then," she said a little more calmly and asked, "How do you plan to help him?"

"I don't know."

"Then don't go!"

"No, I must go to him."

Several times, almost without changing a syllable, we exchanged the same remarks, till Anka, tired of arguing with me, offered no more objections. When I was about to leave, she said:

"Wait a minute . . ."

She went away, evidently to the kitchen, rummaged about there for a long time, and finally came back carrying something wrapped in a piece of newspaper.

"Take it for the road," and she put the parcel near my sack.

When I was about to leave, she stopped me once more.

"Wait another minute," and she disappeared again.

While she was gone, I tore a page from her notebook and quickly wrote:

"Dear Father and Mother: Egor, it seems, is a revolutionary, and is in prison. I am going there to help him. Don't be angry. I had to do it. Your loving son, Kolya."

Anka was back now, holding a tiny key. She got a small, polished, wooden piggy bank from a chest and opened it.

"It was all I could do to get mother to give me the key," she said with a mischievous smile as she emptied her savings onto the table—a little heap of silver coins. "I meant to save up ten rubles, but so far there are only four. Here, take them."

I didn't know how to react. I was ashamed to take money from Anka, money she had so painstakingly saved, a twenty-kopeck piece at a time. But neither did I have the right, under the circumstances, to refuse it.

I felt embarrassed just the same and started to stammer, feeling all the time how badly I was blushing. "You understand . . . this isn't for me . . . this is for the cause . . . for Egor . . ." I blurted out, surprised by my reasoning.

"Yes, yes, I understand," she said solemnly

She wrapped the money in her handkerchief, put it way

down in the inside pocket of my jacket, and secured it with two safety pins.

"I'll walk with you a ways," she said, putting the note to my parents in her apron pocket. She promised to give it to them no earlier than ten o'clock that evening, when my ship would already have departed.

The city was now enveloped in the early southern twilight. The first gaslights were being lit on the streets, and in the windows of the taverns and stores, one after another, appeared the dark-yellowish lights of kerosene lamps. When we reached the corner I urged Anka to go home, but she refused and accompanied me to the boulevard. Here, after hesitating for a moment, we walked halfway down the wide, steep stairway leading to the harbor, and said good-bye on the landing.

"Be careful, Kolya, don't do anything foolish," Anka advised me in a grown-up tone, sounding like a mother. I couldn't see her face in the deepening dusk, and it seemed to me that I was really hearing my mother's voice.

"Let's kiss good-bye," Anka suggested, simply and very seriously.

My hands were occupied, so, bending down slightly, I touched my lips to hers and, as if possessed, bounded down the stairs two at a time, hearing her words following me:

"Don't do anything foolish! Come back soon!"

I didn't turn around but ran on and crossed Primorskaya Street, the railroad tracks, walked under the wooden booms, and, bypassing the railroad depot, soon found myself at the right wharf.

The large steamer *Russian Company* was being loaded. The third-class passengers with their small children and large bundles were making their way up the gangplank in a single file, but before stepping onto it they had to show their tickets to the captain's mate standing at the foot of it. I tried to sneak through with a large, noisy family of six but failed—as it was, they were short three tickets. At my second attempt the mate spotted me at once:

"Get away from here! I won't let you through!"

When I heard the first steam whistle, I realized that I would not succeed in getting aboard without paying my fare. With a heavy heart I went toward the ticket window, but at the last moment noticed an aging sailor with a stack of some ship's documents in his hands. Assuming that he was in charge of something or other, I turned to him and said:

"Uncle, I must get to Sevastopol. I have a brother there, a seaman from the *Pyotr Regger*—he's sick . . . in the hospital. Take me along with you."

"A seaman, did you say? He's sick?" he verified, not trusting me, but smiling in a friendly way. "Are you sure you're not fibbing?"

"Cross my heart, Uncle," I hurried to assure him. "Egor Egorov from the *Pyotr Regger*. Come, take me along—I'll tell you everything later. See—I'm taking some food to him, and a change of clothes."

The sailor looked at the flour sack, at the parcel, at me, and narrowing his eyes with understanding but also with some remaining suspicion, repeated:

"And you're not fibbing?"

"May thunder strike me dead if I am, Uncle."

"Well, all right, come with me."

At the freight gangplank he put me in the care of another seaman, one somewhat younger, saying to him in an undertone:

"Take him to the poop deck. He's a seaman's brother—going to visit a patient."

The two of us quickly mounted to the deck and went toward the stern. Here, in the greenish late twilight, hardly penetrated by the shore lights, I made my way between the windlass, the hawsers, and the chains, stumbling over a large coil of very thick cable smelling strongly of pitch. I sat down on it to rest.

A cool dampness rose from the water, hundreds of white lights winked along the boulevard, a hissing of steam came from somewhere, and it all seemed to me unreal, that I was part of a fairy story or a dream.

The steam whistle made me start—it was much louder when heard from the deck. It blew several times, then there was other whistling mingled with the captain's loud orders, and the steamer pushed off slowly.

The flares of the lighthouse were soon behind us. The night hung low, covering the ship, engulfing everything, even the nearest shapes, and blending with the blackness of the invisible sea. Beyond the stern, somewhere below its outer walls, the wide blades of the propeller slapped tirelessly against the water, and their incessant, monotonous noise, together with the rhythmic rocking of the steamer, gradually soothed and lulled me. I wanted so badly to stretch out right there on the deck and go to sleep! But the cold wind blew over me, the clammy dampness crawled up my sleeves, inside my collar, and chilled me to the bone.

I got up and, hugging my parcels, tried to feel my way to some sheltered corner where I could take cover from the wind and fog of the open sea. But there was no such spot at the stern. Returning to my coil of cable, I settled down on the lee-side, but I jumped right up, stung by the icy cold of the wet metal floor.

Where could I go? I would have tried the third class, but I was afraid I'd run into some inspector.

The wind grew stronger, the cold became unbearable. My cap kept flying off my head and I had to hold it under my arm while holding onto my bundles to keep them from scattering.

Soon a storm blew up in earnest.

Any moment I could have been lifted, thrown against the side of the ship, blown into the sea.

Ignoring caution and with the determination of despair, I went toward the third class. Picking my way past the ballroom of the first and second class, I saw, through the glass of its large windows opening onto the deck, the brightly lit restaurant with its neat rows of small tables covered with snowy-white cloths, decorated with flowers, and glistening with china and with bottles displaying colorful labels.

At these tables sat richly dressed men and women, and over the red carpet hurried waiters wearing white jackets and carrying silver trays from which rose the appetizing vapors of hot food.

How light and warm it was inside! And how good it would feel to have a filling meal there! It would also be nice to sit down on that velvet settee and listen to the piano. The playing could be heard only faintly on deck, through the thick windowpanes.

At that moment the figure of some petty officer appeared in the shaft of light.

"What are you doing here?" his angry voice burst out. "Get back to the third class at once!"

I quickly hid in the darkness, and heard him call after me:

"Do you have a ticket? Hey, you, passenger!"

I bumped into some door and saw a dimly lit sign: "Fourth class."

Evidently there was even such a thing as fourth class!

Without stopping to think, I put my frozen foot down the first step and began to walk down into the semi-dark quarters below. At first I felt nothing except damp warmth, but soon it was mingled with a foul stench. The smell was so overpowering that I turned around at once and started up the stairs to escape from it. Then, remembering the frigid wind,

I stopped, and, struggling with a feeling of nausea, forced myself to go down the remaining steps.

I found myself in an enormous hold. A brown-gray haze hung under the low ceiling. All over on its floor, from wall to wall, women, men, and children lay crowded together. The place was strewn with bundles, parcels, baskets, and boxes. The sleeping, almost naked children, and the adults in tattered half-dress, looked like a stirring heap of rags. There were sounds of throaty breathing, moaning, weeping, coughing. Someone was cursing vilely in his sleep, others were muttering drowsily.

All that I was seeing, hearing, and smelling down there was so unbearable that I hurried back upstairs as if pushed by some intangible force.

The chill that immediately hit me seemed welcome after the horrors of the fourth class.

I groped my way to the coil of cables, consoling myself with the hope that I would somehow, in the course of the night, sneak into the third class or the stokehold. But during my brief absence the situation had changed for the worse. The storm was now in full force! The waves, invisible in the black darkness, buffeted the ship, lifting it very high and instantly dropping it low. There was one big swell after another.

Dropping my possessions, I grabbed at a hawser, trying not to be thrown against the side of the ship. I felt dizzy and seasick.

The wind raged from all sides, blowing the ship about furiously as if it were merely a small barge, and it seemed to me that at any moment I would go down together with it into the turbulent deep.

But at that hopeless moment someone's large figure bent over me. It seemed to be that of a seaman. He held up his lantern.

"Yes, here you are. You are my lad—aren't you?" I heard

the familiar voice of the aging sailor. "Forgot all about him, and he's perishing out here! Are you able to stand up?"

"I'm dying . . ." I answered in a voice not my own.

"God is merciful—you won't die," the sailor laughed. "Grab me around the neck."

He lifted me like a baby and carried me down some steps.

"My things!" I gasped, hardly having the strength to talk, "the sack . . . my parcel . . . my cap."

"Everything is safe," he laughed again. "They're bringing your luggage after you, like for a first-class passenger."

Having caught my breath, I was beginning to feel embarrassed and asked him to put me down, but the seaman held me even tighter in his powerful arms.

"Be still, you Sevastopol hero, don't squirm so. After we pass the Tarkhankutsky lighthouse you'll be able to stand on your own two feet."

We now came into a low-ceilinged, stuffy cabin resembling Egor's quarters on the *Pyotr Regger*. There was the same smell of cheap tobacco, sheepskin, and rye bread. The sailor laid me down on a cot and covered me with a gray quilt.

"Let the lad lie down here for a bit," he said to someone. "He's a seaman's kid brother."

Another sailor left my things at my side.

"Here is your sack and your parcel—the cap wasn't there, it was probably blown into the sea."

The ship continued to rock violently. I still felt dizzy, and my empty stomach ached, but my whole body responded to the bliss of warmth and shelter, and I sank into a light, restoring sleep.

"He's a nice kid," I heard through my sleep. "He's trying to get to his older brother. That poor fellow has wound up in the foe's lair." How did they know that Egor was in prison? . . .

19

IN SEVASTOPOL, after leaving the steamer, I stood on the quay, bewildered by the noise and the commotion. My head felt heavy, and the people and objects kept swaying, as if I weren't yet on firm ground but still on the ship battered by the storm.

But this soon passed.

I found the prison without any trouble. I recognized the dismal building even from a distance, seeing its small, barred cell windows.

There was a crowd of women with bundles at the large iron gates. They explained to me that parcels were accepted for the prisoners only on a certain day of the week, but the first parcel could be left there any day.

The small square window fixed in the narrow door to the side of the gate was opened wide, and the red, mustached face of the guard stared out at me.

"Egor . . . Egor Dormidontovich—is he here?" I inquired in a voice faltering with emotion.

The guard took a long time locating the name in his thick register, moving his yellowed finger with a large black spot in the nail slowly down the page, and finally answered with a lazy indifference:

"Cell number thirteen."

"May I leave him a parcel?"

"Let's have it."

"I'm going to buy him some things—will be back right away."

There was only half an hour left before they would stop accepting parcels for the day. Following the women's advice, I crossed the road, found the grocery store and bought everything that one was allowed to bring for a prisoner. Turning away from the counter, I hurriedly removed Anka's safety pins, took out the money and reluctantly, like a peasant at the market, counted off one silver coin at a time, the amount of the purchase. Then, removing the mandolin and my personal things from the flour sack, I packed it full with the things I had just bought for Egor.

I was soon at the prison again, and my sack disappeared through the small window. Content, I stepped away from the gate.

I hung around for a long time, waiting for them to return the empty sack and give me a receipt signed by Egor himself. In the meantime I kept overhearing the talk among those who also had come here to deliver parcels or to visit imprisoned relatives.

"Mine has been shut away here for six months now," a shrunken woman with tired, sunken eyes was saying, "he's being tried under Article 102, Part 1."

"And mine has been buried here for nearly two years," sighed a sickly short woman with a puffy bluish face and faded eyebrows. "The trial is coming up soon, and how much longer he'll be given, only God knows . . ."

"According to the law, except for hard labor they don't give anything else," an old man reassured her. He had a matted reddish-gray beard and teary red eyes, and was wearing a worn cloak shining with grease spots. "Under this accursed Article 102, Part 1, they sentenced my oldest son to eight years and the younger one, under Part 2, they gave the full twelve. And now I keep coming here and asking them when they plan to drive my poor boys off to Siberia."

I listened with growing panic to the unfamiliar, cruel words: "Military District Court," "One-hundred-second Article of the Law," "hard labor," "twelve years," "shaven head," "chains," "Siberia," "under police escort."

Was it possible that Egor was facing many months in this prison, followed by a trial before the Military District Court, and years of hard labor, in irons, in the far *taiga*—the frozen and marshy Siberian forest? My legs nearly gave way at the thought of what Egor was facing.

The empty sack was finally returned and with it came a crumpled signed note. On the reverse side of it I read in Egor's large rolling handwriting: "I received everything. Thank you. For God's sake, return home! I respectfully bow before you. Egor."

But how could I leave him here, alone? I would gladly have left this grim and gloomy place, but I couldn't forsake Egor.

The rest of the day I wandered through the streets, went up to the Malakhov Hill from where I saw a view of the city, and toward evening, hearing snatches of distant music, I followed the sounds and soon found myself in the public park. The central area was bright with electric lights. A gleaming white shell overhanging the round platform of the stage enclosed it on three sides. A large naval orchestra was playing. There were many rows of benches crowded with listeners. A crowd of people for whom there were no seats left stood in back and along the sides.

I stayed there for the rest of the evening, listening to the concert from my comfortable perch on a high tree stump.

Night approached. The concert ended, the audience dispersed, and the lights went out.

I was now alone in the pitch dark park.

A heavy exhaustion made my shoulders feel as if they were carrying sacks of wet sand, my feet were like lead and felt cemented to the ground. Scarcely able to move, I ambled to a bench in a nearby alley and stretched out on it with great relief. Holding the neck of my mandolin securely in my fist, I immediately fell asleep.

Once or twice during the night I woke with a start from some kind of shaking, which seemed to be caused neither by cold nor by any internal jolt. I couldn't remember where I was. I saw over me the stars shimmering in the dark-blue velvet of the southern sky, heard the monotonous crackling of the crickets, and, unable to keep my eyes open, fell asleep again.

I was wakened by the sunlight streaming into my eyes. The purple-gold, gently warm sun had just risen above the trees. The sky, exceptionally blue and transparent—I had never before in my life seen such a sky!—was very high. The green things—trees, flower beds, grass—were still covered with droplets of dew and gave off a faint, slightly bitter scent. Thousands of birds were chirruping lustily.

I sat up and remained on the bench, overwhelmed by the bright, soothing sun, the happy chatter of the birds. I didn't want to leave the park. I didn't want to think about what was ahead of me—not having a roof over my head, visiting the jail in which Egor was suffering, having to provide the things he so sorely needed. I wanted to be able to forget what I had witnessed the day before at the prison gates and had heard from the mothers, wives, and fathers of the prisoners. Here it was so joyous, so spacious. Above me was such a marvelous sky and around me such gay music that I couldn't quite believe that there were such dreadful things as dark cells, underground dungeons, penal servitude. But I knew these were not fiction, not fantasy—they really existed, and, in fact,

I had to get over to the prison right away. And there, as
yesterday, I would again plainly see the gray building with its
barred cell windows and the huge iron gates designed to deprive people like Egor of the radiance and delight that surrounded me here, in the park.

I had to get up, go to the market and buy more things
for Egor. He had been in jail for a long time and must lack
the very necessities of life. Today was the day for the
weekly delivering of parcels and I had to get together enough
things to last him at least a week.

Giving up the idea of staying on in the park for a while,
I rose reluctantly from the bench. I noticed a silver twenty-
kopeck piece slide down my trouser leg and drop soundlessly
in the dust at my feet. Where did it come from? I didn't
bend down to pick it up but, in surprise, kept examining my
clothes. In the left side of my jacket I saw a long, thin
vertical cut. Frightened, I stuck my fingers into it—my inside
pocket, the one that Anka had secured with the safety pins,
was empty. Not only was all the change gone, but also the
crisp three-ruble note from the pawnshop. I was about to look
into my trouser pockets for the few small coins I had put
there, but found them both turned inside out.

I was stunned! What now? What was I going to use for
money to buy the things Egor needed? How was I going to
buy food for myself? Where was I going to sleep? How would
I get home?

20

I WALKED BEWILDERED through the city till about noon, looking into the store windows, visiting the market place. The
counters were full of meat, butter, fish, and rows of French
rolls and square loaves of bread. There were large baskets
heaped with bright-red tomatoes, yellow pears, and fresh red-
cheeked apples gleaming with juiciness. I was hungry and the
sight of all this food sharpened my appetite, which was big
enough at all times. But I had only twenty kopecks now, and
thirteen of these had to go for a roll and sugar for Egor.
After long deliberation, I bought a pound of dark bread and
two cucumbers, ate them on the spot, and, buying the two
things for Egor, set off to deliver this modest gift to him.

At the prison gate I met yesterday's acquaintances and
found out from them that today was not only the day for
bringing parcels but also for visiting the prisoners.

I instantly decided to pose as Egor's brother so as to be
allowed to see him.

I stood in line, and when I came to the little window, I
named the prisoner I wanted to visit:

"Egorov, Egor Dormidontovich."

"What relation?"

"Brother."

"Identification?"

"I don't . . . have . . ."

"Without it you can't come in."

"I'm too young—I don't have a passport."

"Let's see your birth certificate."

"My birth certificate . . . it was stolen . . ."

"You're lying."

"Honest . . . cross my heart . . . Look, Uncle, they cut into my pocket. You see, my mother fastened it with pins and the thief cut it . . . They stole it, and all my money, too."

A police officer overheard this conversation. At first I couldn't see him. Then an enormous head with a new cap, a bushy red mustache, and a large red nose appeared at the window.

"How old are you?" he asked in a booming bass voice.

"Thirteen," I lied by only a year and a half, and, to play safe, I shrank myself a little.

"Just a pup," he commented, turning to the guard. "Let him in."

They allowed me to go in through the narrow entrance at the side of the gate, and I soon found myself in a small building where several visitors were already waiting. The room was divided into two equal parts by a double-mesh metal partition and behind it, through a side door, the prisoners were coming in, one by one, and at short intervals.

They stared intently through the dense sieve-like partition and called out:

"Mama! . . . Come this way!"

"Glasha, I'm over here!"

"Hey, Dad, don't you know me?"

I, too, looked through the metal veiling into the dimly lit space on the other side of it, and suddenly heard a well-known voice call out:

"Kolya, my friend!"

I ran along the iron net and stopped in front of a thin and pale Egor, his face seamed with the shadows of the partition's mesh.

"Welcome, Kolya!" he shouted, trying to be heard over the noise the others were making. "How did you manage to get through?"

"I'm your brother . . ." I tried to tell him in time about our new relationship and motioned to him to put his ear against the mesh. "I'm your brother—Nicolai Dormidontovich Egorov."

"Ha-a . . ." He nodded his head to tell me that he understood, and immediately greeted me loudly: "Welcome, little brother, how did you come here?"

Speaking fast, so as to have time to tell each other as much as possible, I reviewed everything—from the minute I had received his letter to this day's events.

"Go home, for God's sake!" he pleaded. "Get away from this place or you'll come to some harm."

He looked to the right and to the left, waiting for the moment when the guards, pacing on either side of the partition, would be out of earshot, and, lowering his voice, he said:

"*Emerance*, when it docks in Odessa, tell the stoker, Petrov, that they interrogated me about him, and that I knew nothing. He should change ships. Can you remember all this? *Emerance*—Petrov."

He was going to add something else, but looking around, he saw the guard approaching.

"Give my regards to Father and Mother."

A shrill whistle pierced the air, followed by a harsh order: "E-e-nd of vi-i-si-ting!"

Egor managed to toss out:

"An early trial. They'll give me a long sentence. Leave this place, for God's sake! Return home!"

He was saying something else, but the guard was already pushing me away, and, without hearing any more, I found myself at the door.

Getting back my mandolin and book, I left through the prison gates, and for a long time wandered through the streets.

All around me were the houses of strangers, strangers' windows and doors, and people to whom I was a stranger. To whom could I turn? Where was I to get clothes for Egor? He was wearing a miserable-looking shirt with a big tear and dirty, tangled string lacing. Where could I get even a little money for food? Egor's face was thin and ashen, his cheeks were hollow, there were black rings under his eyes. How was I going to manage to bring him all the supplies he needed for the long trek to Siberia? The poor man would have to travel, mostly on foot, perhaps for several months, across all of Russia, to dozens of way-station jails and police-escort transfer points.

Not finding any answers to these questions, I continued to walk through the city, hungry, tired, without a kopeck, and without shelter.

Toward evening an idea struck me—maybe, luckily, the *Emerance*, with Egor's friend Petrov on board, had docked in Sevastopol.

I went to the waterfront.

But, alas, the *Emerance* wasn't there, and uneasy at the approach of night, I turned back toward the city. My sense of smell, sharpened by hunger, was enticed by the scent of fried food coming from a garden adjoining a tavern. I turned back and, following the scent, soon found myself inside the waterfront tavern. Almost every table was occupied by seamen, longshoremen, and draymen. There were also quite a few women. The air was heavy with the blue smoke of strong tobacco, the fumes of vodka, and the thick vapors of hot food.

I was dying of hunger.

Feeling dizzy from the smoke and the tantalizing smell of food, I turned back toward the door and was about to leave, when I heard a woman's voice call out:

"Hey, urchin, play us something!"

"Yes, come on, give us a song!" a hoarse and rude masculine voice chimed in.

From a table near the wall, a plump, pretty woman with lightly rouged pale cheeks and unusually large eyes smilingly beckoned to me with her finger.

"Come over here, sonny, come on over, don't be bashful," she said softly, in a special singsong tone.

"Yes, come on!" her hoarse neighbor continued to bawl an immense, red-bearded seaman in a white blouse—banging the edge of the table with his thick, toil-hardened fingers. I walked over to them.

"Play us something . . ." the woman almost begged.

She was obviously drunk, but her face was so kind, her large moist eyes looked at me so pleadingly, that I didn't have the heart to refuse her, and I mechanically pulled the mandolin out of the sack, although I had never before in my life played for strangers.

"What would you like me to play?"

"Do you know many songs?"

"Yes, I do."

"Do you know 'Stiojki-Dorojki'?"

"Yes."

"Oh, Lord, then play it, why don't you!" The excitable woman gushed, moving her chair closer to where I was standing.

My mouth was dry, my throat was tight, but I couldn't get myself to ask for food. I kept wetting my palate with my tongue as I played the first chords. I saw the woman move still closer, to the middle of the table, and look avidly at the mandolin with dilated pupils. I began hesitatingly:

> On that path we shall never meet —
> Where once trod my dearest one's feet . . .

My voice vibrated with feeling, especially on the last word of each sentimental line and, without actually intending to, I sang that word with great anguish. It was this that moved the woman so. My voice was thin, unsteady, and I expected it to crack at any moment, but I kept on with deep emotion, as only he can sing who is dying of hunger and knows that in payment he will soon get a plateful of hot rich soup. But, strangely, at the same time I was beginning to forget that I was starving. I was now enjoying my singing, feeling almost inspired, and the pleasure I saw in the eyes of my listeners stimulated me further.

The woman was lost in the romantic words of the love song. Her chin and lips were trembling and the tears were running down her cheeks in two small streams. I was almost ready to cry myself, moved by the song and the woman's weeping and my own troubles. My voice shook and I kept overdoing it in the most maudlin lines.

Moving the dishes to one side, the woman covered her face with her hands, lowered her head to the table, and sobbed uncontrollably. When I was reaching the end of the song, repeating the refrain for the last time, she lifted her face, and, wiping the tears carefully so as not to smear her rouge, waited a moment for the applause to subside. Then, as if afraid that I would leave, she begged me, sniffling:

"Sing it . . . again . . . sonny, once more—please!"

"All right."

"What's your name, dearie?"

"Kolya."

"Sing it once more . . . Kolenka . . . be a lamb!"

And I rendered the song for the second time, from beginning to end, and saw how the woman was weeping again, letting the big tears drop to her dress through her puffy fingers studded with rings.

When I was through, she took a twenty-kopeck piece from her purse and, smiling through her tears, offered it to me:

"Here, take it, Kolya, take it, my pet. You touched the wound in my heart . . ."

I accepted the wet coin with some embarrassment, and put it in my pocket.

"But where is your cap?" thundered her red-bearded companion. "What are we to throw coins in?"

"I don't have a cap—it flew into the sea."

"Ha-ha-ha-ha!" the sailor roared with laughter, his huge frame and spade-like beard quivering as if someone were shaking him from inside. "Did you say it flew away? Ha-ha-ha . . . Ha-ha-ha!"

He pulled a red kerchief from his pocket, clumsily undid a knot in it, and took out a fifty-kopeck piece.

"Here, young fellow, buy yourself another cap, otherwise there is no place to put your wages. And, now, sing me a song! A good one! A song of freedom!"

At first I couldn't think of what to sing for him, but then I remembered the song Egor had taught me. I still knew it well and loved it, and I began to sing it willingly— the song about the endless steppe.

My voice kept breaking and I hardly had any breath left. But the huge sailor would not let me stop, urging me on to sing some more. And when I was completely exhausted and sang barely audibly and very hoarsely—

> *I have no father, no mother,*
> *All I have is one bosom friend . . .*

the sailor, sitting up abruptly and stretching to his full gigantic height, raised his arm and slammed the table with his fist, thundering:

"A-a-a-h! That was good! Real good! It gripped your very soul!" And, turning to me, he added a little more calmly, "Come on, little brother, sing us another!"

Completely worn out by now, I finally refused:

"No, I can't any more. I'm dying of hunger. Haven't eaten since yesterday."

"Oh, my God!" the woman exclaimed. "What fools we are! The youngster is starving and we make him sing! Come over here, sit down, my dear, we'll get you something to eat."

I devoured a whole mackerel, then a bowl of beet soup with meat. All at once the place felt unbearably hot and airless. I couldn't wait to get out into the fresh air and to get far away from the greasy fumes, the stuffiness, and the drunken hubbub. But they wouldn't let me go. Someone pulled me back by the hand roughly, others pulled at my clothes, everyone asking for his favorite song. Having lost my voice completely, I concentrated on the mandolin. Only the expectation of getting money—which from time to time my listeners threw into a bosun's cap lent to me for the purpose —money that Egor needed so badly, made me remain there. Finally, frightened by a fist fight that unexpectedly flared up at one of the tables, I profited from the confusion and escaped into the street.

It was cool and easy to breathe here, as on the open

deck of a steamer after one had been in the red-hot heat of the stokehold.

I went to the docks and sat there alone on the passenger quay. Rows of lights glided noiselessly in different directions over the dark sea. They were evidently the lights of departing and arriving steamers. Ships' bells sounded, the hissing of steam came from somewhere, the hawser of a tardy windlass clanked, and music could be heard from the park, drowned out now and then by the loud neighing of the cab horses on the embankment. I was dead tired and all this was reaching me as if from another world. I was indifferent to everything around me and felt as if I were already asleep. Only one anxious thought kept harassing me—where could I spend the night? I was terrified to return to the park, where I was sure I would be robbed again. And there was no other place.

I could hardly keep my head up, my lids grew very heavy. I would start, sit up stiffly, force myself to keep my eyes wide open, but nothing helped, I dozed off just the same.

"Hey, you!" someone yelled right in my ear, and followed it up with a blow on my shoulder.

Jumping up, I saw an old man with a heavy stick in his hand, evidently he was the night watchman.

"Off to the devil with you!" he shouted meanly. "He's found a bed for himself, the tramp!"

I left, and in the dark I saw the outlines of piles of empty sacks I had noticed in the daytime. There were many of them, stretching for yards in high, neat, square piles with a narrow space between them. The bed-like softness of the sacks was inviting; to the wanderer it even held out the promise of a kind of homey coziness.

Attracted by this tempting comfort, I held, between my teeth, the bag with the mandolin and book, and without further ado made for the opening between two mounds of sacks and scrambled up a ten-foot-high pile.

Someone was already asleep on this one—I could hear his guttural snore. Next to him another sleeper issued a whistling snore. I crawled to the next pile, which seemed to be unoccupied, and settled down, tucking my precious possessions under my chin. I fell asleep instantly.

But I didn't sleep long at all. A sharp blow on my leg made me fly up from my bed. Some people holding up large lanterns and carrying sticks were chasing off the night's lodgers with loud curses.

I slid down quickly and left in search of another refuge. The park gates were locked, and every other nook where one could rest was already occupied. I spent the rest of the night on my feet, tramping through the large town.

21

The military circuit court had sentenced Egor to eight years of convict labor for organizing waterfront workers. I went to visit him in jail for the last time.

As I was nearing the prison, about two hundred paces from the gates, a stranger approached me. He had a long dark square beard—although in appearance he was not at all old—large brown eyes, heavy black eyebrows. He wore a shabby seaman's jacket and a seaman's cap. An anchor was tattooed on his left wrist.

"Hi, there, Kolya!" he called to me.

"Hello," I answered in a more reserved manner.

"Are you a brother of Egorov's?"

"Egorov . . ." I mumbled, uneasy and puzzled. "How do you know this?"

"I was hanging around at the gates when you were here yesterday and heard you talk to the guards. Remember? 'I'm Egorov's brother,' you said."

"Oh, I see."

Then the man took me aside, and, looking about him first, pushed a red note into my hand. He then explained that the money was from Egor's comrades, that it had somehow to be delivered for him at the jail so that he could buy himself whatever he needed in the prison store.

"And when you visit him, tell him," he said, "'regards from the Beard.' Say it softly so that only he hears it. Do you get it?"

"I get it. And what is your name?"

"That's how I'm called—'the Beard,' that's all."

"All right."

"And don't breathe a word of this to anyone. Understand?"

"I understand."

"That's good. You're a youngster with brains in his head! I'll come again next time. When you see me—don't come over. If necessary, I'll come up to you. Understand?"

"I understand."

"Well, so long."

He shook my hand with his rough, toil-calloused one. It felt the same as Egor's. Without looking back, he walked away rapidly.

And I hurried to visit Egor.

He came out with his head shaven and wearing sackcloth convict's clothes. On his feet were heavy chains strapped to a wide, canvas belt.

"Look at the way I am now, Kolya," he said with a bitter smile, as if ashamed of his garb and irons. "Before, I was as free as a bird, and now look at me!"

"Never mind, Egor, it won't be for long," and I wanted to smile at him, but instead of a smile—and I felt it—I managed only a pitiful grimace, and the words stuck in my throat.

"Return home now," Egor pleaded with me. "Why hang around here any more? They'll soon send me off."

"After they take you away, I'll leave." And then I suddenly remembered, and shouted, "Best regards from the Beard."

Egor opened his eyes wide with astonishment.

My words were drowned in the loud clanking of the convicts' chains. The prisoners were coming out into the visiting room to take leave of their relatives. Their every step produced a loud racket. Mothers, wives, and children, seeing their loved ones for the first time in irons, sobbed with anguish and fright. The prisoners, to make themselves heard over the noise, tried to outcry each other. And all this produced a dismal din.

Egor no longer looked like himself. Gone was his wavy hair, and his badly shaven head now looked strange and ugly. His face that used to be smooth and clean-shaven was now covered with tufts of reddish blond beard. Only his eyes, kind, light-blue, and always smiling, were the same.

I wanted to say to him something especially pleasant and affectionate, so that he would feel the sincerity of my friendship, but I couldn't find the right words. It was painful to see Egor in chains, so humiliated and abused. And when he shifted from one foot to the other and I could detect in the general clatter of the irons the rattle of his chains, anger boiled up in me and I wanted to scream with rage. I kept quiet but couldn't control the tears that were brimming in my eyes—tears of exasperating helplessness.

"What's the matter with you, Kolya!"

Egor was straining his voice to make himself heard above the others, and I could see he was forcing himself to smile at me. "What's the matter, kid? Come on, let's not act like women! Things will improve. We'll live it up yet! We'll put up a stiff fight!"

The piercing whistle and the guard's order: "End of visiting!" seemed to incite Egor. More loudly and with fiery passion he shouted through the metal partition:

"Soon, Kolya, things will be better! Much better! The storm will break! The sun will shine upon us . . ."

The guard dragged him away, but he managed to add:

"They can't put all the people in irons!"

Twelve pairs of chained feet moved toward the door, filling the room with a grim noise. It mingled with the cries and laments of the relatives, making inaudible the last parting words of the individual convicts as they left the room to be led away to their cells.

I took the ten rubles the Beard had given me for Egor to the prison office and got a receipt for them, which I carefully put away in my jacket pocket.

I found out outside the prison that the convicts were allowed to receive a large parcel before their departure for Siberia—several pounds of sugar, a side of bacon, biscuits, tobacco, soap. The exiles were also permitted to receive warm clothing.

Egor might need all these things at any time now—it could be within a week, within three days, even tomorrow. I had to earn more money!

From morning to late in the evening I roamed the market places, visited taverns, public gardens, the beaches, singing everywhere and reciting verse. After finishing a number, I held out my new cap without any shame, and collected in it my listeners' donations, coins of different values, from half-pennies to five-kopeck pieces.

After sunset I "performed" in the public parks. Here, in the blue dusk and in the descending evening when the darkness was barely lighted by the dim street lamps, on the rare benches in the out-of-the-way alleys sat couples wanting to be alone. I suddenly cropped up before such a pair like an apparition and, as if it were the most natural thing to do, I began to serenade them with some romantic tune or a Neapolitan love song:

> *Oh! Sing to me! Sing to me once more*
> >   *my de-ea-ea-r,*
> *In our sad hour of parting, I so crave*
> >   *to he-ea-ea-r,*
> *Your voice, like the music that in heaven a-b-ou-ou-nds,*
> *To remember all my life its heavenly s-ou-ou-nds.*

For some strange reason this song was a favorite with the men, especially the military.

The women adored sad, heart-rending ballads about "being madly in love," "cruel separations," "conscienceless deception," and sorrowful memories of a happy past.

A very young girl with languorous eyes, in which shone the golden reflection of the setting sun, sat on a bench with an officer. As I was finishing the first line of the love song, she took from her little purse a twenty-kopeck piece and held it ready in her hand as if afraid that I'd otherwise not finish it and disappear. To reassure her I continued faster:

> *Of their late fall beauty*
> *The fall wind the trees ber-ea-ea-ves . . .*
> *And over the garden paths*
> *Scatters their dead, dry l-ea-ea-ves . . .*

The girl lowered her eyes self-consciously, turned her head slightly to the side not to show that she was crying, and quietly passed a handkerchief over her wet cheeks.

A few minutes later I would stand in front of another bench and with a weary voice sing another romance.

Over the park hung the oppressive Crimean heat haze, the foliage gave forth a bitterish aroma, the crickets chirped monotonously, and high above me was the endless dome of the darkening sky, in which each moment appeared thousands more glimmering dots.

How lonely and sad sounded in this setting my silly little mandolin and small inexpressive voice. It seemed very odd to me that anyone could actually enjoy listening to this silly music, and even pay for it. I therefore never felt hurt or angry when some unwilling listener shouted in response to my sentimental rantings: "Why do you howl like a jackal? Get away from here!" But more often people listened to me quite willingly.

Only once in a while, in the waterfront saloons, instead of the old love songs they would ask for something new.

"Don't you have, little chum, something fresher?" once asked a broad-shouldered, thickset sailor, with a turned-up nose and gay, childish eyes.

"What do you mean by 'fresher'?" I was puzzled by the nature of his request.

"You can guess for yourself, little brother."

But I didn't know what he meant.

"Well, let's say, for example . . ." and he lowered his voice a trifle, "there's a French song—we heard it in Toulon—in France. And now many of us sing it."

"The Marseillaise?" I guessed easily.

"That's it—the Marseillaise!" The sailor grinned happily. "It is a French song, but in a way it speaks for the whole world. For all those who toil."

"I know," I said not without pride. "A stoker . . . a friend of mine . . . taught it to me. It is the national anthem of France—it was written during the French Revolution. The same stoker taught it to me who gave me this mandolin."

I moved closer to the sailor's table, and after looking around cautiously at the few daytime customers, began to sing in an undertone, bearing down on the mandolin so that the forbidden words would not be heard by the others. I sang in Russian:

> Come children of the fatherland,
> The day of glory now is here,
> By tyranny against us
> The bloody banner is raised . . .

"That's the one, the very one!" the sailor's eyes glowed with excitement. "I've never heard the words to it. They sound like our own, like Russian ones."

Alas, I knew only the first four lines and had to make that
do. The sailor offered me a five-kopeck coin but, to my own
surprise, I refused to take it. I pushed away his hand and
said firmly:

"I don't accept money for this kind of song."

"Good boy!" The sailor grinned at me with approval.
Then he added solemnly: "That's the way it should be."

He treated me to a mugful of cider and a large *bublik*—
a Russian doughnut. As I was leaving, he whispered:

"You must understand, my young friend, these are not
times for songs about lovers' trysts and hugs and kisses. These
are different times!"

But I continued my wanderings through the city, singing
the same sentimental songs. Occasionally I'd sing the other
kind. I felt good when a young seaman, aroused by my song,
burst out: "It's good to listen to something like that!"
banging the table with his fist so hard that the dishes
jumped high and fell to the floor. But I sympathized with
the women enraptured by my sad melodies and by the pretty,
perhaps empty, words about unhappy love. I was pleased
when all kinds of people in the taverns, forgetting their drinks
for a while, listened avidly, their eyes filled with sorrow, joy,
tenderness, anger—every emotion with which music has the
power to move us.

I often went down to the waterfront to watch the sunset.
Over the fine ripples ruffling the entire expanse of sea, endlessly
stretched a wide path of gaily shimmering water looking like
golden fish scales. And on this golden path, as though determined not to leave it, glided the dark silhouettes of sail-
boats.

At dusk, the lights of the warships riding at anchor shone
dully in the distance, like the fading stars at dawn. Farther
still, nearer to the horizon, moved two rows of white dots—

probably the lights of a large passenger steamer that recently
left the harbor.

The colorful dresses of strolling women glimmered on the
embankment. Soft singing and hushed laughter could be heard
from there. The breeze carried the damp fragrance of the
newly turned earth of the shorefront lawns, and from the
nearby gardens came the faint scent of fruits, almonds, and
flowers. And all these scents mingled with a light salty wind
blowing softly from the sea, blending into the deliciously
perfumed air of the magnificent Crimean night.

As I was starting for the city the moon rose at the
horizon. Its red disk glided slowly and with a kind of dignity
up from the purple whirlpool of the sea. The sky and water
were ablaze, and the recently sparkling golden path turned a
dull pink. There were no boats in sight. The damp sultriness
changed to a cool sea freshness. The brightly colored dresses
on the embankment could no longer be seen, the singing
had stopped, as well as the laughter.

My mandolin was also still now. Alone on the deserted
shore, I now felt overcome with fatigue after the long days
of unusual and disturbing experiences. My whole body ached,
my throat was parched, my head felt very heavy, and I
couldn't keep my eyes open. I was ready to flop down on
the first empty bench or crawl under the first overturned
boat to fall asleep. But, afraid that I might be robbed
again, I steeled myself, and, using the last ounce of my
waning strength, I forced myself to go on.

I kept my hand over the pocket where I had hidden the
precious bills—I had exchanged the heavy copper coins for
paper money—and held the change I had earned that day
tightly in my fist. Tomorrow or the day after the money
would come in very useful. To lose it would mean to be
unable to help Egor. No, it would be better not to close
my eyes all night, or even for the next several nights, if

necessary, than to pay such a high price for the mere pleasure of sleeping.

I trudged on. Soon I noticed a log cabin to the side of the road. It was nearly as small as a watchman's booth. Peering through its tiny window, I saw a gray-bearded old man in a white Russian shirt sitting at a table. He was bent over a book. Through his glasses his eyes were glued on the page barely lighted by his little kerosene lamp. I knocked on the door.

The tall old man appeared on the doorsill. Removing his glasses, he looked at me closely.

"What do you want, little grandson?" he asked in a mild high-tenor voice.

I felt reassured by his natural and friendly tone.

"Let me spend the night here, Grandpa," I begged him.

"Spend the night? But who are you?"

He asked the question not with the distrustful and annoyed curiosity of a person whom one had disturbed, but with genuine interest. His question was simple enough, but how was I to answer it? There wasn't enough time to think of a careful answer, and to tell him all about myself in detail made no sense, under the circumstances. I blurted out the first thing that came into my head:

"I'm a wandering musician!"

"Oh! So, that's it? A musician? And even a wandering one! And why do you wander?"

"I earn my bread that way. I play and sing. Here, see?" And I showed him the mandolin.

"Ah . . . does that mean you are an actor or something?"

"Yes."

"Of a burned-out theater?"

"That's right."

The old man laughed good-naturedly, but he didn't yet let me in.

"And your parents—are they dead?"

"No, my parents are alive but they are very poor."

"So, that's how it is. Well, come on in."

He bolted the door, and, putting his hands on my shoulders, led me to the table. Sitting down on a stool, he looked straight into my eyes, seemingly deciding still whether I had told the truth. Then he let me go, saying:

"All right, sonny, stay the night."

He removed his sheepskin from a nail, spread it on the floor, and took a large pillow in a pink cotton case from his bed and placed it on the coat.

"Lie down."

I threw myself down on the soft sheepskin.

"Maybe you're hungry?"

"No, Grandpa."

"It seems you're very sleepy. Well, go on, have a good sleep."

Shading the lamp with a piece of cardboard, the old man returned to his seat, put his glasses on, and resumed reading.

I glanced at his pale face with its deep wrinkles, his kind eyes with the crow's-feet spreading fan-like around them, his very thin brown fingers on which he propped his silver-gray head. In an instant the old man's face began to fade from my vision; the low light of the lamp dimmed.

22

THE DAY OF EGOR'S DEPARTURE for Siberia came.

How lucky that I was able the day before to get him some of the things he would need so badly for the long hard journey. Egor's acquaintance, the Beard, had waited for me not far from the jail. Together we went to the store, bought a sack and filled it with sugar, tea, salt pork, soap, tobacco, and biscuits. The Beard gave me another ten rubles for Egor. I delivered the things and the money at the prison and got a receipt for them and also for a pair of felt boots which the same savior, the taciturn Beard, had brought for the prisoner.

There was a crowd of the convicts' relatives and friends at the prison gates. The guards and the police kept dispersing them gruffly, but they would regather in small groups and resume their long, gloomy vigil. They were waiting for a last glimpse of their kin or friend about to be sent off to some Godforsaken convict center in Siberia.

I recognized in the crowd the woman with the hollow cheeks and weary eyes, whose husband had gone out on strike and had been sentenced for it to eight years at hard labor. I also saw the short woman with the puffy face and faded brows, who had complained that her husband "had only hung around with those good-for-nothing workers' groups" but had been sentenced, just the same, to ten years. Here was also the old man with the reddish-gray matted beard and bloodshot, teary eyes, whose oldest son got eight years and the younger one the full twelve. He stood at the side of the old woman whose boy, "quiet, gentle, and obedient," got six years.

They had all been standing around near the prison since the night before. Only now, late in the evening of the second day, were they about to see their dear ones. Pushing the crowd to some distance from the gates, the guards herded the convicts into the prison yard, in two lines. The space between the prisoners and their relatives was lit by smoking torches held by policemen.

Suddenly the air was filled with the clanking of irons, and out into the lighted space, four abreast, came the shadowy figures of the condemned. They were chained together at their hands and feet. By fours they formed a long column, and were surrounded on all sides by soldiers with bared swords. The column moved forward slowly. From a side street came about twenty mounted Cossacks who quickly formed a second ring around the convicts.

The crowd broke up and walked alongside the column as close as the rings of soldiers and Cossacks would allow, and looked into the faces of the prisoners, trying to find their own. But from such a distance the prisoners, who were dressed alike and all of whom had unshaven, bearded faces, were not recognizable in the dim light of the torches.

I also moved along with the column, running from one end of it to the other, peering at every face, but, like the rest, couldn't find the one I was looking for.

I began to wonder if Egor was there at all. Perhaps he was left behind to be sent off with the next convoy.

Then, before quite realizing what I was doing, I shouted with all my might into the semi-darkness:

"Egor, are you there?"

"Here! little brother, here!" I heard the reply in Egor's familiar voice. "So long! Take care of yourself!"

"Shut up, youngster," an old man said, nudging me in the back. "Be quiet, or they'll beat him up because he answered you."

I was appalled and scared. Could it be that for such a thing they would hurt a wonderful person like Egor?

I gritted my teeth and continued to move alongside the column.

In this fashion the unusual procession continued to the very ship, piercing the night's blackness with the smoky light of the torches and breaking the soft silence of the sleeping city with the cruel music of the prisoners' shackles.

On the pier the police, after allowing the prisoners to pass, held back the others. The chained men went up the narrow gangplank in two's. They soon disappeared into the hold of the ship, together with their guards.

I stood around waiting to see what would happen next. I saw the late-arriving passengers rush up the gangplank, and managed to slip on board with them.

The ship didn't pull away until late in the night. But the dark, motionless, silent mass of the prisoners' kin remained on the pier to the end.

A hushed stillness reigned on deck, in the passageways, and in the common third-class cabin, broken now and then by someone's moan, by the heavy snoring of an old man, or by the crying of a baby.

At the stern, about twenty feet from the opening to the hold into which the prisoners had been herded, the guard called out to anyone approaching: "Halt! It is forbidden to come closer."

A dim brown light shone from the few lanterns inside the hold. There, in the foul-smelling depths, usually filled with crates, barrels, sacks, iron, and tiles, hundreds of men tired unto death now suffered in the suffocating darkness.

And among them was Egor.

I saw clearly in my mind his shaven head, sallow face, sunken eyes. I saw the heavy chains on his sore legs, the handcuffs that tied him to his fellow prisoner. I saw him lying there on the filthy boards of the ship's floor, down there, on the very bottom of the ship. And I felt such pity for my friend that I could barely hold back the tears. I wanted to comfort him, to send him a kind word, to raise his spirits with some reassuring act.

But how was I to do this?

I took up my mandolin and began to sing softly the song that he loved so much, and which he had so patiently taught me long ago.

I wasn't sure that Egor could hear my low singing and the soft sounds of the mandolin. I moved closer to the opening of the hold and sang a little more loudly. With each word I sang louder. I wanted to make sure that Egor could hear me.

But the hold was not so close and its bottom was deep down. I stole up still closer, leaned forward, stretched my neck and sang in full voice:

> Oh, eagle, don't fly so close to earth,
> Cossack don't walk so close to the shore . . .

My song was interrupted by a rough shout from the guard: "Beat it, you singing scum!"

Near me had gathered a small crowd of listeners. One of them, judging by his familiar thundering voice, was that very same redheaded bosun for whom I had sung in the Sevastopol tavern. Taking advantage of the darkness that was obscuring him, he objected angrily:

"It's none of your damn business! Let him sing—he's not one of your convicts. He's a passenger! He paid his money."

"Get away from here, I tell you!" snapped the guard. "Leave, or I'll shoot!"

"You lie, you dog! You have no reason to shoot! You have no right!"

In the pitch-black darkness a white flame suddenly burst forth and a shot was heard, followed by a second and a third.

"The villain is shooting from his revolver," the same deep voice said calmly.

"He's shooting into the sky, to scare us," another said.

The air was pierced by a series of sharp whistles accompanied by an exchange of calls by the guards, and I sprang back like a ball and hurried away. The others followed my example—my listeners, the sailors, and the deck passengers.

The bosun turned to us and took charge of the retreat:

"Save yourselves! The fool may start to shoot in earnest. I know these 'heroes'—I spent five years under their heels."

While we were scurrying off along the deck strewn with crates and sacks toward the prow of the ship, the bosun was swearing heavily at our enemy.

"The damn dog!" he kept repeating with bitter contempt. "The mad dog! It's not enough for him that he's guarding those chained wretches, he has to throw himself at free people as well."

"Soon we'll be throwing the likes of him into the deep sea," predicted a man invisible in the darkness. "In Odessa there is a general strike. In Sevastopol the sailors at the naval base have mutinied. And they are not yawning on the ships either."

The seamen and the passengers gradually dispersed, and I settled down for the night inside a folded tarpaulin.

Came the dawn. The stars faded quickly and the dark-blue sky turned a dove gray. The horizon began to blush. The edges of the silver clouds were dipped in crimson red. Over the water blazed the long stripes of the brightly glittering gold of the sun, and from them stretched light-blue and emerald ribbons. The sky was suddenly in full conflagration and up from the horizon rose the edge of the huge red sun. It rose higher and higher, spreading over the sea a wide purple path. The crimson turned into a flaming yellow pouring a blinding light over everything.

Sunrise over the sea is unforgettably beautiful. The water, which only an hour ago couldn't even be seen—for it merged like thick ink with the night's blackness—is now light-blue with a greenish shading and shimmers with millions of gay sparkles. And in the sea, as in a mirror, is reflected the bright blueness of the sky, the slowly gliding roseate clouds, and the golden rays playing in the air.

Near the ship, large dolphins with white undersides and dark backs were diving in and out of the water. Keeping up with the steamer, they followed it tirelessly. At regular intervals and in uniform rhythm, they repeated their graceful jumps.

The ship was gradually coming to life.

The seamen began to wash the deck with sand and soap, hosing it down, and they polished, to a brilliant brightness, the copper fixtures.

From all corners, first came the passengers of the third class, then, about an hour later, appeared the fashionably dressed, scrubbed and well-slept occupants of the comfortable cabins. The waiters dashed to and fro carrying heavy trays.

Only at the stern was there no activity.

On orders from the chief officer of the convoy, the area was blocked off with a low barricade of crates and sacks.

After midday the dim outlines of the distant city appeared on the horizon.

I began to feel the usual chill of worry. What was happening at home? How will they receive me? What will Anka say? Has Reggio returned yet? Will they rehire me at the theater?

But most of all I worried about Egor.

Now the clear outline of the miles-long dark-green shore of Odessa could be seen. Again, as two years ago when I was arriving on the *Pyotr Regger* from Mariopol, I now saw the ruins of the ancient fortress in the Aleksandrovsky Park, the columns of the Vorontsov mansion, the wide stairway on Richelieu Boulevard, the palace of the commanding officer of the city, and the London Hotel.

In another few minutes we were passing the lighthouse and entering the harbor filled with dozens of large and small steamers and the gray sails of small Greek and Turkish coasting vessels. Our ship was heaving to the landing wharf.

I ran down the gangplank and kept running along the familiar streets to reach home the sooner. But my happiness to be home was clouded by the harassing thought of Egor's fate. The bosun had explained to me that the convicts would be taken off the ship only in the middle of the night. Surrounded by a double line of guards and police, they would be taken to a relay prison on the other side of Chumnyi Mountain.

23

NOTHING HAD CHANGED AT HOME during my absence. Father was still on the same poorly paid job. He had tried to work on the night shift at the docks and freight railroad depot as a freight handler, but he wasn't strong enough for that kind of labor. His employers soon noticed it and he was fired.

The same poverty plagued our household. Only the cleanliness of the apartment, the scrubbed floors and windowpanes, the carefully washed linen, the starched and perfectly ironed dress my mother wore—the only dress she had—and the neatly patched clothes of the children, lent our surroundings a semblance of well-being.

My return livened things up at home. My brother was impatient to hear all about my trip. Mother cried and through her tears scolded me mildly:

"I was afraid . . . you ran away . . . to America . . ."

Father tried to act the part of a vexed parent:

"You nasty kid! To run away secretly like that! And, pray, where? What for? After all, what business do you have with Egor?"

But his efforts to sound indignant came to nothing. His kind eyes smiled, his goatee shook, and his tobacco-stained yellow mustache bristled from repressed laughter as he kept repeating:

"You scamp! You willful brat!"

My mother was surprised that I looked so well, and she was even more amazed that my hair was cut and that I wore a new cap and decent shoes.

"Where did you get all this?" she wondered. "How did you come by it?"

When I pulled out from the secret depth of my inside pocket and placed on the table two neatly folded ten-ruble notes, there was no end to the general consternation.

"Where did you get that kind of money?" my mother gasped.

"I'll tell you everything later," I promised importantly. "First, let's have some dinner."

"The boss has returned," my father chuckled as he was opening the package of cigarettes I had brought him.

For two full hours, while we were having a tasty homemade meal, such as I hadn't had in a long time, I told them everything that had happened from the minute I left to the moment of my return to Odessa.

"How he has grown!" my mother commented with mixed touches of gladness and regret in her voice. "He has become a man."

"I think he's beginning to speak with a bass voice," my father remarked, and asked, "Do you smoke?"

"Not yet."

After dinner I ran over to Anka's. She received me like a hero and gazed at me with respect and pride. She, too, found me grown and manly.

"How fast some people grow!" she mused. "As fast as a sunflower."

Golden flecks played in her laughing eyes, and her pretty head was covered with thick dark curls, which made her look more than ever like the painting of an Italian boy I often saw on a colored postcard.

She insisted that I tell her everything right away, and in the minutest details. She asked endless questions, now about the beginning of my adventure, now running way ahead, demanding a description of Sevastopol, asking about Egor, about the prison, the irons, the convoy, the steamers. She wanted to know where I had slept, what I had sung, what music I had heard, and she stopped only when Sashka came over, having heard that I was back.

Nothing much had changed with my friends. Sashka was now working at some factory, on the nightshift. He slept till noon, then would run off somewhere and toward evening return with new sketches. By now he had accumulated quite a collection of them—each one better than the next. The best were his drawings of clouds, trees, cliffs, and waves. But particularly wonderful were his sketches of people—fishermen pulling in their nets; an old man bent over as he pulled on heavy oars; a longshoreman carrying a huge crate on his back, mounting a gangplank. I kept wondering where Sashka got all his talent.

Vitka worked now in a locksmith and plumber's shop. He had equipped a model locomotive with a kerosene engine and had attached three coaches to it, and all this could move forward and backward over toy rails. He had wanted to make several yards of track in a wide curve, but his boss had taken everything away from him, insisting that Vitka had made his tiny railroad out of materials belonging to his employer and on working time.

"I don't care," Vitka said. "Let him choke on it! I'll make another one. It will be even better."

Spirka had written a long poem, "The Black Sea." It began and ended with a stanza that I liked very much:

> *I have always adored the sea!*
> *Its stormy noise, its quiet splash,*
> *And in its angry mood or spree*
> *To watch the breakers roar and dash!*

Spirka, such a quiet and mousy boy—where did he get his gift for writing verse?

My story produced quite an effect on the boys, and they wouldn't let me go for a long time.

That night, the first after many nights of homelessness and worry, I slept in a clean bed under my parental roof, enjoying the coziness and peace of home.

Early next morning, I got from Anka the receipt for the pawned cello and went to the pawnshop. Its doors were still closed. Along the side of the building, stretching from the entrance to the end of the block, stood a crowd of people. The crowd was so large that it spilled over onto the pavement. Women, men, and children carried bundles, coats, suits, samovars—Russian tea urns—and portable sewing machines, and everyone was trying to get nearer to the pawnshop doors. A hefty, mustached policeman rudely pushed back the crowd as he kept shouting:

"First those who are here to get their things out of hock, then those who are here to pawn them."

I couldn't understand for a long time why there were today so many who wanted to pawn their belongings. But, getting inside the crowd, I soon found out that many of the factories and plants had been struck. The flow of people to the pawnshop kept increasing. They now spread to the opposite sidewalk, and around the corners. Many had also come the day before and the day before that, without getting into the shop to receive money for their things.

"They're doing this on purpose, to force us to go back to work," said an elderly laborer with a worn face. "We know their tricks!"

"Maybe they've run out of money?" suggested another. "You see how many people there are—thousands have joined the strike."

"Don't worry, they have more rubles than there are people in this city. It's clear—they're in cahoots with the bosses."

At last the doors to the pawnshop were opened, but the police roughly chased away the people carrying things. The doorman let in only those who held receipts for things they came to redeem.

Receiving my cello, I quickly carried it home. Then I went to the theater to find out if Reggio was back from Italy.

But all that I had seen and found out at the pawnshop and what I now observed in the streets filled me with a new but still vague uneasiness. I felt that something very significant was happening. I suspected that Egor and his friends had something to do with it. And as I kept thinking about this, I observed closely the familiar streets and houses, the faces of passers-by, and saw in everything a strange change.

The streets were filled with people who had never before appeared on them. There were large groups of men and young people gathered on the corners. I could tell they were workers. Everyone was talking excitedly. The corner policeman tried several times to disperse the crowds, but he was ignored or mocked, and, losing courage, he went back to his beat.

Having found out that Reggio had not yet returned, I went down the stairway leading to the harbor, to find at the docks the stoker Petrov about whom Egor had spoken to me in the jail. Here I saw even a more unusual scene.

Large and small ships beached for loading or unloading stood paralyzed in a dead quiet. There was no hissing of steam, no rattling of the windlasses, no smoke came from the stacks. No half-naked stevedores, black with coal dust, red with tile dust, white with flour, moved up and down the freight gangplanks. There were no fast carriages speeding and clattering on the cobble-stoned embankment, there was no whistling of locomotives along the wooden platforms of the depot, no grain poured down the chutes to the grain elevators.

The harbor was slumbering or it had died.

Only across from where some ships were lying at anchor, small groups of agitated strikers sat or stood around and in the shade of the warehouses sprawled many idle longshoremen.

Not far from the strikers were deployed detachments of foot and mounted police and jaunty Cossacks with their flashing red-banded caps and striped trousers. Some bored soldiers stood guarding sheafs of rifles.

The steamship *Emerance* was in dock. It sat low in the water, obviously still unloaded. The same silence reigned on its deck as on most of the moored vessels. No gangplanks had even been placed for the unloading. Instead one could only see Jacob's ladders suspended from the steel riggings. I carefully examined the faces and garb of the striking seamen, trying to pick out among them the stokers. I noticed one such seaman. He was either a stoker or a ship's machinist, or, as it often happened on freight ships, he might have been both. The man stood surrounded by a cluster of people to whom he was saying something, speaking heatedly.

This seaman was squat and stocky. He had a powerful neck and a broad chest, and as he spoke his huge dark brown fist kept flailing the air like a heavy hammer.

"Don't worry, Petrov, we won't give in! We won't be cowed," several voices cried. "We'll hold out!"

When this seaman finally left the group and walked toward the ship, I soon managed to catch up with him.

"Could you tell me where I could find the stoker Petrov of the *Emerance?*"

"Stoker Petrov?" he asked, surprised. "What do you want with him?"

"I have to give him a message from a friend."

"From whom?" he asked guardedly, and seeing that I was hesitating to reply, he reassured me:

"Go on, tell me, don't be afraid. I am Petrov."

"From Egor."

"Egor who?" he wanted to know and looked at me sharply.

"Egorov."

"What ship?"

"The *Pyotr Regger*."

"And where is he?"

The stoker, as he walked alongside of me, heard the story about Egor. He had known only about his arrest. The news about the long sentence, the irons, and the exile to Siberia stunned him. He stood stock-still. His eyes took on a hardness; his soft red lips no longer spread in a smile and he tightened them more and more, as if trying to hold back some strong word he wanted badly to utter.

"A curse on them!" he said just the same. "May they be thrice damned!"

He questioned me further about Egor, and then with a kind of deep outrage he exclaimed:

"What a pity! And to get caught at a time like this! To be exiled now, when the most fateful days are so near!"

But in another minute Petrov had himself under complete control, saying with a tone of finality:

"No! We won't suffer much longer! Time is running out for the bloodsuckers!"

When I was about to leave him, he asked me to find out where Egor was now.

"If he is still near this city, please come and tell us—we'll get some money to him."

A company of soldiers with two officers at the head passed us.

"Go on, my young friend, go on home," Petrov said to me meaningfully, not taking his eyes off the military. "Go on, you see, any minute there may be a clash here."

Petrov's face looked concerned. There was a special meaning in its expression and a special caution in his movements, as if he expected any minute to have to meet some danger. I left, and kept looking around for a long time until I lost sight of him, the groups of seamen, and the *Emerance*.

The harbor was still ominously quiet. Nothing moved here now, where usually there was such a noisy confusion of activity.

Only the police and the Cossacks were moving about to different spots along the waterfront, deploying themselves in various formations, like an army choosing the best positions for an impending battle.

24

EGOR WASN'T IN THE ODESSA PRISON.

His convoy from Sevastopol, including among its political prisoners many sailors from the navy and seamen from the merchant marine, had been transferred from the ship directly to a train. That same night the whole contingent was sent on to an unknown destination, most likely Siberia.

I now lost all contact with Egor.

The city was full of disturbing rumors, of talk about the disastrous war with Japan* and the heavy losses on the battle-front, as well as about strikes, workers' uprisings, and peasant rebellions. Everyone seemed to be waiting for something catastrophic to happen. Informing one another with great agitation about the unusual happenings, people would express amazement, then hurry off somewhere. They were still telling each other about the terrible February rout at the battle of Mukden, although it had taken place three months before.

The newspapers gave meager news and distorted accounts of important events. Anyone who had returned from the Far East was questioned eagerly. Usually the narrator, despite his efforts to hold back the awful truth, reluctantly admitted that tens of thousands of soldiers had perished, that there was

---

* The Russo-Japanese War of 1904.

shocking embezzlement of public funds by top military officers, as well as inexcusable drunkenness, gambling, and corruption. He would also tell about the lack of preparedness and the bungling of the high command.

At the entrance to the building of the *Odessa News* there was always a crowd reading the latest edition posted on the wall.

One day someone recognized the local physician who had recently come back wounded from the front. The people turned from the wall newspaper and began to question him about the war. He answered reluctantly, pulling nervously at his pince-nez string:

"It's a disaster! A catastrophe! A hopeless situation!"

"Then, what's to be done?" someone asked in a business-like manner.

"What's to be done?" the doctor answered. "Kick the scoundrels out! Throw the embezzlers in jail! The traitors! Elect a people's government!"

I never before heard such talk in the streets. But now there was a great deal of it, and there seemed to be no fear of persecution.

A tall, light-haired student in a school-uniform jacket and black shirt had mounted the stairs to the entrance of the City Theater, and was shouting to the gathered crowd:

"What is it that's still not clear to you? Our fleet at Port Arthur was sunk the first day of the war. The warship *Petropavlovsk* went down together with Admiral Makarov. The fortified encampment at Liao-Yan has been devastated. Our army was put to rout at Mukden. Thousands of Russian soldiers have been killed. Hundreds of thousands of the nation's money has been stolen. What more are you waiting for? What are you hoping for? Brothers! Russia's patience is at an end! The nation is rising in revolt! Nothing—no threats, no prisons—will stop us!"

At that moment someone wearing a derby hat and blue glasses began to pull at the student, trying to get him down from the top of the stairs.

"Get down, mister. It's forbidden to talk like that here."

The man wouldn't let the student finish his speech. He kept inviting him to follow him to "the proper place"—probably the police station.

"Get away from here! Vanish!" the crowd shouted. "Provocateur! Spy!"

Someone grabbed him and warned him:

"You'd better go while you're still in one piece! Go on your way! Your time has passed!"

"Knock off his glasses. Let's see who he is!" people in the crowd were shouting.

A youngster moved quickly toward the man, snatched off his glasses, and disappeared with them into the crowd. The frightened spy grew pale, as if he were left on the street without clothes. Pulling his derby over his eyes, he made a quick getaway, as the crowd laughed and whistled in derision.

Every day brought new events. There were demonstrations in different parts of the city. There were rousing speeches. Leaflets were given out everywhere.

And when the first news dispatches reached the city about the terrible destruction of the Rojdestvensky and Nebogov fleet squadrons, the city was seized with panic, and indignation. The horrifying figures were passed around by word of mouth.

"Just think of it, the entire fleet!"

"Dozens of ships going down to the bottom of the sea!"

"Several thousand sailors perished!"

"The bulk of our naval officers has been destroyed!"

"The commanding officers of our squadrons are prisoners of war!"

"What a disgrace!"

"It's unbelievable!"

Now everyone commented on the frightful situation. People were talking openly, bluntly on the streets, in the market places, in stores, in cafes. Everyone was searching the papers for the latest figures, details, explanations. But there were none. Then they tried to guess them. One heard different opinions: fifteen, twenty, thirty large and medium-sized warships; ten, twelve, eighteen thousand sailors; twelve hundred officers.

In front of the bakery on Deribavskaya Street, a middle-aged man with longish hair—probably an artist or teacher—angrily crumpled up his newspaper and, flinging it to the ground, shouted in a powerful voice:

"The papers lie—the censors are strangling them! What happened at Mukden was not only a military disaster! It was the collapse of the regime!"

No one seized this speaker. No one even attempted to restrain him. He instantly disappeared into the crowd, and his place was taken by another who spoke just as openly and as daringly.

In those disturbed days it was impossible to stay at home.

No matter how hard I tried, I couldn't concentrate on music, and putting my cello in the corner of the living room, I rushed out into the streets.

The general strike kept spreading. There were more and more throngs of strikers in the streets, marching to factories and plants to get their fellow workers to join them.

The crowds grew like a snow avalanche. They joined others, forming a swift current of people moving forward.

The police tried not to let them pass and to disperse them, but they gave way before the pressure of the mass of marchers.

Together with a large company of boys from our courtyard and from the neighborhood, my friends and I tried to be at every spot where something out of the ordinary was happening.

25

I STILL WANTED VERY MUCH to find the senior cello student at the music school, the one who had promised to teach me. But I didn't know his home address. Since I had been forbidden to enter the school building, there was only one thing left to do—to go to Yamskaya Street and watch for him at the school entrance.

I looked with bitterness at the boys and girls arriving at the school with their instruments and scores. The confidence with which they opened the doors, their loud conversation and happy laughter irritated me. But at the same time I felt the strong desire to begin to learn, to become a regular student, to mingle with this noisy and lively crowd.

It was almost noon. I was still pacing in front of the building, looking closely at every approaching person. And although I was repeatedly disappointed, I did not leave but continued endlessly to hang around the fascinating and forbidden yellow-gray building of the Russian Musical Society.

Then it was suppertime. I was limp with hunger and exhaustion and had a nagging pain in my legs.

Finally I decided to ask someone about the youth for whom I was waiting. Unfortunately I didn't know his name or which class he belonged to. I tried to describe him by his appearance.

"He is . . . you know . . . pleasant-looking," I said to a boy violin student. "Kind of tall, thin, very pale . . . with dark eyes . . ."

"Oh!" How amazing that the boy immediately guessed whom I meant. "Everyone knows him," he said, "he's the best cellist! It's Volodya Rensky! He's Brambill's student!"

My heart skipped a beat with happy anticipation. Think of it—the best cellist! Was it possible that he'd be my teacher? He promised!

"Where does he live?"

"On the Moldovanka."

"On which street in that district?"

"This I don't know."

I must have looked very disappointed. The lively boy quickly reassured me:

"I'm going to ask, right away. Wait here a minute." Gripping his notebook and scores in one hand and his violin in the other, he sprinted into the building and in a few moments popped out again, and running toward me, cried on the way:

"On Hospital Street near Stepovaya." He didn't know the number, but explained where the house was so clearly that I knew exactly how to find it.

At that very moment I suddenly saw the tall, pale, dark-eyed youth leave the building carrying his cello.

I ran to meet him with great glee, as if he were the very closest person to me—someone whom I had for a long time hopelessly sought. He didn't recognize me at once, but then, remembering, asked:

"Where did you disappear to? I thought you wanted to study. Well, do you?"

"Yes . . . I'll tell you everything later. May I come to see you at home? With my cello?"

"Let's go into the classroom now. I'll listen to you play."

In the classroom he checked my ear, and assuring himself

that I could repeat from memory sufficiently complicated musical phrases, he said with genuine satisfaction:

"Well done! You are very musical. And you have good hands. We'll work together. Come tomorrow and bring your cello."

"Where?"

"Right here."

I was somewhat confused. To come here! That was such joy! I hadn't even dared hope for such a break. But that was impossible! They would immediately throw me out. It would be especially risky to come face to face with the old school custodian.

"Can't I come to your home?"

"If you prefer, please do. But we have no piano and that will be a drawback. Is it too far for you to come here?"

"No . . . but they'll chase me out . . ."

The young man laughed.

"Don't worry. Just say you came to see me, and no one will bother you."

From that day, twice a week, I came to the school of the Russian Musical Society, just like the real students and coeds. I tried not to be seen by the school officialdom, avoiding the corridors and visiting only my teacher's classroom. In that room I experienced great things. I listened to the playing of the students—violinists and cellists—to the criticisms of the instructors, noticed the placement of the fingers and the position of the hand. I was learning everything there was to learn in this class. I therefore came to the school not only on my assigned days but every day, and spent many hours there, sometimes from morning to late evening.

There was lots of music at this school!

It came from all the classrooms, from the auditorium, from the teachers' room, even from the corridors and the lunchroom, where the students practiced some difficult passages before going to class.

I particularly enjoyed the class of the older students who played the complicated and long compositions like professionals. In the first days I heard the strange music for clarinet and orchestra by Mozart, a concerto for flute by Keller, a violin piece by Mendelssohn, and, finally, Tchaikovsky's Variations for Cello on a Theme by Rocco, played by my own instructor.

I felt deep affection for my teacher. He was a kind, calm, gentle person who treated me with friendliness and warmth. He was really the best student. He was going to graduate that year and had already been invited to perform at concerts in Odessa and other cities. He didn't play often at the school, but when he did I listened with such rapt attention and evidently, with such a dumb expression on my face that he would pause for a moment and tease me:

"Please close your mouth, Nikolai, or a fly will take up residence in it."

It seemed to me that no one played the cello as well as Volodya Rensky. He produced with his instrument deep-throated, wonderfully fine, and at the same time transparently clear sounds. Always after a lesson the melodies he had played continued to resound in my ears. I was always sorry to see him put his cello away in the case and vacate the platform for the next student. I would have liked to listen to the next musician as well. I knew that he would play Bach's "Chaconne" while he waited for his instructor. But I wanted even more to walk with my teacher and left the classroom with him.

26

EARLY ONE MORNING Sashka called through my window:

"Get up, Kolya! Hurry up! Let's go into the city. Lots is happening!"

Schools were closed, also many offices, stores, and banks. It was useless to go to the music school—it, too, would be closed.

Our usual foursome rushed to the center of town.

I don't think there ever was such a wild excitement in the city of Odessa.

On the corner of Richelieu Boulevard and Greek Street, a pale young fellow with burning eyes, lifting his arm high— it was bare to the elbow and stained with machine oil and brown varnish—was courageously scattering packets of leaflets into the crowd. The people caught them in the air and read them on the spot, exchanging remarks about the content:

"That's the truth!"

"There must be unity—a general political strike!"

A tall man with a scraggly beard and a trembling pince-nez on a short copper chain suspended from his ear, called out in a voice choked with emotion:

"Friends, break up into flying squads. Proceed to the plants, factories, and workshops. Pull the workers off their jobs."

And strangely, as if it had all been planned beforehand,

certain individuals advanced to the head of small groups and promptly led them away into the side streets.

The same tall man continued to give precise instructions to other small squads:

"You go to the Dikler printshop and to the newspaper *Progress*. You—to the Visotsky tea-packing house. You—to the Southern Trading Company."

The squads departed expeditiously. They were at once replaced by new ones. After a brief consultation, we boys chose the farthest destination, following the second group, to the tea-packing plant. We were very anxious to see how they would "pull people off their jobs."

But we got there too late. All work had already ceased there. A noisy bunch of girls, the majority in their teens, pleasantly excited by the unusual events and singing loudly, were hurrying to the Kulikova Ground where the Vakhovsky Tobacco Factory was located.

The sun was especially brilliant that day. There wasn't a cloud in the sky. High, transparently blue, clear as a calm summer sea, its dome spread over the houses, trees, people, over the girls in their little slippers worn on bare feet, their patched light blouses and aprons, and their uncovered heads— without hats or kerchiefs—and their thick braids and slender arms.

And in this shining, happy brightness of the day, overwhelmingly sudden and cruel were the volleys of shots and unbearable were the moans of the wounded.

From two sides simultaneously appeared two detachments of police. Without any warning and *without any* orders, they bared their sabers and rushed into the stunned crowd of young women and men.

The sabers, cutting the air with a whistling sound, fell on the dark shirts of the men, on the girls' light blouses, on the braided crowns of their heads, on the bare arms raised to shield their faces, and in the same instant the heads, faces, shoulders, light dresses, and shirts were covered with wet red stains. The horrible screams of the women, the loud cursing of the men, the bang of revolver shots, the thud of the policemen's boots, the cries and moans of the fallen on the pavement and sidewalks—all mingled in a frightening uproar.

Vitka and Sashka were pushed aside by the rushing crowd. I lost sight of them. Spirka hid behind a wide drainpipe. I pressed against the wall of the corner building of a factory. I saw a beefy purple-faced policeman with fiercely bulging eyes bring his saber down on the head of a man, knocking him down to the sidewalk. The same policeman then pursued a slender, short young girl whose face was white with terror. Her young eyes were wide with panic, her mouth was open as if to scream but no sound came from it, and with her sun-tanned arms outstretched she ran straight in my direction, looking pleadingly at me as though asking me to save her.

Feeling desperate at my own helplessness, I closed my eyes for a moment. I then heard a piercing cry. Opening my eyes I saw the girl on the ground two feet away, the blood trickling down her neck from a cut at the ear. Her thin little shoeless feet thrashed with the pain.

The policeman who had struck her down was now after another victim.

I rushed to the wounded girl. Using all my strength, I lifted her helpless body, holding up her bleeding head. I carried her around the corner of the factory. She moaned barely audibly:

"Help . . . help. Oh! Mommie . . ."

With the aid of some women who had run over to us, I placed the girl on a shawl that someone had spread out and put my cap under her head.

Other wounded were already lying in the same enclosure. The nurse from the factory clinic arrived and two students with Red Cross armbands appeared, bringing bandages.

"It's Katya!" the girls cried.

"Katenka, can you hear me?"

But Katenka closed her eyes, her face was turning blue, and her dark, almost black, lips did not move. They carried her off somewhere.

For a while I stood there glued to the spot. Then I picked up my cap. It was covered with bloodstains to which clung a few golden hairs. I walked into the street.

There were no longer any crowds of workers or the police. I saw only someone's hat looking abandoned as it stuck between a drainpipe and a wall. A woman's white kerchief lay on the curbstone. Where Katya had fallen lay a pair of old slippers with worn-down heels, and near them was a large, dark spot of drying blood.

A little way from there, a yard porter in a white apron on which a copper badge had been pinned was carefully covering something with gray dirt.

And over all this, as though nothing had happened in the last half hour, was the bright blue sky, and in its transparent depth serenely hung the blinding sun.

I walked along Kanatnaya Street. From around the corners, first looking carefully in all directions, strikers and passers-by were slowly emerging. On the next block I ran into Vitka. He was pale, scared, and grim. With him was Sashka, looking upset but fearless. A number of boys from our neighborhood were also there. Spirka looked crushed and he was speechless and bewildered.

"They are murdering the people, the villains," Vitka muttered.

"Just wait!" Sashka said, his eyes flashing with outrage. "Their turn will come, the dogs!"

Vitka suggested that we all go home, but Sashka objected.

"No, let's go back to Richelieu Boulevard."

We all followed Sashka to the center of town. Soon we

heard volleys of rifle shots. The corrugated iron shutters were being hastily lowered over store windows and doors with a lot of banging. Groups of people were regathering, but no police were visible at their usual beats.

Some men came running, among them the same thin, pale young fellow with burning eyes who an hour earlier had thrown leaflets to the crowd.

"Brothers!" he cried, addressing the strikers coming into the square from the neighboring streets. "The soldiers are coming! Put up barricades! There is no time to lose!"

The people responded as if all their lives they had been occupied with nothing else. They instantly stopped the horse-drawn trolleys going in both directions. Untying the horses, they turned over the trolleys, placing them between two parallel street corners. A boy of about fourteen or fifteen, in a blue jersey and wearing a soft cap on his shaven head, climbed onto one of the trolleys and shouted in a cracked voice:

"Come on, boys! Help the grown-ups! Let's help put up the barricade!"

"Let's go, fellows!" shouted Sashka in response. "We'll give them a hand!"

From around one of the corners appeared a tall, handsome old man in a long black coat and a soft round hat on his gray head. Leaning on a cane with a rubber tip, he slowly walked toward a man with a scraggly beard, who seemed to be a leader.

"Here," he said, taking a pistol from his trouser pocket, "take it—it may come in handy—a spoon for the stew the devils are brewing."

I recognized the old man and was stupefied by his appearing so unexpectedly.

It was Reggio!

"Aleksandr Nikolayevich!" I gasped. "Where did you come from?"

"Oh, it's you!" he said, equally surprised. "How you've grown! I just got back from Paris—hurried back home—didn't want to miss anything. But why do you stand there? Build the barricade! Drag out everything from the yards." Then turning around abruptly and facing the other boys who were staring at him, old Reggio shouted, shaking his cane at them, "Go on, work—don't stand there gaping!"

He gave orders with such authority that we threw ourselves as one man against the nearby kiosk for billboards, knocked it down, and dragged it to the barricade.

Seeing that the work was going well, Reggio shook hands with the scraggly bearded man and went on his way.

There were now about fifteen of us boys. Under the command of the fellow in the blue jersey, we rushed into the courtyards of the nearest houses and brought out lumber, wheelbarrows, and sheets of iron. A few men came dragging a whole cider-vending booth and a newsstand. Some appeared with a variety of other objects. Everything was piled up.

It had taken us only a few minutes to build the tall, jagged barricade which now obstructed access to Richelieu Boulevard. And at once, as if they had waited impatiently for our task to be completed, not far from behind the barricade came an uneven rattling of shots. The wounded began to fall, and some slid down the side of the barricade and dropped to the pavement.

"The Cossacks!" the youth in the blue jersey shouted, climbing to the crest of the barricade. "The Cossacks are galloping here!"

"Get down from there, boy!" yelled an unshaven man with prominent cheekbones. He looked like a peasant and wore a peasant shirt. "Get down, I tell you! Don't push your luck! And you brothers who are armed, stand over here at the loopholes. The others get back and dig up the cobblestones. We'll defend ourselves!"

The Cossacks were very near now, ignoring the stones and occasional pistol shots. The bullets from the Cossacks' rifles easily penetrated the flimsy wooden obstructions and the thin sheets of iron, and flew without hindrance through the many holes and niches in the fragile barricade.

The pale youth kept shooting from a long, clumsy revolver. The man in the peasant shirt calmly let the bullets fly from his pistol, and the tall man with the scraggly beard and the old-fashioned pince-nez was busily firing from a Browning revolver.

"Uncle! Uncle! More Cossacks are coming from Pushkin Street!"

This news was brought by a freckle-faced boy, pale and breathless from running.

"Uncles . . ." he continued, catching his breath once in a while, and in a trembling voice: "There are cannon over there near the Stock Exchange and near the Bristol Hotel— the Cossacks are there! And their chief came galloping and he shouted to them: 'I command you to take the barricade on Richelieu Street! To crush them like flies! Annihilate them!'"

"Are there many of them, sonny?" the man with the pince-nez asked the boy.

"Oh, my! Uncle, a full hundred! The 8th Don Regiment!"

From fright and the strain of running and his rapid speech, the youngster's thin chest and ribs heaved, the small nostrils of his freckled nose flared weakly, and from his shaven head dirty little streaks of sweat trickled down to his face.

"Brothers!" the man in the peasant shirt addressed us. "Abandon the barricade! Disband along both sides of Richelieu! Reassemble on Bazarnaya Street!"

Most of us left, but some remained and continued to shoot. The youth in the blue jersey also didn't abandon his position.

"Get down!" the men shouted to him.

"Hurry, hurry!" commanded the man with the scraggly beard. "Come on, boy, get down, that's enough!"

But the youth didn't seem to hear him. He had gotten hold of a revolver, here on the barricade, and stubbornly went on firing.

"Pull him off from there!" irritably cried the man with the beard.

Then the youth was wounded. He rolled down the side of the barricade. Sashka, Vitka, and I ran to him. The three of us lifted him, and we were about to carry him to safety when the powerful arms of the man in the peasant shirt took the wounded youth from us and carried him easily toward some shelter.

We now heard the familiar dry rat-tat-tat-tat of rifle shots. It came from the direction of Pushkin Street. Soon we saw a horizontal line of mounted Cossacks rushing at us, letting go one volley after another.

The man in the peasant blouse dropped the wounded youth and ran down the street toward the theater. Others scampered away in the opposite direction.

Again the four of us lost one another. We later reassembled on Preobrazhenskaya Street.

Here a new barricade was being put up. Several dozen boys had gathered and we joined them in helping the grown-ups.

But we were no match for the Cossacks. The defenders of this barricade, too, finally abandoned it, scattering to reassemble at another spot, there to build a new one.

Toward evening we met the man in the peasant shirt. On his chest, on the embroidery, was a dry brown stain.

"Where is that youth?" we asked him.

"He's safe," the man answered, "he'll recover. He's quite a fellow!"

Before leaving he pulled out from inside his shirt a batch of leaflets, and, handing them to Sashka, asked us to distribute them to the people on our block, but not before it was quite dark.

The leaflets were signed: "The Russian Social-Democratic People's Party."

Proud of the task entrusted to us, we walked swiftly down the now silent street.

27

Next day, no sooner did we go outside our yards than we heard the astounding news. Everyone in the streets was talking about it.

"Have you heard?"

"You bet!"

"It is incredible! One can hardly imagine it! Mutiny on a battleship!"

"A thousand sailors!"

"Fifty guns!"

"That's not bad!"

"They've raised the flag of the revolution, and are supporting the strikers."

"Where is the ship now?"

"Right in the harbor, across from the Boulevard."

"Have they really raised that flag?"

"The very same!"

"Listen, are you sure you're not exaggerating?"

"So help me God! I saw it with my own eyes. You can go see for yourself!"

Like hundreds of other boys, we too raced to the waterfront. There were groups of agitated people at almost every house gate. Throngs of workers were streaming toward the harbor, exchanging the latest news and rumors on the way.

"Hurry up!" the tireless Sashka kept prodding us, speaking his native Ukrainian dialect in his great excitement. "You're dragging along like dying cats. Even the horses are moving faster!"

At last we reached the end of the Boulevard. From its elevation we could see, to the left, in the center of the large green lawns and flower beds, the building of the English Club. On the right, between the club and the columns of the City Court, was the bronze bust of the poet Pushkin. And right behind it, beyond the docks invisible from this cliff, was the wide blue expanse of the sea.

The main avenue leading to the waterfront was dark with a swarming crowd of people. Everyone was gazing into the silver-blue roadstead of the sea, where the large ships lay at anchor. And on this roadstead, about a quarter of a mile from the mole, its right broadside facing the city, stood the immense, grim battleship. It was dead still, as though rooted to the sea bottom. The long stems of the guns were pointed threateningly at the city. Thousands of its polished metal parts, the glass of its bull's eyes, and the colored lanterns sparkled in the sunlight. And over all of it, from the tall second mast, the flag of freedom waved defiantly.

"There it is! There it is!" Sashka whispered to me in a voice unsteady with rapture, as he poked me in the ribs with his sharp fist. "Look at it!"

"Yes," Vitka agreed, "it's surely not the old Andreevsky flag, it's not white and there's no blue cross. It's surely different!"

"And look at that small armored cruiser, farther away," Spirka pointed.

"That's not an armored cruiser," laughed an elderly man in a merchant-marine uniform, who was looking through large binoculars. "It's a torpedo boat. You can even see its number —267."

"That one's also flying the new flag! Look, look!" Sashka was beside himself with glee.

"You're right!" Vitka agreed with him again, not taking his eyes off the two ships.

A uniformed old general was standing near Sashka and Vitka.

"Un-han-ged vil-lains!" he said gritting his teeth, stressing each syllable with venom, and shaking his walking stick in the direction of the ships. The general's cheeks were flabby, he had big pouches under his colorless, faded eyes, and altogether he bore an amazing resemblance to a bulldog. "You just wait!" he continued. "You'll get it from us for that flag, and the uprising, and the revolution! We'll hang all of you bandits from the sail yards!"

"I shouldn't talk this way now if I were you," a youth in a threadbare blue school uniform said to the general, "or someone might be tempted to string you up—not from a sail yard, but right here, from the nearest lamppost."

"Go away, Your Excellency," a petty civil servant urged the general with great delicacy, looking nervously around him. And speaking in a loud whisper into the general's ear, he added: "Be good enough, sir, to go home. They may allow themselves, some . . . some rudeness, even . . . pardon the word . . . some roughness . . . like, you know, in France . . . At the time of the . . . pardon the word . . . revolution."

"Yes, yes . . . these bandits are capable of anything . . ." and the pale general began to push his way through the crowd, leaning on his heavy cane. "What scum!"

We didn't miss a single detail of this scene. Someone mimicked the solicitous civil servant, calling after the departing officer:

"Please, Your Excellency, to scurry off home. Here they may . . . you know . . . get even with the likes of you . . . pardon the word . . . bloodsuckers . . ."

The crowd laughed appreciatively. The frightened civil servant skulked away on his tiptoes.

There was much activity in the vicinity of the *Potemkin*. A variety of small craft kept approaching it—steam-cutters, sloops, yawls, and even rowboats. Sailors and civilians darted up and down the trap-ladders of the battleship.

But the harbor itself, always so bustling and noisy, was sunk in silence. A magnificent view of the harbor and the roadstead could be seen from the top of the sweeping stairway leading to the waterfront. The hundreds of steamboats and their many-colored stacks, the numerous schooners with their tall masts and cobweb-fine black rigging, the massive warehouses, the green customs building, the sharp lines of the booms, the loading cranes, elevators, the railroad tracks— everything was hushed this sultry June day.

The workers had abandoned their jobs and the harbor had died.

"Over there, at the edge of the New Breakwater, in a tent, lies the murdered sailor," a wrinkled, suntanned old fisherman pointed. He was carrying in his brown hands a string of wriggling mackerel he had just caught.

"Who was he?" people in the crowd asked him.

"A Ukrainian, they say . . ." the fisherman answered in a slow old-man's drawl. "Vakulenchuk . . . Gregory . . ."

"Who killed him?"

"An officer killed him . . . with a rifle . . . because he would not eat their rotten meat . . ."

"Come on, fellows, down to the harbor," Sashka called to us. "To the New Breakwater!"

We ran headlong down the immense stairway. Across the entire width of the middle landing stood a row of soldiers blocking everyone's way to the harbor.

We retraced our steps, and, circling the City Court building, descended to the waterfront along the steep, overgrown cliff.

The port was as full of people as the Boulevard, and more were coming from all approaches—everyone intent on reaching the breakwater and seeing the mutinied warship more closely.

On our part, we raced to the New Breakwater, and, reaching it, we pushed our way to the very edge, where, as the fisherman had said, lay the killed sailor Gregory Vakulenchuk.

"There he is!"

Before us was a small tent hurriedly put together from sails. At the entrance a naval guard—four sailors with weather-beaten faces—stood with rifles in their hands.

A tight crowd surrounded the tent. Inside, on an elevated platform, lay the massive body of the sailor, half-covered with a red cloth. In his hands, which were folded on his chest, was a piece of paper on which was written:

"Brothers! Before you is the corpse of the murdered sailor, Gregory Vakulenchuk. He was shot to death by the senior officer of the battleship *Count Potemkin Tavrichesky* for saying that the meat the crew was fed was rotten. Let's make the sign of the cross and say: 'May he rest in peace!' We'll get even with the bloodsuckers, the bloodthirsty vampires! Long live freedom! One for all, and all for one!"

Dock workers, sailors, townspeople, and women filed past the body, the men reverently removing their caps. The message was read, everyone crossed himself, bowed his head, knelt for an instant. Some sobbed, others wiped away silent tears. A girl leaned over the body of the victim and kissed his hand.

There were speeches by orators who mounted onto a large box placed close to the tent. One of them was Egor's friend, Petrov. He spoke briefly, yielding his place to another—a stocky man with large gray eyes and a blond beard. Raising his hand, this man called out:

"Brothers! The brutalities of the Czarist government, the endless exploitation of the working man by the bosses and

the peasant by the landowners, the ruinous war with Japan—
have reduced the nation to despair. The people can bear it
no longer and are rebelling. Brothers! The peasantry is joining
the workers! Also the Army and the Navy! You are witnessing
the first naval mutiny in the history of Russia! See for yourselves. The rebels in military and naval uniforms are of
the common people. Jointly with their brothers—the workers
and the peasants—they are rising up against the autocracy!
Down with the Czarist government! Long live the people
and the people's democracy!"

A thundering "Hurrah!" rolled from the crowd over the
sea. And like an echo came the answering "Hurrah!" from
the mutineers of the *Potemkin*. We saw hundreds of hands
waving white sailor's caps.

The speaker left the box. He was hugged, some shook his
hand, others kissed him. A sailor went over to him and
asked his name.

The speaker whispered something in the sailor's ear, and
asked, in his turn, "And yours?"

"Matiushenko. You've come to us from . . ." The sailor
bent down to the orator and said something in an undertone.

"You're quite right."

"And the password?"

Having heard the right password, Matiushenko spoke in full
voice, saying to the speaker: "In that case, please get into
our boat and visit our ship. And you, too, dear brothers!"

The sailor carefully helped the important speaker step into
the rowboat. They were joined by a handsome student, blond,
with large gleaming blue eyes, whom someone had called
Feldman, and by another, whose name was Ivanov, and by
a third man in civilian clothes whom people addressed simply
as Boris. The large boat, under the power of three sets of
oars pulled powerfully by three hefty sailors, moved smoothly
toward the *Potemkin*.

"Darn it, in a minute they'll be on the battleship," Sashka said, his eyes following the boat with envy.

"We should have asked to be taken along," Vitka whispered. "Maybe they'd have let us come."

"You don't say!" I disagreed with him. "Why should they allow us on a battleship?"

"But there are civilians among those."

"They're not ordinary civilians—they're members of the Social-Democratic Party."

"You saw, didn't you?" Sashka was impatient with Vitka's ignorance. "Evidently you saw, but understood nothing. The password—they gave the password. Only then did the sailors trust them."

We felt an irrepressible urge to participate in the dramatic event of the mutiny, and hung around hoping that someone would need our help.

We looked on as coal barges pulled by tugboats drew up near the battleship, and rowboats filled with produce—bread, potatoes, meat, and fish. Dockers and factory hands, fishermen and seamen took care of the unloading.

Evidently we boys weren't needed over there.

We were happy therefore when we saw a wagon piled high with freshly picked cabbages arrive at the mole and a sloop from the *Potemkin* draw up to be loaded with them. Spreading ourselves out in a line from the wagon to the water's edge, we began, like real lightermen, to pass the large green cabbage heads from one pair of hands to the next. The lighterboat was filling up rapidly.

"Thanks, fellows," the sailor on the boat said, smiling and saluting us.

"You might need some help in unloading them over there," Sashka suggested diplomatically, his khokhol accent thicker than ever. "We could come along with you to the ship and help. May we?"

"Why not?" the good-natured sailor said, his eyes twin-
kling boyishly. "Make yourselves at home—get in."

Sashka was the first to jump into the boat, without even
holding on. Then I followed, Vitka was the third, climbing
in carefully, and the shy Spirka fairly rolled in.

The boat pushed off, and, accompanied by the envious
looks of the boys who remained on shore, we quickly approached the fateful warship.

They were waiting for us at a trap-ladder. But, alas, we
weren't lucky enough to get on board. They had us pass
the cabbage heads along in the same manner as on the
mole, handing them to a row of sailors on the steep trap-
ladder. The unloading finished, the enterprising Sashka tried
to win the day yet with his gift for diplomacy.

"We can carry the cabbages right into the pantry for
you. We can . . ."

But the sailor at the top of the ladder—he was not the
chap with the boyish twinkle—this one was older and more
stern, said:

"Outsiders are not allowed."

Within only a couple of minutes, before we could really
profit from the situation and get a good look at this close
range at the ship's gun turrets, stacks, masts, and decks,
and after barely glancing at the naval heroes filling every
inch of the tremendous ship, huge as a tall building, our
boat was rapidly departing.

About midway between the *Potemkin* and the shore, our
boat stopped abruptly. The sailors rested their oars and
peered at what was now happening at the trap-ladder. An
armed guard of the mutineers had stationed itself on its
rungs.

Our sailors began to row back to the battleship.

A tugboat full of gendarmes had approached the *Potemkin*.

"Who are you?" asked Matiushenko, who was standing on the bottom rung.

"Police," answered a police officer.

"What do you want?"

"To conduct an investigation."

"So, an in-vesti-gation?" Matiushenko repeated grimly, and, turning suddenly to the sailors, he cried:

"Attention! On guard!"

"What's that? What are you doing?" the frightened officer muttered. "Why 'on guard'?"

"Throw your swords into the water," Matiushenko ordered the police.

The men hurriedly unfastened their swords and cast them into the sea.

"Your guns, too."

Their large, blue Nagant revolvers went flying into the waves. Then the silver glint of a small Browning flashed in the sun, and like a fish that got off the hook, it, too, dived into the water.

"Away from the ship! Full speed!"

The tugboat with the gendarmes, who looked scared to death, retreated at full steam back to the harbor, amid the roaring laughter and catcalls of the sailors on the decks of the *Potemkin*.

28

IN THE BRIEF TIME THAT WE WERE AWAY from the breakwater, the crowd had increased. We barely stepped on land
when we saw a tiny white tugboat speeding to the shore,
with a sailor in it waving his cap to attract the crowd's
attention.

"Brothers! Cossacks, soldiers, and police have appeared at
the harbor. Disperse! We might be forced to open fire."

The sailor on duty at the tent with the corpse of Vakulenchuk, noticing the new flag raised on the warship, announced:

"We've raised the signal of alarm!"

"Brothers, disperse quickly!"

"We are opening fire!"

"Inform the workers at the docks!"

"Warn everyone!"

The people scattered in all directions. They soon encountered large squads of police, foot soldiers, and mounted Cossacks. Some managed to by-pass them and leave without
trouble, but many others got hopelessly caught among the
warehouses and tall piles of freight.

"Let's go to the beach!" Sashka suggested.

We went there in a round-about way, to avoid the armed
squads, and reached the Langeron without incident.

Here there were no signs of disturbance. Old fishermen

were spreading pitch over some overturned boats, and fisherwomen were mending nets or cooking mackerel stew over
open fires in kettles suspended from iron tripods.

We could see the *Potemkin* quite well from here, and
kept watching its gun turrets, expecting to see action at any
moment and to hear the boom of the firing. One hour passed,
another, and a third, but there was no firing. From the harbor
to the battleship, and in the opposite direction, scurried many
cutters, rigged yawls, and ketches, and other small craft.

Tired with the tension and the heat, we limply climbed
a hill, crossed the "Consolation" resort area, found ourselves
on the French Boulevard, and went to our homes.

Once there, it would have been impossible for me to get
away again before late in the evening if something else quite
unusual hadn't occurred. This new development so upset everyone in the household that I had no trouble slipping out.

A gigantic fire, covering half the sky with black smoke,
was spreading from the port to the southern segment of the
city.

The whole neighborhood had gathered outside. The frightened people were asking each other:

"Heavens! What's happening?"

"The harbor is on fire!"

"It's not the harbor! They've set the city on fire. Can't
you see?"

"It's on the Boulevard."

"No, it's much nearer than that, on Deribasovskaya and
Pushkinskaya streets."

"That's right! Look how close!"

It really seemed as though the flames had spread over
the entire city—over the houses, roofs, the very sky. Black
columns of smoke edged with fiery purple spiraled over the
embankment. Huge tongues of flame soared toward the sky,
their reflections playing over the surface of the sea.

The flames encircled building after building. Along the endless stretch of the embankment, as though over rails, farther and farther, rushed the raging fire. The dry wood of the structures cracked, and the burning train coaches and girders collapsed with an awful crash.

Everywhere the roofs of burned-out homes and warehouses were coming down with a malevolent hissing sound. Storage houses, office buildings, piles of lumber, crates, and barrels were in flames. The acrid smoke from burning paint, varnishes, and tar burned our throats.

The sound of shots continued, and we could hear the desperate cries of the people caught in the fiery chaos.

"Look, look!" someone called out, pointing to the sea. "A ship is on fire! Over there!"

The blaze at the ship's stern flashed over the whole ship like lightning. The dark outlines of the masts and rigging looked yellow-orange on one side and the other side was sunk in the blueness of the mist. The ship had obviously been deserted, for there seemed to be no one aboard to put out the fire, and the hungry flames soon swallowed all of its decks.

A man appeared over the steep cliff from the harbor. He was still breathing hard. He was trembling, and answered in a broken and hoarse voice the questions put to him by the people in the street.

"The police organized a provocation—they gathered a bunch of hoodlums, got them drunk—incited them against the strikers . . . allowed them to loot warehouses and stores and then set them on fire. When the harbor was aflame and the people tried to get away . . . to save themselves . . . the police began to shoot them down . . . from all sides. The people threw themselves into the sea, some into the flames, or buried themselves in the mounds of coal . . . But there was no firing from the *Potemkin* . . . they were afraid they'd hit the fleeing people. There is panic and chaos."

And, as though to prove the truth of his words, we once more heard volleys of shots from the port, and they repeated themselves again and again.

The crowd on the cliff was shaken.

From the *Potemkin* suddenly flashed a gigantic searchlight. It swept the sky and swung over the harbor, pausing at the most distant corners, stubbornly trying to spot something in the remote alleys, bywalks, and slopes. Then, swiftly drawing an arc in the sky, it was lowered once more and continued to bore frantically into the dark areas of the wharfs not lighted by the conflagration.

Then the searchlight was extinguished as abruptly as it had been turned on.

Another man came panting from the waterfront.

After asking for a cigarette and drawing on it hard to steady his nerves, he reported the same horrors as his predecessor, adding:

"Thousands have been killed down there . . . there's no one to help the wounded."

The harbor burned all night, now inflaming half the sky with the ill-omened flares, now spreading a black smoky mist like mourning crepe. All night we heard the din of the conflagration, volleys of shots, heavy sniping, and the cries and wailing of the victims, invisible in the inferno.

Not before daybreak, when the impenetrable smoke had overcast the entire harbor and many of the neighboring streets, did we return to our homes.

The harbor smoldered all day.

Later in the morning, we could see from a distance, through the thinning brown-gray smoke, the dark remains of the burned-down wooden booms, the skeletons of the consumed stores and warehouses, the grim islands of the cremated ships. We saw the police and troops hurriedly gather up the killed and the burned, placing them on wide horse-drawn, sideless wagons and hiding them from view under tarpaulins. The casualties were carted away to some unknown place.

In the afternoon, people were saying that the Military Governor, fearing the *Potemkin* guns, gave official permission for the public funeral of the sailor Vakulenchuk, guaranteeing safety for those attending it.

We looked for a long time for the procession and finally came upon it at about five o'clock, on Preobrazhenskaya Street.

Twelve sailors walked right behind the cortege. After them came columns of workers, university students, high-schoolers. Soldiers were lined up at the curbs, shoulder-to-shoulder, evidently to keep the onlookers on the sidewalks from joining the procession. But the soldiers themselves, forgetting for the moment the purpose for which they were there, snapped to attention, without orders, saluted the dead man, removed their caps, and crossed themselves.

Suddenly, from Uspenskaya Street, a squad of soldiers tore into the marching column and, separating it from the funeral cortege, shot a volley into the air. The people dispersed and we boys ran with them. But after circling three blocks, we came out again on Preobrazhenskaya Street, and saw that a considerable crowd had regathered and was again marching behind the coffin.

The procession approached the cemetery. The column of marchers had become much longer. The coffin was lifted out of the carriage and carried by students, workers, and girls. The familiar man in the black hat and the pince-nez, the same one who had been in charge of putting up the barricade on Richelieu Boulevard three days before, made a speech. When the coffin was lowered into the grave and covered with spadefuls of earth, many, especially the women, wept.

Having paid their last respects to their mate, the sailors got into cabs, and, telling the drivers "to the port," departed.

They were soon stopped by some troops whose officer ordered the sailors to leave the cabs and proceed on foot. Anxious, evidently, to avoid trouble, the sailors complied. But when they had gone about half a block, the signal was given to fire and there was a salvo of shots. The sailors darted into the side streets. One of them must have been wounded, for two red blotches could be seen on the sidewalk, and near them a sailor's cap with a bullet hole in it. Sashka quickly crawled over to the cap, snatched it up, and as quickly returned.

"Villains," exclaimed an old man, trembling with indignation and shaking his clenched fist in the direction of the soldiers. "The dirty liars! They didn't keep their word, they shot at unarmed men! They'll pay for this!"

"The soldiers didn't want to kill. They shot above their heads . . ." explained a student youth. "All the sailors, thank God, got away unharmed."

As we were coming into the city, way above us, as if in the very sky itself, something was bursting with a frightful force, the first shuddering crash always followed by a second, third, fourth.

People ran in panic, paling and crossing themselves.

"That's from the *Potemkin!*" Sashka guessed right. "What do you know! They've finally done it!"

"You're right! That did come from the *Potemkin.*"

"Let's go, fellows, hurry up!"

And once more we raced to the harbor.

But Cossacks blocked our way on Ekaterinovskaya Street. Here people knew all about it. They were saying that the first two shots were blank, but one of the next two shells fell somewhere on Yamskaya Street, the other on Bugaevskaya. There were no casualties.

The city was in full panic.

The corrugated iron window and door shutters of the stores were closed with the usual metallic clatter, the trolleys stopped running, yard gates were bolted.

A whole naval squadron appeared in the sea roadstead. We could see clearly from the Boulevard that at first it drew up near the *Potemkin* then left and sailed off toward the horizon, with the fateful battleship lifting anchor and starting in pursuit. All the ships disappeared into the horizon, one after another. No one could tell what was happening there.

The people on the Nikolayevsky Boulevard, on the stone walks of the Aleksandrovsky Park, on the crests of the slopes leading to the waterfront, kept gazing at the distant line where the sea merged with the edge of the blue sky.

"There will be a battle."

"Without doubt."

"No, the squadron will not fight, it will surrender."

"It'll return to Sevastopol."

"The *Potemkin* won't let it."

"What can it do—one against a whole squadron?"

"It's the most powerful and fastest in the whole navy, isn't it?"

"Everything depends on the mood of the crews."

"It's too bad they didn't agree in advance, so that they'd all act now in unison."

"Of course, if they had agreed, then things would be different now."

"A collision is inevitable. They may be shooting it out right now."

Soon we could see the outline of the *Potemkin* once more.

"There it is! Look!"

"And another is following."

"I recognize it. I worked on it five years, at Sevastopol. It is the *Georgii Pobedonosetz.*"

We saw this battleship solemnly salute the *Potemkin* and draw up alongside of it. Then a number of men descended the trap-ladder and entered a transport boat, which immediately pushed off. These were evidently the ship's officers, now under arrest. The flag of the revolution was raised on the *Georgii*.

What joy!

But, alas, it wasn't of long duration. The *Georgii* wavered. Abruptly the new flag was lowered and the battleship proceeded at full steam into the open sea. The *Potemkin* pursued the runaway ship, aiming its guns at it. Realizing the danger it was in, the *Georgii* turned around and made for the harbor. It came at such a speed that its prow cut deep into the breakwater and the ship couldn't extricate itself.

The crew was evidently divided. Those who were for the uprising got into lifeboats and turned back toward the *Potemkin*, those against hurried to land on shore.

"It's plain as day what has happened," said an old man in a black Russian shirt, looking anxiously at the boats coming toward the wharf. The *Potemkin* had not returned.

Of the hundreds of speculations heard in the crowd, one was probably the most likely:

The *Potemkin* was not being joined by the rest of the squadron, and, realizing the hopelessness of the situation, its leaders decided to escape on the ship to Bulgaria or Rumania, and to disband there. Others supposed that the *Potemkin* had sailed to Sevastopol to try once more to win the whole fleet over to its cause.

In the dusk appeared the large naval transport *Prut*, flying the revolutionary flag. It came from a distant port to join forces with the *Potemkin*. But the *Potemkin* was no longer there, and, like the battleship, the *Prut* also left for some mysterious destination.

29

THE STORMY DAYS OF THE POTEMKIN had passed. The battleship had escaped to Rumania to be separated there from its rebel crew.

The heroic sailors of the Black Sea! Hundreds of them now lay in unmarked graves, hundreds more were perishing in Siberia, some were in prisons, awaiting sentence, some had escaped to foreign lands where they were yearning for their native land and waiting for the hour when their victorious countrymen would summon them home. Others, having already secretly returned, were living under assumed names, or hiding in distant corners of the country.

The peace treaty with Japan, sighed at Portsmouth,* had been announced. There was little talk now about the war. People mentioned it only when they saw the soldiers come back from the battlefields and from Japanese war-prisoner camps—the emaciated, ragged soldiers in their soiled fur caps, torn uniforms, and broken boots.

News releases, falsified and distorted by the censors, had now become commonplace. They described uprisings, barricades, strikes; the execution of hundreds of rebels in Poland;

---

* President Theodore Roosevelt used his influence with the Russian Czar, and with himself as mediator, the Treaty of Portsmouth was signed in New Hampshire on September 5, 1905, ending the Russo-Japanese War.

the pogroms against Jews perpetrated by the Black Hundred; the murder of workers in Nizhnyi-Novgorod, Baku, and St. Petersburg; peasant rebellions; the burning and sacking of landlords' estates.

The nation-wide railroad strike was over. Then came to an end the general strike which had paralyzed all transport, factories, postal and telegraph services and had closed the schools, government offices, banks, and city courts.

One early October morning newsboys appeared in the streets, shouting extras:

"Constitution! Constitution! Constitution!"

"Czar's *Manifesto!* Freedom of speech! Freedom of the press! Freedom of religion!"

The papers were immediately snapped up. The people read them in the street and discussed the astounding news, repeating out loud the new, incomprehensible words.

"Consti-tu-tioul"

"What is this constitution?"

"Limiting the autocratic power."

"Then what?"

"It grants freedoms."

"Are they giving land?"

"It doesn't say."

"To the devil with such a constitution!"

"Today they're scared, so they yield a little, tomorrow they'll be scared about yielding and will take it all back."

Some lord, smoothing his beard with his lily-white hand with a large emerald ring on the little finger, said in a velvet-smooth baritone:

"This is a great kindness on the part of the Monarch. This, you know is . . ."

"Go away, mister, with your 'kindness'!" answered a middle-aged man in a shabby black coat that had turned green with age. "The strikers scared him and the uprisings, and he wants to hide his sins and the blood that's been shed, so he gives a constitution . . ."

"This is an insult to His Highness, this . . . I'll not allow it! I . . ."

"Go home, mister, with Your Highness! Now it's freedom of speech, you say, so if you don't like it, you can lump it."

An hour later, the streets were overflowing with a sea of festive human columns. Red banners were everywhere. The marchers were singing the "Marseillaise" and the "Varshavyanka." The people were ecstatically happy. They were celebrating the Constitution. Only when darkness came over the city did they begin to disperse, as if fearing that another such glorious day would never repeat itself.

And, indeed, the morrow brought frightful and cruel events.

The walls were covered with an ultimatum from the military commander of the Odessa district, Baron Kaulbars:

"I warn the city that it is under martial law. In view of the heavy disorders provoked by certain criminal revolutionary elements, the public is forbidden to appear on the streets after six o'clock. The gates to yards and window shutters must be closed. In case of sniping from a house or the presence of arms, the place will be instantly destroyed by artillery fire. Anyone found with arms will be shot on the spot."

Following this, we witnessed an incredible scene. From the police station emerged a motley crowd—owners of cab companies, saloon keepers, bartenders from the waterfront. They carried a large portrait of the Czar; others, looking like petty merchants from the market places, held the tricolored Imperial flag and icons. All were singing "God Save the King."

These were followed by a mob of waterfront tramps, hooligans from the worst slums, young pickpockets with disfigured drunken faces, and heavily rouged women with ugly bags under their dissipated eyes. And at once we heard the clatter of the iron shutters banging open, after the locks were forced, and the crash of broken store windows.

We walked nearer to the corner of Skobelev Street, and saw cartons of tea, biscuits, and chocolates come flying through the broken windows onto the sidewalk. Sugar, coffee, and nuts were strewn on the street, the sacks having been torn by the looters.

The mob, protected by the police, greedily snatched up and made off with all they could carry—on their shoulders, in carts, in cabs—everything they could lay hands on.

I stood there rooted to the ground, appalled and perplexed. "What's happening, Sashka, how come?"

"They are from the Black Hundred. The police arranged all this," he explained, watching the scene as if hypnotized. "You saw, they all came out of the police station."

"That's right," Vitka agreed forlornly. "It's right. Look, there is our corner policeman, in civilian clothes, with an apron on and a yard porter's jacket."

"Yes, that's him." Spirka recognized him, too. "And he has a club in his hand."

Near us a drunk driver was busily loading his cab with crates of sardines.

We saw similar scenes in other streets—hooligans helping themselves to everything, with the police standing by, not interfering.

The same was happening in our neighborhood. Dozens of dwellings, small stores, and workshops were looted. The mobs of degenerates, carrying the Czar's portrait and holy images, and protected by the police and Cossacks, moved on to do their evil work in other places.

An onlooker commented:

"Here it's not so bad. Here in the center of the city, they're only looting, here they don't allow them to kill, but in other sections, in the Moldavanka, for instance, there they can go to it . . ."

Another man added:

"Orders from the Czar. He has given three days for this sort of thing."

"My teacher lives there," I whispered to my friends.

And we ran to the Moldavanka.

At the hospital a Red Cross flag hung on the gate. A number of doctors and nurses were at the entrance, receiving the victims. Here from all over the Moldavanka were brought the killed and the wounded.

What we saw on the streets of the Moldavanka was more horrible than any nightmare. Wherever we turned, on every street, we came upon brutal scenes of violence and pillage.

To call out a workers' defense squad was unthinkable. The place was thick with troops and Cossacks. We saw a small group of armed printers trying to protect their shop. They were pursued by a bunch of Cossacks with their sabers bared. The Cossacks seemed to be everywhere, attacking the innocent and aiding the rampaging mob.

Weary and in a state of shock, we silently started toward home, keeping to out-of-the-way, usually quiet, streets. But everywhere we found the same horror. The violence had spread to a large area and all of it was engulfed in the marauding and killing.

My parents didn't allow me to leave the house for several days, and when I finally went out, with Anka, she told me that the pogrom had lasted three days. The papers reported similar massacres in other cities, where many workers, revolutionaries, civic leaders, and students perished.

The violence had been plotted by the police, on orders from the government. The police had recruited the worst reactionary and criminal elements for the evil job. The purpose of it all was to stem the revolution. The Czar of the *Manifesto* had changed his mind.

30

I COULD NO LONGER REMEMBER when I last held the cello in my hands. Wrapped in a yellow cloth, it stood like a forsaken orphan in the corner of our living room.

My cellist-teacher was far away in France now. He had begun to be involved in the student underground in Odessa, and his worried parents had moved heaven and earth to send him to Paris for safety. He was now pursuing his musical career away from his native land.

By what means would I be able to resume my cello lessons?

No new drawings had been added to Sashka's folder in the past three months. And Vitka's models hadn't been improved with a single new detail. They remained on the window sill of his basement home and were now covered with a layer of black dust that had blown in from the next yard where coal was sold. Nor had Spirka read any poems to us for a long time, neither his own nor those of a favorite poet.

The paler and thinner Sashka was now drawing sketches on long sheets of metal for an "Atelier of an Artist of Signs." His pay was all of twenty kopecks a day! Vitka was still apprenticed to the locksmith-plumber and breaking his back working in the smelly workshop or in various cellars, laundries, and washrooms. He was working just for his keep. Spirka went to work with his father who was a clerk in a warehouse.

I now worked at a newsstand. Several times a day I would go down to the railroad station in time for the arrival of trains from St. Petersburg, the capital, and from Moscow. These trains brought the newspapers and magazines which I picked up for my employer. Part of my job was to sneak from under the noses of two perpetually drunk censors—Avdeenko and Kukharsky—sacks of printed matter "subject to confiscation" and to distribute them among neighboring newsstands and vendors. For all of these "brisk" services I received from my satisfied boss a fifteen-kopeck silver coin a day.

Many satirical political magazines were now being published. Among them *The Machine Gun* stood out sharply for its colorful illustrations and daring mockery of the authorities. For the time being this publication kept coming on the mail trains of the St. Petersburg-Odessa run, although it was usually outpaced by the official telegram: "All issues of the journal *The Machine Gun* are to be confiscated." My employer had received notice of this order simultaneously from a friend in the capital and from the local censors themselves. To the latter I often enough bore "gifts" from my boss—usually they were two-gallon kegs of Bessarabian wine. And it was the custom, before the arrival of the trains, for the newsstand owners to amiably invite the censors for drinks, reassuring them:

"Gentlemen, we still have eight minutes before the train arrives. Please allow us to treat you. Wouldn't you like to fortify yourselves . . ."

And while the officials fortified themselves, the St. Petersburg train snappily drew into the station. The respectfully greeted, well-known-to-us freight conductor immediately opened the mail coach and the delivery boys quickly and with great agility pulled off the mail sacks. After finding what we were after, we piled the long sacks into cabs and hurriedly left the station.

I was anxious to see what *The Machine Gun* looked like.

As soon as we left the station behind us, I tore open the top of one of the sacks and pulled out a copy of the outlawed magazine.

It looked like an ordinary thin journal. But I was spellbound by its cover. On it was printed a manifesto from the Czar about a constitution: "With God's blessing, we, Nicholas the Second, Emperor and Autocrat of All the Russias, Czar of Poland, Grand Duke of Finland, Czar of Astrahan . . . Kazan, etc., etc., etc., recognize as necessary to grant the basic freedoms of speech, of the press, of religion, of assembly . . ."

Above this text, printed in large black letters, were added in red ink, the words written in natural size by a masculine hand: "To which I affix my signature: Major-General Trepov "* And from this signature, spreading over the page, was a stain of blood-red ink, the same color as that of the signature. I found it impossible to tear my eyes from this magazine cover. It produced on me a shattering impression. With amazing force it summed up all the events of the past days: the Czar's manifesto—a lie, the bloody acts of Trepov—the reality.

The Machine Gun and a number of other publications that were clearly against the regime kept appearing. Often, despite the "freedom of the press," they were seized. And every day we had to solve the complicated problem of how to "soften" the censors the evening before by "soaking them in liquor" and how next morning to "lure" them at the depot to a bar, and, as soon as the trains pulled in, to unload the mailbags and make a quick getaway with them, leaving for Avdeenko and Kukharsky a few token copies to enable them to comply to a minimum with the official orders for confiscation.

On one such day, as I stood on the platform waiting for the train, I was approached by a tall, spindly student in

---

* Trepov was the country's police chief.

an old school uniform coat and a wrinkled, faded cap barely covering his thick hair. Smiling pleasantly, he said:

"May I ask you, my friend, for some friendly advice?"

"If I am able to . . . please . . ." I muttered, embarrassed by the unaccustomed respectful address.

The student laughed. "Oh, I'm sure you're able to—I've no doubt about it. I've been watching you for a long time—your work, that is. You're a very capable young man!"

He then explained that a sack of student papers had arrived for him from St. Petersburg, but since he didn't know how to go about claiming them personally—wasn't acquainted with the rules and regulations—he hesitated to proceed.

"Especially since," he added, bending down to my ear, "it seems that these issues are subject to confiscation."

"I see," I responded casually and in a business-like tone. "How long ago were they received here?"

"Three days ago."

"That's too bad. Now they look through all mailbags, especially those that are not claimed at once!"

"That's exactly it."

"What time is it now?" and I looked at the large station clock. "We have thirteen minutes before the train will arrive. There's time."

Taking from the student his freight receipt, and, for emergency, a three-ruble note, I told him to stay where he was and to watch me from a distance. If anything went wrong, he was to disappear immediately.

"What about . . . you?" The student was astounded.

"They won't touch me. If necessary, I'll say that a stranger asked me to do this for him."

In the freight section, the weigher, barely looking at me, asked:

"Newspapers?"

"Probably."

"After the St. Petersburg train arrives Kukharsky will examine them."

"Hasn't he seen them yet?"

"No, he examines them at the time they are picked up."

"Listen," I said to him secretively, "when the train arrives I'll be busy. You understand. My boss is very strict. And here is a bonus—some of it is for you."

He quickly accepted the three rubles and gave me the student's papers.

The student took a cab. Before departing he shook my hand and at the same time tried to give me a ten-ruble note. I jerked my hand away:

"I don't need it," and speaking into his ear, I added, "This is for the cause."

He stared at me, obviously surprised by my reaction.

"How do you know?"

"Let's go!" I shouted to his driver, and, waving at the student, I went away and reached the platform just in time to meet the train from St. Petersburg now clattering into the station.

I had no doubt that in the student's mailbag there were not only censorable magazines but outright underground literature.

The days wore on in the usual way—newspapers, magazines, books, customers: five-kopeck, twenty-kopeck, fifteen-kopeck coins; spies, censors, police.

Occasionally the routine would be changed. To the newsstand one day came a young man in a derby and a carefully trimmed black mustache, and equally black, shaggy, as though pasted on, brows. He bent down and stuck his secret-police badge right through the small newsstand window.

"Open up!" he ordered.

Soundlessly, like a rat, he slipped inside, quickly passed his spidery fingers over the shelves, found several copies of an illegal magazine and left, brusquely saying on his way out, "Appear at the Boulevard police station."

Limping lightly and leaning on a cane, the detective was off to the police station, carrying there his plunder.

I caught up with him to make sure that he wasn't an impostor. After me followed a whole flock of newsboys, greedy for something sensational to happen. Among them were the desperate mischief Senka, the reserved Petka, the lanky, with a long dark neck and a tiny, serpent's hairless head, Lenka, Glista, and Motka. Here also was the freckled and fiery redhead, Shlemka. Shlemka not only sold the papers but read them from the first page to the last, telling everyone their contents—the ones who asked for it and those who didn't.

There were about ten of us, and we kept pestering the detective.

"Give back those magazines, you hobble-footed devil!"

"If we ever catch you, we'll shave your stupid head!"

"You'd better give them back!"

"Come, sell them to us for three rubles. Here they are—cash."

"Give them back, you toad. Your time has passed. Now it's freedom of the press!"

The limping detective increased his pace, but Senka stole up from behind, grabbed him by the leg. The man fell flat on the sidewalk. Shlemka snatched away his cane, broke it in half over his knee, and threw each part in a different direction. The rest of the boys quickly gathered the scattered copies of the magazine and scampered off with them, telling me as they went that they'd be back later in the evening to settle accounts "honestly" with my employer. Separated by a safe distance from the detective, we watched him pick himself up, and, without removing from his mouth a large whistle, keep blowing it shrilly to attract the attention of a policeman. Not waiting for one to show up, he gathered the halves of his cane and scuttled into a nearby courtyard.

But in the midst of the various incidents accompanying my employment, I couldn't rid myself of the nagging and bitter feeling of loss at not studying and not becoming a musician.

Now I didn't even have the opportunity to listen to music. There were almost no concerts of good music in the city. Most of the posters announced lurid night club programs and displayed pictures of indecently dressed pretty women. Other advertisements featured "beauty queens," circus "queens of the air," "goddesses of fire," or "princesses of flowers."

Evenings our group gathered somewhere on a staircase or on a street corner, and in case of extremely cold weather in someone's home. There we would tell each other the day's news, read books and newspapers out loud, and have song fests.

Sashka, who had grown almost into manhood, showed us his drawings done from memory. Most of them were of the people and scenes at the barricades and the waterfront. We were very impressed with his picture of the armored cruiser, its guns pointing at the city. In the foreground he had drawn the New Breakwater, the tent with its red banner, and lying in the tent was the killed sailor.

When we gazed at Sashka's drawing of the massacre, Anka's light brown eyes, usually so merry and full of laughter, filled with tears. I tried to take her mind off the picture and showed her a model of a flying balloon Vitka's skillful hands had made.

Turning to the would-be engineer, she said, "You must become an engineer, Vitka. You must!"

"And on whose money?" Vitka said irritably. "An engineer . . . they don't teach mathematics and physics in a plumber's shop."

Anka looked away, feeling somewhat guilty for giving Vitka

advice he couldn't possibly afford to follow, and she said no more on the subject.

Spirka read one of his new poems. Together we put it to music. Feeling quite satisfied with our collective composition, we sang the song over and over again. It was a sad and at the same time stirring song about Russia's yearning for freedom.

We separated late that evening. As she was leaving, Anka said to all of us:

"Tomorrow evening my father will be away at a teachers' meeting. Come over at eight. We'll sing with piano accompaniment."

"Now don't forget the time, fellows—on the dot of eight!" Sashka issued the order in his usual tone of a chieftain. "No one is to be late. Let's all arrive together."

31

I NOW OFTEN HELPED THE STUDENT with the thin, pale face and mop of black hair, picking up at the freight counter packages of newspapers addressed to him. I was well aware of the contents of this secret cargo—hidden inside the parcels of uncensored newspapers and magazines was underground literature. The receipts for this material were sent ahead by registered letters addressed to the student. He received them in time for him to present the receipts when he called for the packages. There was danger both in receiving these letters by mail and in calling for the parcels. To lessen the danger for the student, I took turns with him in picking up one or the other.

I would go to the General Post Office, proceed to the second floor where the "claims" section was. The letters were usually given out by a girl with large gloomy eyes. Occasionally there was a grim, unpleasant postal clerk in her place. At first I would calmly saunter through the large room, casually chat with the post office boy helpers who were removing mail from "American" iron boxes, in the meantime taking stock of the people present. When I didn't see anyone suspicious-looking, I went over to the right window.

"Would you kindly tell me if there is a letter for Pyotr Ivanovich Scherbakov?"

The girl with the gloomy eyes efficiently went through the cubbyhole marked with the letters "sch" and soon handed me a thick blue envelope with the imprint "A. C. Suvorin, Publisher." This was the publisher of the newspaper *New Times*, St. Petersburg, 11-2 Ertelev Lane.

Hiding the letter in my pocket, I immediately left the building. I was intrigued with the shrewd use of the imprint of the *New Times*, the most "respectable" newspaper, the mouthpiece of the Black Hundred, which was the most violently reactionary organization in Russia.

"Pretty clever," I said to my student, when I brought his mail to the university. "Suvorin! *New Times!* Not bad!"

"Yes," he smiled somewhat stiffly, "next time it might be from the Government Bank. But, be careful, Orlov, I beg you! Not a syllable of this to anyone, not even to your family."

I felt insulted.

"Aren't you ashamed to say such a thing to me, Pyotr Ivanovich? You know I am . . ."

"Now, don't be offended, my friend. These are the rules of the underground. I treat you like one of us—like a fellow student. I repeat the lesson with you. And remember, in case anything happens—you don't know anyone. Not anyone!"

Sometimes I visited my student friend at the university. Here everything was new to me, and extremely interesting. A new world opened before me—a world I knew nothing about. The young people led their own lives here, had their own morals, customs, and rules. But the general unrest had penetrated even into this unique atmosphere from the outside. Hundreds of young people in uniform and in ordinary clothes —some quite young and others already quite mature, some lively, vivacious like high-schoolers and others staid like professors—passed through the halls and along the stairways.

"Attention, law students! Find your representative! Send him to the council meeting!"

"Attention everybody! In two hours there will be a meeting of the natural science student-body in the large assembly hall!"

"Is there anyone here from the history and philosophy departments? Send your chairman for literature! He knows where to go!"

"Physics and mathematics students! There will be a meeting at one in the small assembly hall!"

At noon that day I observed the meeting in the vast, round assembly hall. There were many speakers, and I listened with rapt attention. One of them, a tall, very blond young man was particularly striking. His mustache was golden on top and silver on the bottom, his eyebrows and eyelashes were the color of straw, and his eyes were green, with yellow flecks. Only his nose, long and with a small hump, made him look not Russian. As soon as he uttered his first word, I knew he was a Georgian. He spoke with the sharp Georgian accent, and although his sentences were absolutely correct, precise, and were impressive for their clarity, they at first seemed to me foreign. But only at first. Soon I was totally absorbed in the convincing reasoning of his speech.

"Fellow students! Although our university has been officially declared autonomous, we see that this, as well as everything said by the Czarist government, is false! If a besieged fortress is autonomous, then, of course, there is no argument—then we'll consider that we, too, are self-governing. But, friends, let us remember the events of the past week. Let us remember how our dear *alma mater* was surrounded by the Czar's military forces of all kinds and types! Our autonomy, like an enemy fortress, was under siege for three days by artillery, cavalry, and infantry!"

The speaker's comparison of the university to a besieged fortress met with approval from the audience; laughter for a

long time drowned the sounds of the orator's voice. He re-
stored silence with difficulty.

"Fellow students! We have long ago graduated from swad-
dling clothes. We are adults and must regard everything with
mature eyes. We must show our unity with the common
people. When cannon, rifles, and bayonets are used against us,
if we don't want to be corpses or slaves, convicts in chains,
we must defend ourselves and join with our brothers . . ."

"Down with him!" someone yelled in a shrill voice. "This is
heresy. He's . . ."

Others supported the objector and also shouted, "Down
with him. He's causing dissent!"

But the crowd's approving shouts drowned the outcries of
the small opposition, and through the tumult could be heard
snatches of the ongoing speech:

"The time has come . . . We must take a stand . . . On to
victory!"

My friend, the student Pyotr Ivanovich, walked up to the
speaker and whispered something to him. The Georgian
nodded, then announced to the audience:

"Friends! Information has reached us that large detachments of police and armed soldiers are again stationed opposite the university."

The audience responded with a howl of indignation. The
speaker remained on the platform, his arm raised to indicate
that he was not through.

"Everyone please return to your classes! Wait for orders
from your representatives! Brothers! Remember—discipline,
self-control! Outsiders, please leave the university grounds!"

I left, and my student friend came away with me.

In the streets, on the nearest corners, were detachments of
police. A short distance farther back were soldiers, mounted
Cossacks, and not far from them were men in military uni-

forms setting up some ammunition that looked like small cannon or a new kind of machine gun.

"Artillery, cavalry, infantry . . ." the words of the Georgian student kept sounding in my ears.

With whom have they come to do battle? Why have they singled out the university? How come they were displaying their readiness for warfare here, bringing their bayonets, spears, sabers, and even machine guns?

That evening I had arranged to meet Pyotr Ivanovich at the Civic Theater. The St. Petersburg Drama Theater had come to Odessa and was giving performances with the most celebrated actress of the day, Komissarzhevskaya, in the star roles. Tonight she was appearing in *The Girl Without a Dowry*. Anka and I were happy to have the opportunity to see something worth while again.

The famous actress was my newest enthusiasm, and I attended almost every play in which she appeared. Thanks to my old connections with the box-office attendants, Anka and I were admitted free.

The beautiful acting of the star, her delicate face, the expression in her lovely eyes, and her emotional voice captivated me from the moment she came on the stage. I even forgot the matter that had brought me there that particular evening. Anka and I were both moved to tears at the suffering and nobility of the heroine.

The final curtain came down, hiding from view the dying Larisa, and her last words echoed in the hushed auditorium: "I love everyone . . . the whole world . . ." The curtain came down for the last time, but Anka and I remained in our seats, shaken from the effects of the tragic ending.

"Have you decided to sit here all night?" my student friend asked us. We got up, and lowering our heads so that he couldn't see our tear-stained faces, we followed him outside.

On the street Pyotr Ivanovich handed me an envelope and, as though he were talking about the most ordinary errand, said briefly:

"You mustn't bring the papers to the university any more. Take the parcel to New First Street—I'll meet you on the corner of Ekaterinovskaya."

We shook hands and he left.

All the way home Anka and I were silent, still under the spell of the wonderful actress's performance.

When we arrived at her house, Anka finally spoke:

"I didn't know it was possible to become someone else. You know, she was really dying. I felt as though I actually saw the blood, drop by drop, leave her broken heart."

We stood at the gate for a while, then passed into the courtyard, reviewing one scene after another in which the talented actress had appeared.

Anka and I parted late. We said good-bye so solemnly, as if we weren't going to meet again for a long time. Anka's eyes under the small light at the entrance to her house looked unusually dark and mournful, and her mouth, when she tried to smile, trembled.

32

NEXT MORNING MY FATHER TOLD ME THAT Egor had paid us a visit the evening before.

I was so surprised and happy at the news that I couldn't utter a single word.

Later that day I found out that the amnesty for political prisoners had reduced Egor's eight-year sentence by half. After he served an initial period of "probation and punishment" his irons had been removed. He was to have remained in exile for the rest of the shortened sentence of four years unchained. Taking advantage of being out of their irons, he and a few other political convicts escaped. One of the men was killed, two were caught, a fourth died in the *taiga* wilderness, and only three managed to get away.

Father told me that Egor had aged very much, was gaunt, and wore a heavy beard.

"And do you know," my father said, choosing his words carefully in order not to upset me too much, "he has a large scar on his head . . . and it seems he can't use his left arm . . . he must have been beaten over there . . . You'll see for yourself. He's spending the night at his buddy's house on the Slobodka-Romanovka. He'll come over again tomorrow, after dark."

My mother informed me the same morning that her cousin

Gregory was back, that he planned to live in Odessa now, and that he wanted me to come and see him, without fail, and that I was to bring my cello with me.

"When he heard that you had an instrument, he said he would now give you lessons himself."

This was indeed a happy day for me!

It was Sunday, and I could have gone to see Gregory Mikhailovich at any hour, but I had an important errand to take care of first. I had to go down to the railroad station to pick up a parcel and then meet my student friend to give it to him.

I planned the day carefully: after delivering the parcel to Pyotr Ivanovich, at about four in the afternoon, I'd return home toward five, pick up the cello, and half an hour later I'd be at my unexpected—as if he had dropped from the sky—teacher's. After that I'd get back in time for Egor's visit.

Very excited, I ran to Anka's, but I was cautious and told her only about the return of my relative and that he would teach me.

"You know," I tried to impress her with the significance of this news, unwittingly exaggerating, "Gregory Mikhailovich himself will teach me! A celebrated cellist, a conductor of a symphony orchestra, a composer!"

In Anka's lovely eyes appeared thousands of tiny flames.

"This would be wonderful!" she said moodily, looking past me into the distance.

"Why do you say 'would be'?" I objected with annoyance. "It certainly *will* be! I'll never again abandon my cello! You may be sure of that!"

Just then Anka's father came home. He was a forbidding, cold person. He always wore his long teacher's frock coat with two rows of gold buttons and shiny yellow braid on the dark-green velvet collar, and the white and blue university crest was pinned on his chest. He had a high white forehead, a straight handsome nose, a long bushy mustache and a light brown beard, and wore a pince-nez on a wide silk ribbon. He was very impressive and picturesque, but I didn't like him because he didn't like me. He talked to me condescendingly and always called me a *bashi-bazouk*—the name by which Turkish irregulars, notorious for their brutality, were known in the nineteenth century.

"Well, how are things, bashi-bazouk? Have you killed anyone yet?"

"Not so far," I answered casually, trying not to show how offended I was.

"When will you?"

"Any day now."

"Who will it be?"

"The Chief of Staff, of course."

He stopped and looked penetratingly at me.

"I bet you could, too," he said slowly, as if he were carefully analyzing my character, and his eyes kept peering at me. "You are the type. If not the Chief of Staff it will be someone else."

After saying this, he engaged Anka in conversation, deliberately leaving me out of it. I left.

I had an errand to do at the railway depot. There things were the same as always: the usual red-faced policeman on the platform; the gray-bearded snack-counter waiter; the same assistant in a flashy red cap, holding a signal flag in his hand; porters in their white aprons with the brass numbers pinned to them; carts piled with luggage on which brightcolored labels from Russian and foreign hotels were pasted; and, finally, the baggage room which faced the platform on one side and the street on the other.

I entered the large baggage room and went to the claim window. The clerk was sitting over his greasy hand-sewn ledger, his back to the window. I attracted his attention to

offer him the receipt. He turned around, and I saw that
he wasn't the old clerk whom I knew and from whom I
always received my parcels of papers.

"Newspapers?" he asked very casually.

"Yes, I think so."

I expected him to refuse to give me the parcel before
Kukharsky or Avdeenko had a chance to examine it. I was
about to leave, thinking it would be better to come back for
it the next day. But, to my surprise, he immediately left his
desk, went to the adjacent room, and quickly returned with
my parcel.

"Here it is."

A porter helped me carry it to the street and put it on
the coach box of a cab, beside the driver.

We left the station without any trouble, but it seemed
suspicious that at the same minute two men, without any
luggage, left the baggage room and got into a cab which
immediately followed mine.

Maybe I was unnecessarily anxious? Perhaps these men
had called for their baggage, it had not yet arrived, and they
were now merely returning empty-handed?

Looking behind me as if I were only satisfying an idle
curiosity, I took a good look at the suspicious characters.
They wore identical black derbies pulled down over their eyebrows and their chins were buried in upturned collars. They
had the typical coarse faces of policemen and the same steely
look. These were, without doubt, detectives. They were following me to find out where I was going to deliver the parcel.
And the fact that the new clerk had let me have it so
readily, and without a bribe, strengthened my suspicions.

I told the driver to take me along an out-of-the-way route,
to avoid the corner where my student friend was waiting
for me.

The other cab turned to follow. It was all plain now!

But to recheck my suspicions, I asked the driver to stop, telling him that I wanted to get a drink. I went into a cafe and ordered a glass of cold soda water, and as I was drinking it I looked through the window, watching the movements of the detectives who had halted their cab across the street. One of them was watching the door of the cafe, evidently intent on not losing sight of me.

Now I was absolutely sure. There was no doubt about it. I had to get away! But how?

Going over to the proprietress, I said:

"Please, madam, may I leave through the back door?"

She looked at me distrustfully:

"What for?"

"Some boys are after me—they want to beat me up. They're hoodlums."

The old proprietor said, "Let him pass." But at that moment the door was opened and one of the detectives entered. He ordered a glass of soda with lemon.

I thanked the owners, said a quick good-bye, and dashed out into the street, intending to disappear in the crowd. But my pursuer apparently understood my maneuver, and, leaving his drink, followed me out.

I had no alternative but to return to my cab.

"Let's go," I said to the driver.

The two detectives continued to follow me, staying twenty to thirty feet behind.

Now what? I thought. At any rate it was fortunate that I was managing not to expose the student. He at least was not in danger. Now, first of all, I must avoid going to the university. The detectives must not even remotely guess the connection between the school and the addressee of the parcel. Or, maybe the contrary would be best—to drive to the campus, leave the newspapers there to their fate, hide myself in one of the buildings, and then leave through another street. I convinced myself that the detectives would not dare enter the university proper. Perhaps some student or a whole crowd of them would come to my rescue. But, then, they would be detained together with the papers. What was I to do? I simply had to find some intricate arcade or a yard with two opposite exits. But where? We were approaching a large building in a curving arcade. I'll enter on Preobrazhenskaya Street and leave on Deribasovskaya.

"Driver, stop! I'll get out here and send someone out for the parcel."

I paid him off in full view of the detectives. Let them think I was actually delivering the papers here.

"Someone will come out right away to get it," I said loudly, and immediately disappeared around the arcade.

"The devil take you!" I said to myself, "just try and catch me!"

I knew that arcade as well as I knew the five fingers of my own hand. This was where I had worked for the *Odessa News.*

The building was L-shaped. I ran along the shorter end of it and streaked around the corner to its longer side. My spine was tingling with fright. Are they chasing me? I was too scared to look around.

Now where? . . . Should I run down Deribasovskaya Street or seek cover in some store? Of course, it was safer to hide somewhere here. I'll run into the office of the *Odessa News.* From there I'll go down to the basement, and through some dark passages down there get out into the back courtyard. I ran up the steps.

But, to my horror, I saw on the door of the *Odessa News* the sign "Closed." Of course, today was Sunday. How could I have forgotten this? And it meant that everything was closed and the people moving along in all drections were merely Sunday strollers.

I ran into the street, turned left, and, trying to lose myself in the crowd, dashed down Ekaterinovskaya Street. I
couldn't tell whether or not my pursuer had lost sight of me
or whether he was right behind me. I was too scared to look.
In any case, I felt it was better to run on and then suddenly
turn into some courtyard. I was approaching a square building
with a yard that I knew had three exits.

One couldn't ask for anything better. In order not to have
to cross an exposed empty space, I ran to the corner, intending
to turn back sharply and race into the yard. But at that
moment, just as I made the turn, I saw my detective standing beside the corner policeman. He was pointing in my
direction. The policeman came toward me. I tried to make
my getaway but it was too late.

"Halt! Hands up!"

I was petrified with fear. The policeman forced my arms
up, pulling my hands out of my coat pocket. He ran his hands
roughly over my whole body, checking for weapons. Then,
squeezing my wrist painfully, he dragged me toward my cab,
pushed me into it, and sat down at my side.

"To the police station," he ordered the driver.

"They've got me! It's the end! I'm caught!" the words
kept beating in my head.

The policeman held on to me, his arm around my waist,
but my right arm was free. My hand was in my pocket. There
was some piece of paper in it. I realized it was the envelope
in which my student friend had gotten the receipt for the
confiscated parcel. The envelope had to be destroyed. They
must not find out the address. With my fingers, I very quietly
began to tear up the envelope. The coins got in the way.
But I stubbornly continued to destroy the envelope, not stopping until we got to the police station.

Inside, we walked along a dimly lighted corridor. I tried,
without dropping any coin on the cement floor, to get rid

of the shreds of paper in my pocket. I did this a few pieces at a time, and entered for the cross-examination with empty pockets.

They searched me, finding nothing except some change and two or three meaningless shreds of paper.

"What is your name?" asked the district police inspector.

"Orlov."

"Christian name?"

"Nikolai."

"Patronymic."

"Ivanovich."

"Age?"

"Fifteen."

"Eastern Orthodox?"

"Russian."

"From whom is that parcel?"

"I don't know."

"To whom were you taking it?"

"I don't know."

"To what address?"

"The arcade."

"Exactly to whom? What person?"

"I don't know."

"How come?"

"I was hired."

"So?"

"They promised to pay me."

"So?"

"I brought it, but he wasn't there."

"Who wasn't there?"

"The man."

"What's his name?"

"I don't know."

"What did he look like?"

"Blond . . . short . . . stout . . ."

"You're lying. He was probably dark, tall, and thin."

"No."

This kind of exchange continued for a long time, sounding like a broken phonograph record.

The inspector's assistant then joined the cross-examination.

"Don't you play the fool with us! You're beating about the bush, but your eyes look sly and burn like a fox's at bay! Tell the truth—who sent you for the papers? If you tell us, we'll let you go home. It's not you we're after, you know that yourself, we want those others. You understand! The others!"

"I don't know."

"Tell us, you scoundrel, or you'll get the beating of your life—then, you won't only talk, you'll scream!"

"I know nothing to tell."

I could hear someone's cries from the corridor and I realized that the policeman's words were not an empty threat.

"Do you hear that? You'll get the same."

"I don't know anything else."

"Don't bother with him," the chief inspector said, "save your health. After all, we've done our part. The rest is up to the guards—let them take care of him. Our job is the preliminary cross-examination. They'll do the rest."

I was led away and pushed into a cell.

33

It was a cold, dirty cell with only a small, high window. Hardly any light came through it because of the grimy window-panes and thick iron bars.

I shivered from the dampness that rose from the cement floor as from a cellar. My feet and back became stiff with the cold and my head burned. I got up from the floor and started pacing the small room, from corner to corner, but I soon got very tired and sat down again.

It grew dark. There was no light in the cell. There was no cot, table, or chair. There wasn't even a bed of straw. Two or three cells from mine someone was being beaten. I could hear the sound of the blows and the screams of the prisoner.

All night long, one after another, they kept bringing in drunkards, and the corridors were filled with sounds of shoving and heavy cursing. But things quieted down toward morning. Completely exhausted now, I stretched out at the door of the cell where there was a little less filth and fell into a troubled sleep. I had a nightmare: Anka was seized by a policeman; the plainclothesman who had arrested me took my cello away. I tried to grab it from him but he ran away with it. I tried to pursue him but my feet would not move and I fell down. Then I woke up.

It took what seemed a long time for me to figure out where I was. The greenish light of the beginning sunrise penetrated the small window. The door was soon opened and a large figure entered my cell. Unable to see me, the man stepped on my leg. I felt a sharp pain in my knee.

"Who is it?" the man said drawing back when I jumped up, nearly knocking him off his feet. He tried to see my face in the gray-green semi-darkness of the room.

"Have you been here long?" he asked in a matter-of-fact way.

"Since yesterday."

"But you're not even a grown-up!" he said, hearing my voice. "Heavens, you're just a boy!"

The man put his hands on my shoulders and turned me toward the window.

"Of course you're just a boy," he said, now quite convinced of it. "Why did they throw you in here?"

My cell mate had an unusually pleasant face. It seemed strange to see such a good-natured, smiling person in a place such as this, and to hear him speak in so friendly a manner when he himself had just lost his freedom.

"Why don't you say something?" He insisted on knowing why I had been arrested. "I'm surprised, because I thought they locked up only political offenders in this cell."

"Yes," I said, "I am a political prisoner."

The words sounded odd to me and they seemed even stranger to my cell mate. As a matter of fact, judging by the broad grin on his face, he could hardly refrain from laughing. But he offered me his hand, saying:

"Well, how do you do, pal! Pleased to meet you. I'm also political."

I was sure that he identified himself with me only to ease my embarrassment at his recent amusement—in everything else we certainly didn't resemble each other. He was about thirty-five, I was only fifteen. He was a tall, bearded, and powerful person. I was just a kid. He was evidently an experienced revolutionary. I had fallen into the hands of the police by accident because I was a mere amateur in underground activity.

Without mentioning names, I told him what had happened. When I finished, he said very seriously:

"This won't do at all. You mustn't remain here. Not under any circumstances!"

"I don't know what you mean . . ." I said, hesitating to reveal my ignorance of the reason for his opinion.

"I'll explain. The fact is that despite the existence of special statutes of law for the safety and circulation of printed matter —these are Statutes No. 129 and No. 132—you will most definitely be accused of violating Statute No. 102, that is, you'll be accused of aiming to overthrow the existing regime and will be sentenced to four to eight years of penal servitude. The city, as you must know, is under martial law."

I felt a chill in my heart, and my knees gave under me.

"We must not allow this to happen!" the man continued. He said this more slowly, as if he were considering an alternative. "No, we mustn't allow that!" he repeated.

"But . . . how can we prevent this from happening?" I asked forlornly.

"If they transfer you to a prison, things will go badly with you. There is no escaping from there."

"Then what am I to do?"

"You'll have to start thinking of escape—either from here or on the way to the prison."

At first this seemed to me sheer fantasy. Later, however, after he described in detail three of his own escapes, I began to understand that before me was a responsible man and that he was sincerely urging me to escape and was not fooling.

The man promised to study the surroundings and to suggest a workable plan of escape.

By now the cell was unbearably cold, and I was faint with hunger. Because of the filth I couldn't make myself lie down again or even lean against the wall. This was torture to my exhausted body. I kept shifting my weight from one foot to the other. My neighbor paced the cell as he talked. He didn't stop for a second, and it occurred to me that he must have formed this habit over his years of repeated imprisonment. I was sure that he had paced hundreds of miles inside tiny prison cells.

"You're right," he suddenly said as if he had read my thoughts. "This way you cover a distance of three miles in one hour and fifteen to twenty miles a day. It means that in a month you can pace a thousand miles and in a year twelve thousand. And throughout all the years that I've been shut up in jails, I believe I've paced fifty to sixty thousand miles."

The man's name was Prokopy. He was obviously a laborer. In the past few years of his life he must have spent more time in prison and in exile than at home and at work. He had a wide face with slightly prominent cheekbones, a square blond beard, a long mustache, and, although I couldn't see their color in the dim light of the cell, I was sure his eyes were blue. His speech was clear and precise. He was very likely a good orator.

"How well you speak!" I said without meaning to, aware that this was hardly a time for paying compliments.

"That's exactly why I'm here," he laughed. "The police are prejudiced against orators."

Seeing that I was shaking with cold, he at once unbuttoned his coat, took it off, and wrapped it around my shoulders.

"What are you doing?" I said, trying to object, but he assured me that when he paced like that he felt hot and that he had been about to take off his coat anyway.

"Come on, walk with me and you'll feel a lot warmer," he suggested.

"I'm dizzy."

"You must be starving!" he guessed. He quickly untied a small bundle he had brought with him and offered me a piece of bread.

He got angry when I refused it. "Eat, I tell you! One can die of hunger before they feed you here."

While I was eating the bread, Prokopy continued to walk back and forth. From time to time he looked up at the window, examining it. When I finished eating he suddenly stopped in front of me and announced with firm conviction:

"I've got it!"

"What?"

"You can escape."

"How?" I felt hope and fear at the same time. "How?" I repeated.

"It's quite simple. Through the window."

This seemed madness to me. The window was very high. Its bars were thick. Below was the main prison yard, and a sentry was probably stationed there.

"Nonsense," Prokopy said after hearing me out. "We'll measure the window at once. I'm sure they didn't anticipate boy prisoners here. You can certainly push through the bars. I'll lift you and help you push through. There's no guard down there. At night the yard is dark and deserted."

I now shook even more with fright than with the cold. "I'll not be able to get through those bars," I said, my voice disgracefully unsteady.

"Very well, let's do some measuring."

He removed his coat from my shoulders, lifted me to the window, and whispered: "Go on, measure it."

Stretching my hand from thumb to pinky, I used it as a yardstick, counting the number of times it took my stretched hand to cover the width and height of the space between two bars. When he put me down we compared the size of our hands and allowing for the difference, we calculated the width of my back, which Prokopy measured. It seemed to me that I was much too wide for the space between the bars.

"That's nothing," he assured me. "You can get through."

"No," I shook my head, "I won't be able to. I'm scared!"

"Don't be foolish," he said with sudden impatience. "You're just a kid, after all. You're facing a long jail sentence. You may never survive it! And here—two or three minutes of danger and you're free! Some revolutionary you are!"

Our argument was interrupted by the arrival of a guard.

"To the lavatory!" he bellowed.

We walked down a long corridor to the lavatory.

"Look!" Prokopy whispered pointing at its window. "This, you know, is not a real prison. It's just a police station. An experienced prisoner can flee from here in a wink of an eye. Just look—this window doesn't even have bars. It's probably a makeshift lavatory and the regular one is most likely being 'redecorated.'"

When we returned to the cell, Prokopy could talk of nothing else but the best way for me to escape. He kept speculating: would it be better to do it through the cell window, or the lavatory one? He explained that the building hadn't always been a police station—it used to house a seminary.

He paced for another ten minutes, then stopped to announce his final decision:

"We'll get you on your way this very evening."

But an hour later everything changed. Prokopy was taken away for interrogation. When he came back, he said nothing about himself but immediately informed me of his new plan for my escape. And this new plan seemed even wilder than the first one.

"In the evening all prisoners will be assembled for roll call," he explained. "There'll be a large number of them. I'll try to stand as close as possible to the door leading to the outside and you'll stand right behind me. When I begin to back up, barely noticeably, and start stepping on your feet, you'll then start backing up too, but more boldly. If you see that the crowd has covered you from view and the police officials in the front of the room can't see you, calmly step into the hall and rush toward the stairway."

"But they'll see me!"

"Don't talk nonsense. I know what I'm saying. This is not a jail, it's a police station—don't forget that. They seldom have political prisoners here and there is no one here except the district police inspector and a local inspector; there are no guards at the entrance. It would be hard for me or another adult to get away, but for you, especially with my help, it'll be simple. Before anyone realizes what's happening, you'll be on the street. Only, be sure not to run, just walk and look relaxed. Dogs chase only those who run from them."

This plan seemed to me alternately quite feasible and totally impossible.

"All right," I agreed reluctantly, almost hoping that before the evening Prokopy would come up with still another plan, perhaps a more reasonable one.

Two new prisoners were brought to our cell. They were students. At first I was worried that they were perhaps in some way mixed up with my affair. I was relieved when I found out that they had been seized near the university at the moment when they were passing to each other some notes on a lecture about ancient Roman law.

Prokopy burst into a gale of laughter at hearing the students' story. "That was sure hot revolutionary stuff. They caught the wrong mice."

For the rest of the day, while the students were having an endless political argument with the eloquent Prokopy, I sat leaning against the wall and thought of home, Egor, the music school and my music studies. Now all has gone to the devil. Even if I succeeded in escaping, where was I to go? I couldn't return home—my name, surname, and address were on the police books. This would force me to leave not only my family but also my city. It was good-bye now to parents, friends, Anka, Egor. And it was good-bye to music.

A thousand obstacles had hindered my becoming a musician. Everything had conspired against me. And now I was trapped by the police.

And in all the obstacles materializing, almost as a rule, just as I was about to move toward my goal, I now began to see not blind fate, as I used to regard them, not as the curse of bad luck, but as a cruel order of things established by evil people and perpetuated by them. It was as hard to bypass this order as it was to pass through barbed wire.

I sorted out in my mind all that Egor had told me and that which I had witnessed recently in the city of Odessa and in Sevastopol. I began to understand more clearly what it all signified. Was it mere fate that my father, an honest and industrious person, remained unemployed for many months and then, finally finding a job, couldn't take proper care of his family on his miserable wages? No, of course, that wasn't fate. In this and in all the other troubles that confronted us, there was some awful consistency, some kind of bond with the evil truth of our kind of existence.

Was it fate that I was unable to attend school only because my father was out of work so much of the time—was this merely bad luck? And was it just bad luck that made it necessary for me to work with all my strength from the age of thirteen, earning three rubles or less a month, instead of being in school? And was it mere fate that there existed not a single music school in the whole city where instruction was free, and that wherever I had turned for musical training they had asked large sums of money for the right to learn? No, all

this was due to our order of things, to the whole system—
and nothing else could be expected as long as it lasted.

Some people had turned away when I had asked for help,
others had wanted to assist me but didn't have the means,
and those who could refused to. Did the goodness or meanness
of people you met depend only on your luck? And why did
my cello teacher have to leave his native land to be safe?
Russia should have been proud of him. He should not have
been hounded out of his country.

All these "accidents," bits of "good luck," or "bad luck,"
all these together added up to our kind of life and no other,
a life in which our fathers didn't earn and their children
didn't learn. Sashka, Vitka, and Spirka were all being raised
in the street, and I had ended up in the clutches of the police.
How good it would feel right now to see Egor and talk all
this over with him!

Thinking of Egor, my thoughts took me back once more to
my home and to music. I could remember without any effort
everything that I had played before the uprising. Without
being aware of it, I began to hum the melodies I loved most.
One after another they rose in my memory, stirred the emotions, and wanted to be sung. And sing I did. I was so absorbed
that I sang louder and louder, not noticing that my cell mates
had long since stopped talking and were listening to me. I
must have sung well and with earnest grief, for I heard one of
them whisper: "Not bad!" and the others agreed.

"Stop it, Kolenka," Prokopy said, putting his arms around
me, "or, listening to you, I'll start weeping."

But he wasn't on the verge of tears. He laughed uproari-
ously. Huge, bearded, bright-eyed, he resembled a benevolent
giant. "I told you, you mustn't remain in this filthy cell—
you're still only a boy. You must regain your freedom. You'll
have another chance, later, to get back into prison. In the
meantime, you must make your getaway."

"What about you?"

"Me?" and he laughed again. "I'll be caught another dozen times and will escape as often. *They* don't allow me too much liberty at a time and *I* can't stand to be locked up."

The students regarded Prokopy with awe.

"And what will become of the students?" I asked.

"Don't you worry your young head about them. They'll let them out this very day. It was all a mistake."

The key was turned in the lock, the door was opened, and a fat, red-bearded policeman shouted:

"Report for roll call."

On the way to the "reception room," Prokopy whispered rapidly in my ear:

"Remember what I told you. Pay close attention—no yawning now!"

Then he turned to the students: "Stay close to me—one on each side, three abreast."

And to me: "Don't go home. Hide at a friend's place. Then leave town."

The room into which the prisoners were herded was quickly filled. The arrested came from all the cells—thieves, drunkards, beggars. In addition to the four of us, there were six other political prisoners—two women and four men. The crowd formed a semi-circle facing the officials. The backs of the prisoners were to the door leading to the exit.

Prokopy, without being noticed, edged backward to the door. I stayed close behind him. The students were on either side of him. Giving the impression that he didn't like his immediate neighbors, Prokopy kept moving away and getting nearer to the door.

In addition to the district and local inspectors who were sitting as in an office behind a partition, there were three ordinary policemen. One of them, by coincidence or on purpose—this I couldn't tell—stood right behind me at the door leading to the exit. I assumed that our plot was now without a chance of succeeding. But Prokopy didn't seem to think so. He seemed not to notice the policeman and kept moving backward and stepping on my feet. I was forced to back up.

Finally I felt myself touching the doorpost. The policeman was almost right at my side, and behind him was the hallway leading to the staircase which took one to the outside door. I felt the draft from the hall on the back of my neck. And Prokopy pressed on. The policeman lit a cigarette. I had only one hope—that after finishing his smoke, he would return to the front of the room. But when he finished, he threw the butt on the floor, stamped it out with the heel of his boot, and remained rooted to the same spot. And Prokopy continued to push back. I was about to shove him forward to get him off my feet, when a scuffle was heard from the stairway. There was pushing and yelling.

"Move on, you bum!" someone shouted. "Get up there! Do as you're told!"

"Why do you hit? Why do you hit?" a desperate voice kept wailing.

"Move, move . . ."

And again there was a struggle, the sound of a boot hitting hard against something, then a hoarse, muffled moan, and cursing.

The policeman who had been standing near me rushed to give assistance and soon reappeared with two other policemen, all three dragging, by his feet, a ragged, half-naked, bleeding man. They were followed by a number of curious spectators from the street.

"Let us pass!" yelled one of the policemen. "Make way!"

The crowd of prisoners parted and I remained alone at the door. The policemen pulled the man to the front and the crowd from the street huddled at the door.

I turned quickly, took a step forward and mingled with

this group of gaping boys and grown-ups. In the next instant I turned to the stairs and, breathless with fear, I barely managed not to run. Slowly, very slowly, I walked toward the exit, down the stairs, through another door, down a few more steps, and out into the yard.

"Oh, God!" I saw a policeman just outside the door. When he saw me, he raised his fist and shouted, his rough, colorless mustache bristling:

"You're going to get it from me, you tramp! I told you not to hang around here any more!"

"What do you mean?" I asked senselessly, slowing my pace even more.

"Scram!" he shouted fiercely "You pickpocket! If I ever see you around here again, I'll box your ears for you. Out into the street with you!" He must have mistaken me for some other boy.

I flew across the yard, dashed through the gate, and, forgetting Prokopy's directions, ran as fast as my legs could carry me. Winding my way past the pedestrians, I kept running until I reached the dimly lit Aleksandrovsky Square and turned into a dark side street.

Where was I going to hide from the police?

I considered the possible places and finally decided to go to Sashka's and to have him summon my father, so that I could ask his advice.

I followed this course.

34

M<small>Y</small> MOTHER CAME WITH MY FATHER. They were both overjoyed to see me alive and unharmed. But when I told them where I had been, they felt distressed that I was now a "criminal," an escapee from the police, a person committed to an illegal existence and to the life of a wanderer in constant danger of being arrested, tried, and sentenced to penal servitude.

"Don't cry, everything will be all right," I said, trying to console them. "Everything will be all right. Just let me have my mandolin, and I will go to the Crimea, to the Caucasus and earn my living. I'll even help you out! You can send me the cello later. I'll learn to play it yet!"

"Where? How?" my mother asked, grieving.

"I'll achieve my goal!" I declared with conviction. "I'll be a musician, come what may! You'll see!"

My mother couldn't tear herself away from me and covered my face with tears, but my father, silent and pale, firmly took her by the arm and drew her away.

"How's Egor?" I barely managed to ask my father as he was quickly leading Mother out of the room.

"Egor found out that you've disappeared and decided not to come around for the present. He also advised that it would be safer for you to go to the Crimea, and best of all to Yalta.

Said it's easy to find work in a hotel, on a ship, or in the theater in Yalta. He asked me to tell you that he'll try to find you there—that he'd find you even if he had to search for you to the end of the earth!" Then Father handed me two blue bills that Egor had given him for me.

My parents left.

About two hours later Anka came over. She informed me of the latest news:

Soon after my parents got home, the police came. They questioned them in turn, first my mother then my father, "on the subject of clarifying the whereabouts of your son." The police officer threatened my father with imprisonment and said, as he was leaving without the information he tried to pry from them: "We'll find him just the same."

"You must get away from here at once," Anka insisted in the tone of an experienced person. "I'll take you down to my grandmother's."

Within half an hour, I found myself in a stuffy room filled to the rafters with rubber and oleander plants. Anka was telling her grandmother, whom we had wakened, that my brothers had come down with scarlet fever and that I had to spend the night away from home before setting out on a long journey to visit distant relatives.

Next day Anka brought my mandolin, a sack filled with my belongings, and someone's sturdy boots.

And the following day, at the dawn of a cold November morning, when the night's darkness had barely begun to lift, I left the old lady's house accompanied by Anka, and equipped with Sashka's birth certificate. I calmly set off on the familiar Nikolayevskaya Road leading out of the city.

With the heavy bag on my back, the mandolin wrapped in a blue cotton cloth in my hand, and the coarse boots on my feet, I looked and felt like a poor tourist or a wandering musician.

Anka and I soon parted. She was upset—her eyes were moist and her lips quivered. But she controlled herself and didn't cry. As several months before, when I was leaving for Sevastopol, she said: "Let's kiss," and after touching my face lightly with her lips, she quickly left.

Sashka, Vitka, and Spirka met me at the turn into the highway. They walked with me along the seashore for about two miles.

Sashka gave me a painstakingly drawn and brightly colored map for the road and explained how it would show me the way to the Crimea. Vitka handed me a shiny compass that he himself had made and showed me how to read it. Referring to Sashka's map, he pointed out how far to go north, where to turn east, and at which point to return southward. "In other words," he said, "follow the coastline—that would be best of all."

Shy as usual, Spirka offered me some of his verse. "Read them later," he said, blushing. I managed to see the title of the first poem before putting his gift in my pocket: "To a Friend at Parting."

We separated at the crossroads.

I went on but my friends stood there for a long time, waving their caps until they could no longer see me.

I walked along the sloping shoulder of the highway, near to the edge of the sea, and looked at the eastern horizon bathed in purple-pink and gold and at the mountains of early dawn clouds filling the sky.

All at once the whole sea was ablaze with the rising sun, and half the sky was aflame with a sudden flush of brightness, as though a stream of fire had been loosened from the horizon and was spilling over half the world.

A huge orange-purple globe was rising over the radiant sea, and with every moment it became more golden and blinding.

I felt good! Warmed by the sun, prodded gently by the

fresh sea breeze, I walked on briskly, clutching hard my mandolin, and, stirred by a mounting feeling of hopefulness, I began to sing at the top of my voice—the song pouring forth from the depths of my soul.

Where had I heard this song before?

I kept trying to remember, but couldn't recall where or when I had heard it.

Then I knew without any doubt that I had never heard it before. Where, then, did it come from?

I realized that the song had been born in my heart and that it had now, for the first time, rung out clear and strong.

Yes, it was my very own song!

It rang out in the pure morning air, taking on volume and depth. I walked to its buoyant rhythm with a feeling of new joy in life and hope for the future.

I knew that there would be more of such songs.

The sun rose higher. Over the sea, from shore to horizon, stretched a golden road, and my path stretched very near, almost alongside of it.

SEMYON ROSENFELD was born in Odessa, in 1891. His father was a clerk, often unemployed, and Semyon could not attend school because of his family's poverty. Eager not to remain illiterate, Semyon studied his friends' textbooks and read every volume his book-loving father brought home. At the age of fourteen, Semyon was drawn into the stormy and hazardous social events of the day. It was the eve of the Revolution of 1905. The youth was soon arrested and spent three years in jail.

From the age of thirty-five, Semyon Rosenfeld devoted all his time to literature. He wrote several excellent books about his youth. *The First Song* was the last of this series, published one month after the author's death, in February 1959.

MIRIAM MORTON was born in Russia and lived her entire childhood there. She has now devoted a number of years to selecting, editing, and translating outstanding works of Russian literature for the young reader. She has been called a "superb" translator by *The Saturday Review*, and other publications have found her translations "excellent," "masterly," and "remarkable."

Mrs. Morton has lived in this country since her early adolescence. She now resides in Los Angeles.